That Which Was

That Which Was

GLENN PATTERSON

HAMISH HAMILTON
an imprint of
PENGUIN BOOKS

HAMISH HAMILTON

Published by the Penguin Group
Penguin Books Ltd, 80 Strand, London WC2R ORL, England
Penguin Group (USA), Inc., 375 Hudson Street, New York, New York 10014, USA
Penguin Books Australia Ltd, 250 Camberwell Road, Camberwell, Victoria 3124, Australia
Penguin Books Canada Ltd, 10 Alcorn Avenue, Toronto, Ontario, Canada M4V 3B2
Penguin Books India (P) Ltd, 11 Community Centre, Panchsheel Park, New Delhi – 110 017, India
Penguin Books (NZ) Ltd, Cnr Rosedale and Airborne Roads, Albany, Auckland, New Zealand
Penguin Books (South Africa) (Pty) Ltd, 24 Sturdee Avenue, Rosebank 2196, South Africa

Penguin Books Ltd, Registered Offices: 80 Strand, London WC2R ORL, England

www.penguin.com

First published 2004
1

Copyright © Glenn Patterson, 2004

Set in 12/14.75 pt Monotype Dante
Typeset by Rowland Phototypesetting Ltd,
Bury St Edmunds, Suffolk
Printed in Great Britain by Clays Ltd, St Ives plc

A CIP catalogue record for this book is available from the British Library

ISBN 0-241-14195-8

Lyrics from "God Only Knows" (Wilson/Asher) © 1966 by kind permission of Rondor
Music (London) Limited

"Lady Godiva's Operation" Words and Music by Lou Reed © 1968, Oakfield Avenue
Music Ltd/Screen Gems-EMI Music Inc, USA
Reproduced by permission of Screen Gems-EMI Music Inc, London WC2H OQY.

For Jessica, whose city it is too

In those days there was no king in Israel: every man did that which was right in his own eyes.

Judges 21:25

PART ONE

PART ONE

I

The *East Belfast Community News* (verified free delivery to 31,094 households) is, by definition, a paper that recognizes its own limits. This is not to say that the paper wants for hard news. Alongside the pictures of councillors squeezed into chicken suits for charity, of local comedians holding basketballs above the reach of leaping schoolchildren; alongside the ads for carpet clearouts, for genuine reductions in genuine pine and genuine leather, and stories of disrepair and disputed access, which – beyond 31,094 households – most people would consider free too high a price to pay to read about, there are, week in, week out, reports of the sort of violence familiar to anyone who has lived in what once could fairly have been called the industrial inner city and of the sort peculiar to a place where, for three decades, everything from an ideological difference through an upsurge in car theft to plain looking at someone funny has been regarded as a cause for paramilitary intervention.

Not even the summer months are slow for the *East Belfast Community News*. Summertime is marching time, the time of bonfires planned and improvised and of confrontations along (a popular summer term) the sectarian interfaces. It is no news then, though it takes up column after column, that east Belfast does not imagine itself a single, harmonious community.

For all that, the paper is not without its own silly-season moments. Among the sillier in the midsummer of 2000 was the feature on the Presbyterian minister who had once been a junior manager with a leading Northern Irish bank, though he had left banking in the earlier nineties and at the time of the feature had been minister to his church, a mile and a half east of the city centre, for close on eighteen months.

Under the predictable heading 'From Savings Accounts to Saving Souls', the Reverend Ken Avery (34) jooks out from behind a stack of collection plates, smiling the smile of those coaxed into such poses by community newspapers the world over – uncertain, but keen to oblige – wearing his clerical collar attached to a light-coloured short-sleeved shirt. It's a light-coloured, short-sleeved sort of piece all round. The minister admits he has yet to get used to being the Reverend as opposed to plain Ken Avery – to his friends he has always been even plainer *Avery* – and later confides (eyes, says the paper, twinkling) that he has never been a great one for quoting chunks of the Bible, beyond the obvious, of course, Genesis 1:1, John 3:16.

It was this last comment that prompted a call the following Monday to the local lunchtime phone-in programme by an adherent to a variant – he would have claimed purer – form of Presbyterianism.

What kind of a man, the caller wanted to know, so badly he could nearly not get the question out, what kind of a *minister* is it makes jokes about not remembering the Scriptures, the word of God as handed down? Did Christ himself not say in Matthew thirteen and twenty-two . . .

And that was the start of it. For the next hour and a quarter every second caller wanted to address the subject of the Reverend Ken Avery. The presenter lamented, as he was often moved to do. Folks, there are wars on out there. There are natural disasters, matters of great po-li-ti-cal moment. Is this really what you want to be talking about?

4

Still, the next day he phoned the Reverend Ken Avery live on air. So what's all this about you not knowing the Bible?

The minister said what he might have been expected to say: that his remarks were being taken out of context.

Never been a great one, the presenter read from the article, for quoting chunks of the Bible, beyond the obvious. That seems pretty clear. Have your congregation not a right to expect a bit more knowledge than the *obvious* from you?

The Reverend Ken Avery had apparently not heard the previous day's programme and might not until that moment have grasped how seriously this was being taken. Knowledge and memory were not the same, he countered. (Those who had seen the photo in the *East Belfast Community News* but had never heard him speak might have been surprised by the sudden flintiness in his voice.) Just because his wasn't a mind that retained things verbatim didn't mean he didn't know where to go looking in the Scriptures for what he needed.

(A concordance, it was called. All clergymen used one.)

The presenter, who was rumoured to have been head of Belfast's drugs squad in a former life and who sounded as though he was already searching through the papers on his desk for the next topic, switched from bad cop to not-so-bad cop and asked the minister, before he went, if he didn't have one – I won't believe you if you tell me there isn't *one* – favourite verse off by heart.

Well, not a complete verse, the minister said, a line, from Paul's letter to the Romans, chapter fourteen, verse five, King James style: Let every man be fully persuaded in his own mind.

A good Presbyterian one, said the presenter. He had evidently found what he was looking for and was able to be attentive, and conciliatory, in signing off.

The Reverend Ken Avery, realizing maybe that he would be addressing more people in these next few seconds than he would address again in his entire ministerial life, said it was how he tried to approach all major decisions and dilemmas. If you couldn't be sure of your own mind, where were you?

Indeed, indeed, the presenter said. There you have it, folks. And if you want to give us a piece of your minds, on the Reverend Ken Avery or anything else, you can ring us on all the usual numbers.

By the next day the topic had been well and truly exhausted, the day after that the new edition of the *East Belfast Community News* was delivered to its 31,094 households, and three days after that again the Reverend Ken Avery climbed into his pulpit a mile and a half east of the city centre to deliver his seventieth Sunday-morning service.

We begin our worship this morning by singing together psalm number twenty-three. The Lord's my shepherd I'll not want, Avery intoned then switched off his microphone as Gregory Martin at the organ repeated the line and gave the congregation, rising to their feet, their note to begin.

The congregation's feet, this first Sunday in August, numbered ninety-five. Michael Simpson arrived and left in a wheelchair, but insisted on standing at every opportunity in between, one hand gripping the hymnal, one hand gripping the pew in front, in defiance of the cowards who had attached a booby-trap to the underside of his car a dozen years ago, robbing him of a leg and an RUC colleague of his life.

Forty-eight people in a church built to seat four hundred and fifty-two more couldn't help but look and sound thin. At this stage of the summer, though, you were grateful for what you got, in general the extremely devout, the extremely elderly, and young couples clocking up the worship hours necessary for their September weddings. Seasonal visitors weren't entirely unknown, though since this part of east Belfast had neither the attractions nor the accommodation for out-and-out tourists, these tended to be individuals back from abroad to see their families.

Into this category, Avery decided, his gaze flitting from face to face as he sang, fell the man standing alone right side of the aisle half a dozen rows from the back, eyes turned towards the ceiling as though on the watch for the oil with which the Lord his head would at any moment anoint.

Avery blinked. Forgive me, he said inwardly. The organ hit the last verse *fortissimo* and he raised his own eyes to the ceiling, letting the words goodness and mercy shape his mouth and his thoughts.

A-, the congregation sang then dropped a semitone, -men.

Avery turned on the microphone. Let us pray, he said.

A motorbike passed on the main road, trailing its noise into the distant silence.

The congregation sat, stood again, sang, sat, put money in the collection plate and listened to Avery preach from Paul's letter to the Ephesians, chapter two: For he is our peace, who hath made both one, and hath broken down the middle wall of partition between us.

It was a minute after half past twelve when he spoke the benediction over them. A moment or two before, the sun had burned through the morning haze to shine directly on the stained-glass window and cast a bright purple puddle on the aisle's carpet of Presbyterian blue. Through this puddle Avery, descending from his pulpit, walked, a nod now to this side now to that; to Michael Simpson, swaying as mildly, as necessarily, as a skyscraper in a hurricane; to Dorothy Moore; to the visitor from out of town who looked for a second as though he was about to speak (thanks were not unheard of) if Avery's relentless, nodding momentum hadn't already carried him a pace too far – yet another pace while he wondered should he have stopped – and then, prevented by the traffic that was building at his back from turning, out on to the front step.

Across the road a boy in a black baseball cap was pulling the push door of the Co-op mini-market. A girl arranging the display outside the neighbouring florist's called to him to push. The boy went on pulling, said he wasn't effing thick.

The freezers are on the blink, Avery heard someone shout from inside the shop. We're not open.

The boy – he couldn't have been more than eleven or twelve – swore again and aimed a kick first at the door, then for no apparent reason at a Volkswagen Passat parked directly in front, setting off the alarm. The boy stood a moment, mesmerized, before fleeing up a side-street. The owner of the Passat ran out from the florist's, stems of red gladioli dropping from the sheet of patterned paper unravelling behind him.

He went up that street there, shouted one of Avery's congregation.

He can't have got far, shouted another, though the Passat owner seemed more interested in the damage to his bodywork than in pursuit.

Three faces now looked out – scared, bashful, indifferent – from behind the Co-op's locked push door.

The girl from the florist's gathered in the gladioli. She placed her feet toe to heel when she bent, balancing as though on a ledge, as though the world beyond her shadow was all traps and pitfalls.

Frances Avery arrived at that point by her husband's side.

By her side, covering her ears with the heels of her hands, was the couple's soon to be five year old daughter, Ruth. On Frances's inside their second child, gender as yet unknown, was fifteen weeks away from birth, God willing.

What have I missed? Frances asked.

Yahoo, Dorothy Moore said, though not in reply and absently taking Avery's hand. Dorothy Moore was more elderly than devout, the imbalance left her a touch crabbed. I recognize the wee fella. Know his father and grandfather. Yahoos too.

The car alarm was deactivated. Somewhere leafier a hedge-trimmer hummed.

Cautiously Ruth uncovered her ears and watched over her shoulder as Michael Simpson was steered backwards down the wheelchair ramp. Every minute was filled with wonder when you were soon to be five.

Avery shook another hand then another, then there were no more hands to shake.

I've the oven and all set, Frances said. Will we see you back at the house?

No, hang on, said Avery, I'll not be a minute.

He walked back through the sanctuary (rarely was word more appropriate) and was half-way along the L-shaped corridor to his room when he met Guy Broudie, the Clerk of Session.

There's a something-or-other something-or-other, Minister, said Guy, in a whisper so low Avery had to ask him to come again. Guy increased the volume the barest degree. A man wanting to talk to you.

Guy's whisper, like his insistence on referring to Avery as Minister, was the legacy of a life of civil service in the rather grander corridors of the parliament buildings at Stormont.

Though he had retired years before to the shores of Strangford Lough he still made the thirty-mile round trip for every service – every meeting of Kirk Session, finance committee, quarterly magazine editorial board – in the church he had attended since he was a boy. Avery had been assured that a look of pained disappointment was habitual to him.

I told him, Guy said, the Minister didn't normally see people after morning service.

Avery sensed that he was being told this too, and while he didn't see people normally there was no rule said he couldn't. That's all right, he said. Guy shrugged, his duty discharged, his advice – not for the first time, his expression said – spurned.

Round the corner, standing before the door of the Minister's Room, hands clasped behind his back, looking at the bare wall on the other side of the corridor, was the stranger Avery had noticed during the service. Middle forties, medium height, hair midway between fair and grey. Avery lengthened his stride. Very sorry to have kept you waiting.

The man turned. There was, Avery thought despondently, effort in the smile.

No worries, he said. Good of you to see me at all.

The accent was more assertively Belfast than Avery had imagined, though there was definitely somewhere else, somewhere Scottish mixed in. A hand came round from behind his back and he seemed to be about to offer it, but slipped it instead into his trouser pocket.

His movements were deliberate to the point of sluggishness and as Avery held the door for him to pass through he involuntarily breathed in a little deeper, though he detected nothing with certainty.

The Minister's Room was not large. A B&Q cupboard, a desk, two chairs, a door in the wall on the right through to

the toilet, added last year in compliance with Church law –
'The Code', a copy of which rubbed boards with *Cruden's
Concordance* and the *Revised Common Lectionary* on the solitary
bookshelf. In the cupboard, along with his suit jacket, hung
Avery's spare robe, his formalwear hood and bands, and the
tan boiler suit he wore when helping Ronnie, the caretaker,
with odd jobs about the church. On the desk were a phone-fax
combo and a leatherbound Bible; in its single, deep, locked
drawer a laptop and a portable printer. The page-a-day calendar on the mint-painted wall was by Gary Larsen and was
three days in arrears.

Please . . . Avery said, leaving room for a name – Larry, the
man said – Larry. He pulled the second chair out from the
wall. Take a seat.

Larry did, awkwardly, and remained sitting in silence, his
smile growing weaker by the second, so that at the end of half
a minute it was hard to imagine he had ever had the strength
to muster it. Something about his appearance – the rumpled
jumper and sports jacket – how would you put it? He seemed
a little crushed, from the inside out. He passed a hand across
his forehead and Avery had to frown to banish the thought of
oil dripping from the ceiling of the sanctuary.

Was there something you wanted to talk about?

Larry looked up at him, looked down, looked up again
and sighed. This time Avery caught the unmistakable smell of
night-old alcohol: jammy, tainted. So that's what this was about.
Morning-after guilt and self-loathing. Where did it all go
wrong, Reverend? In his last – and first – church in Holywood,
along the North Down Gold Coast, most of the crises Avery
had dealt with were more spirituous than spiritual in origin.

We can't offer you the full all-singing all-dancing confession,
of course – he chanced a smile that wasn't returned; sometimes

one approach worked, sometimes another – but if you're in need of a little heart-to-heart . . .

Larry's gaze drifted off Avery's face. Is that there OK? he asked.

Avery looked over his shoulder. The Bible was obscured by his own back. All he could see was the telephone and fax machine. This? He pointed. Larry nodded. You mean the two things together? Do they work all right?

I mean, can anybody hear us?

Avery laughed, nonplussed, picked up the handset. Not unless we ring them first, he said, and tapped the earpiece against his palm. It's just an ordinary phone.

This was a hangover of a wholly different order, he was telling himself at the same moment as Larry sighed again and said, I think I've got blood on my hands.

Avery glanced from the hands in question to the door. He weighed the telephone handset in his palm a second or two longer before replacing it lightly on the cradle. The insides of his mouth felt shrunken. Last night? he asked.

What?

The blood.

For the briefest of moments the corners of Larry's mouth twitched.

When the Troubles were on, he said.

Ah! Avery was almost relieved. Now he had him. I *see*.

For the past two years the prisons of Northern Ireland had been emptying of paramilitary prisoners. Any day now the most famous prison of them all, the Maze – Long Kesh – would close its gates for good. For the past two years Avery, like most members of the clergy, had been attending conferences on issues arising from this early-release scheme. Many of the prisoners had found the Lord while inside, some had even become pastors and in a few cases established their own congregations.

It was expected, though, that for the vast majority the enormity of their deeds would only hit home once they were on the outside again away from their comrades, having to cope on their own.

Avery replayed Larry's words. I *think* I've got blood on my hands. Classic reluctance to accept responsibility.

He leant forward, elbows on his knees, hands loosely joined. Do you want to tell me about it?

I'm dying to, Larry said, and sounded it.

Avery waited, a full minute. So?

Larry was massaging his forehead. I don't remember.

Don't remember what happened? Avery started to say, but Larry cut in.

Don't remember what, don't remember where, don't remember when.

It crossed Avery's mind to ask him was he sure about *whether*, but Larry looked scared. His fingers now held his forehead in a tight grip.

It's OK, Avery said. It's OK.

It's not OK. Larry's voice was rising. It's doing my head in.

There was a moment's silence in the room, broken by a knock without. Avery?

It was Frances. Avery heard Ruth asking what Daddy was doing, when they were having lunch.

You go on ahead, he called. He wanted his daughter well away from this. I'll catch you up.

Larry hadn't moved. Avery sat back in his chair, feeling on the desk for the Bible. He brought it round on to his lap, opened it where it was bookmarked – 1 Peter 2–4 – trying to buy himself a few more seconds' thinking time. *Christ the corner stone*, ran the caption and, facing that, *Rules of Conduct*.

I keep getting these flashes, Larry said without warning. Like waking nightmares. People's faces looking at me like they know they're about to die, like I'm the one's going to kill them.

Avery closed the Bible.

Only somebody doesn't want me to remember. They've been tampering with my brain.

His fingertips had left white marks on his forehead. Avery watched them fill with colour, which was when he noticed the scarring a fraction below the scalp at Larry's right temple. An inch, two inches long. He peered. No, longer, faded to a faint sheen for another inch, but still unbroken.

Oh, no.

His heart closed in on itself leaving his chest hollow and chill. The scarring – the *scar* – ran almost the entire length of Larry's hairline.

Larry was looking directly at him.

Would you like to say a prayer with me? Avery said, grateful for the opportunity to close his eyes. Heavenly Father, he began, who sees and knows the least of our thoughts and deeds, we ask today that you might be with your servant, Larry, in this time of great trouble and confusion.

There was the sound in the room of a chair being pushed back, the door opening and closing; footsteps receded along the corridor. Avery prayed on. And grant us all, O Lord, when we are sure in our minds of the right thing to do the strength and courage to carry it through.

Frances asked him at lunch what was bothering him.

Nothing, he said. Why?

Because I had to ask you three times before you heard me.

2

Monday is as close to a day off as a Presbyterian minister gets in a normal week. That Monday morning, Avery woke late. Frances and Ruth's voices carried to him above the sound of the radio downstairs. It was going to be another warm day. Frances had left the side windows ajar in the bay, and the rise and fall of the breeze had sucked the curtains into the openings.

The house – Avery resisted the word manse – was off the main road, five minutes' brisk walk from the church. With its rustic flourishes and vestigial outhouses, it was still referred to by some locally as Townsend Grange from the days when the city's outward reach was several miles shorter. Now, its tall hedge was broken on one side by the palings of an electricity substation, and on the other by the goods yard of a Tesco Metro. The view over the hedge from the back-bedroom windows was of the stairwell of a block of seventies maisonettes, from the windowsills of which at this time of year a startling array of flags flew: Ulster flags, UVF and UDA flags (though never close together), Scottish flags, Canadian and Australian flags, even the occasional Union Jack. To find anything remotely resembling countryside these days you had to carry on a further mile out the main road and cross the four lanes of the Outer Ring Road, where a glen would take you the quiet and roundabout way to the south-eastern suburbs.

Avery's predecessor had lived here for close on thirty-five years, had died here, and though the house was as well fitted-out as you could want, the decoration left much to be desired for a couple in their thirties with a young child. Young children. There was no end of volunteers to help with the stripping and painting, but Frances and Avery were trying where possible to manage on their own, bit by little bit. Last Monday Avery had repainted the walls of the cloakroom under the stairs and today he was going to put up shelves to take some of his excess videos.

He was glad to have woken into such practical thoughts for he had not gone over to sleep easily last night. He had spoken to Guy Broudie after the evening service, but Guy could add nothing to what he had told Avery in the morning. He had discovered the man in the corridor, looking at the nameplates on the various doors. When he told Guy what he wanted, Guy had tried to persuade him to come back another time, though he might not have spoken for all the notice the man took.

Frances was even less help. As they were getting ready for bed Avery had asked her had she noticed anyone unfamiliar before or after the morning service. But Frances had had her hands full with Ruth. It's no joke, you know, sometimes, she told him, keeping her in check.

Frances was worried she had a haemorrhoid; she was entitled to be a bit short.

Lying in bed, at half past nine the next morning, he listened to her laughing downstairs, more like herself, and might have dozed again but for the sudden klaxon of a lorry reversing through the gates of the Tesco goods yard. The price they paid for being able to run out in their slippers at eight o'clock in the evening for chocolate cake and banana frozen yoghurt.

He thanked God for the blessing of a new day, then swung his legs out on to the floor, jogging them to gee himself up.

Hey-ho, let's go, he chanted, a secular exhortation.

He was supposed to have two weddings that week, but the second cancelled with only forty-eight hours' notice. He spent much of Wednesday afternoon at the family home of the disconsolate groom. No, of course he wasn't a dull person, nobody was, God had made us all individually interesting. Yes, three former girlfriends and his fiancée *could* be wrong.

On Thursday lunchtime he attended a lecture at the City Mission: Facing Up to the Fractions. More than $\frac{9}{10}$ of people on the globe would soon be living in urban areas. More than $\frac{9}{10}$ of the world's current city dwellers attended no manner of religious service. The question was, was the Church driving people away by the slow pace of change, or were the changes too fast, making the Church just another form of entertainment that today's urban population could take or – as it increasingly appeared – leave? The audience of six was split, $\frac{1}{2}$ and $\frac{1}{2}$. Avery leant one way, then the other. He was attached to his collar, if not the title that went with it, and to certain traditional forms of worship, the yeas and verilys of the King James Bible, the hymns of Isaac Watts, while not forgetting how as a teenager those same forms had driven him almost beyond the Church's reach.

As he walked back to the car he was hailed by a group of tourists carrying precautionary Pacamacs. German, up from Dublin for the day, their spokesman explained and handed Avery a map. Waterfront Hall? he asked.

Avery traced the route with his finger. We are here, it is there.

He told them there was an even bigger arena, the Odyssey, now being built just across the mouth of the Lagan from the Waterfront. Worth a look at least.

The tourists thanked him, began moving off, map like a divining rod before them. The spokesman hung back a little.

I was wondering, he said, as awkwardly as if he had been talking to a pimp, not a Presbyterian minister, where is *everything*, you know?

Avery knew. Walk half a mile in any direction from here, he said, you'll come across something.

I'm sorry. You don't mind me asking?

No, said Avery, conscious that in Berlin, Belfast's erstwhile wall-twin, he might ask the same thing.

That night, switching on the news while he worked in his study, he heard that a former loyalist prisoner had been found dead at the foot of a cliff in north Antrim. Police said they were not looking for anyone else in connection with the incident.

The enormity of the deeds come home.

They gave an age, forty-four, and a name, which meant nothing to Avery, though he had no reason to believe that the man who had come to the office had told the truth about his.

He endured another restless night thinking about it, persuading himself one minute that the odds were still stacked against it being his man, the next that it could be nobody else. He hadn't talked like any ex-prisoner Avery had met, it's true, and if he was in denial then he was in a pretty advanced state. Even so, first thing in the morning Avery went and bought both local dailies, flipping through the pages as soon as he was out of the newsagent's door. There was a picture in one, a blow-up from a prison group-shot. The quality was poor, the period detail misleading, but Avery was certain, it wasn't him.

So why after all the worry, he wondered, rising to his feet in the pulpit on Sunday morning, did he feel a momentary relief looking down the sanctuary and seeing only the old familiar faces looking back? The microphone hummed a note as he switched it on, drowning thoughts of self. Let us join as a congregation and pray, he said.

It was a baptism Sunday. Avery came down from the pulpit to receive the baby at the font. He saw Frances smiling at him from the second row, Ruth beside her, chin straining to clear the back of the pew. The baby's parents were scarcely out of their teens. The mother had puncture marks on her right eyebrow, her left nostril, below her bottom lip, from which in deference to the occasion her various sleepers and studs had been removed. The father wore a goatee beard, blond hair with a fringe cut dead straight and dyed orange. Between them they handled the baby with infinite care. The baby was tiny, even a little deflated-looking, but it blinked its eyes open as Avery took it in the crook of his right arm and its face was beautiful. The mother and father smiled, proud and abashed. They were beautiful too. Avery dipped his fingertips in the tepid water, brushing the baby's temple. The baby snuffled into its fists as Avery spoke its name, Marshall. The congregation, according to tradition, sang in an undertone and without prompt or accompaniment the Aaronic blessing: The Lord bless you and keep you, the Lord make his face to shine upon you and be gracious unto you . . .

Avery loved that moment. At that moment no one could doubt that God created all of his children equal. It was humankind's tragedy and sin that it worked so hard at obliterating the fact.

By the time Avery had returned to the pulpit to deliver the next reading, Larry had slipped in and was sitting in the seat he had occupied the Sunday before.

This week Avery did not dally on the front step after service.

He asked Guy Broudie to tell Frances he would follow her home a little later.

I'm glad you felt able to come back, he said.

Larry, looking at the calendar on the wall, now five days behind, nodded. There was none of the stale-drink smell of last week, which was a plus.

I was concerned about you.

I'm sorry. I didn't mean to worry you.

Avery thought better of asking what he had meant to do, confessing to murder, claiming there was something not right with his head. He averted his eyes from the scar snaking across Larry's hairline. How have you been since last Sunday? he asked.

Not good, said Larry, evenly. Not good at all, to be honest.

More flashes?

Larry winced at the mention of them.

They still as bad?

Worse, said Larry. You've no idea.

That was exactly Avery's problem. He didn't want to press, but he didn't see how else they were going to get anywhere.

By worse, do you mean, like, clearer?

Larry looked him in the eye as though trying to uncover there where this was leading.

Avery shook his head to throw off the stare. I'm just trying to understand.

They're clear enough that I know I've done something terrible, Larry said. Believe me.

Avery couldn't find it in him yet to say that he did, so for the moment said nothing at all.

Ronnie passed along the corridor forcing a whistle through

his teeth, straining the tune out of it. Larry dragged a hand across his forehead. There was no avoiding the question.

I don't mean to be rude, Avery said, but I can't help noticing . . . He ran a finger part-way along his own hairline.

Larry sighed. It's what I've been trying to tell you. They did something to my brain.

Avery realized, with a sudden and profound regret, that he hadn't kissed Frances and Ruth before he left the house this morning. Who did? he managed to say.

Larry stood suddenly and flipped the bottom of the Larsen calendar so that he could see the wall underneath, then just as suddenly sat down. The government, he said. Or people connected to it. MI5, elements of the police and army. They were trying to wipe out my memory.

It's a doctor this man needs, Avery thought. Why would they want to do a thing like that? he asked.

Because of what I knew, Larry said, because of what I did for them.

These killings? Avery tried to withhold his consent from the word.

Yes.

Which you don't . . .

Remember anything about, no.

Larry shrugged as if to acknowledge the difficulties Avery must be having with this; as if to say he really wished, for both their sakes, he could tell him more.

Avery had made a steeple of his index fingers either side of his nose. Have you talked to anyone else about this?

Larry became guarded again. Like who?

I don't know. Family, a friend . . . He checked Larry's fingers for rings, saw none . . . Someone you're close to.

Oh. Larry shook his head. There was someone, but I couldn't trust her. I had to leave.

Avery let his eyes close while he contemplated the implications of this. He trusts me. He opened his eyes. Larry, were you – as far as you can remember were you – brought up in the Presbyterian Church?

No, not that I remember.

At this moment, do you consider yourself to be a religious person at all?

Not really.

So why choose a minister to tell all this to?

Larry couldn't seem to think of an answer at once. His shrug this time was a movement away, a drawing back into himself. God knows, he said eventually, and got up from his seat.

Avery put a hand out to stop him. That wasn't a rebuke. I wasn't telling you to go.

OK, but I'm going now anyway.

Avery watched him turn the door handle. He was certain that if he didn't utter another word, he would not see or hear from Larry a third time. The urgency of his own voice took him by surprise. Hold on, it said.

He went to the cupboard and felt in the inside pocket of his suit jacket for his wallet. Take this. He handed Larry a card. It has all my numbers on it. If things get too much for you.

Larry held on to the card with both hands as he read. Thank you, he said, and was gone.

Avery stood for a few moments with his head resting against the door, mind so full it felt blank, then he turned back to the calendar, slipping the tip of an index finger underneath. He tapped. Solid brick.

★

Do you know who we haven't seen for a while?

It was Tuesday night, only just nine, and Frances and Avery were in the sitting room, looking past the TV at a sky turned tangerine to one side of their window frame.

Who?

Frances had been doing the *Belfast Telegraph* crossword, feet up on the settee, when Avery arrived home from his district visits. If it had been autumn he would probably have made an appearance at a church club or society afterwards. Then, it was half ten or eleven most nights before he got in.

Michele and Tony, he said, massaging her feet, lying now across his lap.

Michele and Tony?

Avery raised one foot by its ankle and, bending, kissed the sole.

What brought Michele and Tony up all of a sudden?

Just that we haven't seen them for a while.

We've seen practically nobody since we moved here.

That's what I was thinking. We should ask those two over for dinner, before Ruthie starts school. He laid a hand on his wife's stomach. Before it gets too difficult.

It's not going to be that easy now, Frances said crossly, and made to swing her legs on to the floor, as though she would have to start preparing at once.

Listen. Avery pulled her legs back on to his lap. We don't have to go to a whole lot of trouble. It's summer, people don't expect a big sit-down thing. I can do a barbecue, get a load of salads from next door.

I'm not buying stuff for guests from in there. If we're having salads I'll do my own.

Avery traced firm circles on her heels with the shaft of his thumb. That was a yes, then?

Frances took up the newspaper, frowned at it for half a minute then set it down again. I still can't believe you wanting to see Michele and Tony.

And who was the one was always telling me I never gave them a proper chance?

Frances went back to her crossword.

I was thinking this Friday or Saturday, Avery said. Frances shook her head, an expression of his incorrigibility, not her negativity.

Michele and Frances had grown up a couple of streets apart, but it wasn't until they started university that they became close friends. They were in the drama society together, out of their depth. Avery got to know the two of them at the same time. He was working then in the bank's university branch. He helped Michele open her account. Frances was nabbed by Stu, one of the other clerks, who always fancied his chances with the first-years. Avery could hear him on the other side of the partition flirting with Frances. He heard Frances's bright laugh. Michele ducked her head round a couple of times to see what was going on. God, she said, your account sounds like it's going to be a lot more fun than mine.

Frances, of course, had no memory of this. In all likelihood Michele hadn't either, though at a party once, years later, she commandeered Avery's reminiscence to say what an awful drip he had been back then, how after that day she would see him standing at the counter blushing and drooling whenever she and Frances walked through the revolving door.

Never mind that Avery was almost never at the counter by that stage of his banking career. He saw Michele and Frances all right, but from behind Venetian blinds, from over the top of the bank's one enormous computer. It was two years before he managed to talk to Frances. He had been transferred to a city-centre branch, but was still attending a Bible study group close to the university. Frances turned up with another friend. (Frances was her moral support, though it was the friend who never returned.) Michele was already living with Tony and hanging out with all his friends from Medicine. She and Frances rarely saw each other.

There were a couple of dismal attempts at nights out as a foursome. Tony showed up for one so drunk he actually *talked*, until he threw up. Then Avery started training for the ministry and Tony and Michele, like a good many other people, it has to be said, evidently concluded that his desire for a social life had come to an end.

They had been living in Saudi, where Tony was doctoring lucratively to the oil industry, when Frances and Avery married. They sent a card with the word Commiserations, in Tony's hand, crossed out and replaced by Congratulations!!! in Michele's.

In more recent times, while Avery was still assistant in Holywood, he and Frances had become Friends of the Lyric Theatre and discovered that Michele was a Friend too. They had run into her, though never Tony, at this or that first-night party (we must, must, *must* get together soon) before the demands of ministering to his own congregation here in east Belfast started to tell on Avery. He hadn't been to a play in months and, as Frances said, they'd had precious few people over their doorstep for anything other than pastoral guidance.

Tony had banked with Avery's bank too when he was a student. Avery had had occasion to look at his file. Plenty, in fact. There were stories there he could have told. Could have but wouldn't have. However bizarre his career change appeared to other people, being privy to friends' financial affairs had been the best possible training for his new vocation.

Tony and Michele arrived in a low-slung, showroom-shiny silver Mazda and parked it, like an exercise in stark contrast, parallel with Avery's aged Orion, the joints of which were so stiff that only a qualified physiotherapist could adjust the rear-view mirror without brute force. Tony gripped the Mazda's doorframe with both hands to lever himself out of the passenger seat. His left leg, below the cuff of his three-quarter-length trousers, was in plaster. Broken bone in his foot.

Don't ask, he said, though Michele, handing him his crutch, answered anyway: Chasing next door's cats.

They're stalking our carp, Tony said, in his own defence. You'd need a water-cannon to keep them away.

You can buy special pellets, Frances said.

Tried them, said Tony, and you could almost hear the bugles as the punchline thundered over the hill, but I never managed to hit one.

Michele and Tony, Frances had said last time she met them together, would be a very long time getting old. There wasn't an obvious bit of sag or wear about either of them: they fitted perfectly clothes designed with people ten, fifteen years their junior in mind. It meant they stood out less when they went to their clubs and bars as well.

Avery wondered whether Tony's broken foot accounted for their accepting the invitation at such short notice, though he soon found out they had other reasons for taking things a little easier these days.

He and Tony were down the garden checking the barbecue – Tony had insisted on accompanying him, grimacing every step of the way – when Frances, in the kitchen, shouted: Michele! That's fantastic.

Avery looked at Tony, who nodded. Thirteen weeks, he said. Had the first scan the day I did this. If you'd seen the state of us at the hospital. At *my* hospital.

Avery had charcoal on his hands. Tony waved away his apologies for not shaking. Ach! You know yourself it's not that hard, he said, with as much genuine fellow feeling in his voice as Avery could remember being on the receiving end of.

Tony let his gaze follow the drift of the barbecue smoke over the back hedge. From that spot at the end of the garden only the top third of the maisonettes could be seen, side-on. Satellite dishes and aerials, a commonwealth of flags, a *Jane's Guide* to loyalist paramilitaries. Simply the best, declared one standard.

Nice neighbours, Tony couldn't keep himself from saying, and stumped off back up the garden, calling to the kitchen: Michele, are those beers we brought cold?

Frances and Avery had beer in – three types – and wine besides, though in the end Tony drank less than Avery had ever seen him drink on a night out. No company, of course. Frances and Michele were off it altogether and Avery stuck to his two-drink limit.

Which made it that little bit more awkward for Avery to just happen to mention a medical matter he had been puzzling over.

Memory? Tony said. Well, that wouldn't really be my field. He was perched on a high stool, swirling a half-empty bottle of Budvar, watching as Avery, with Ruth assisting, filled the dishwasher. It depends, though, what aspect of it you're interested in.

Big plates down below, said Avery. Careful, here, let Daddy
– that's a girl. Well done.

He walked to the swing bin, held back the lid with his wrist
as he dumped the uneaten burgers. He rested his back against
the countertop. I'm just interested generally. Where people in
your profession think memory resides, what it's composed of,
things that can go wrong with it.

Tony raised the bottle to his mouth, flipped the base
and gave a loose, wet-lipped smile. Do I feel a sermon coming on?

That's not your sausage, Avery said, darting over to Ruth,
who had picked a half-chewed thing off one of the plates.

I wasn't going to *eat* it, she said, four going on twenty-five.

Tony opened the bin lid for her with his crutch. Ruth was
delighted.

Let's just say I have my reasons for wanting to know, Avery
said.

Oh dear, Frances said, coming in at that moment from the
garden and pretending to go straight back out. Have I walked
in on some secret men's thing?

We were talking about memory, said Tony.

So you heard him on the radio?

No, when?

Were you on the radio? Michele, overhearing, came to
the door.

Only about half the week, Frances said. Where's that
newspaper?

I don't know where I put it.

He was in the newspaper as well? Michele asked, and Tony
added with exaggerated awe, Is there no end to this man's
fame and notoriety?

Oh, wait till you see. Frances was in under the stairs. Where

28

is it? I can't find a flipping thing since you moved this all around.

Tell you what, you can send us a photocopy, Michele said.

Yes, said Tony, and clapped his hands. (Ruth clapped too.) *Do*.

Frances switched off the under-stairs light. She was flushed from bending; and from the way her expression had changed she might have slipped on a mask while she was in there. There was joking and there was joking and Avery knew when she thought a joke had gone too far.

He was very good, you know. I mean it was only a free-newspaper interview, but some of what he said – and on the radio – he was, he was very good.

In the momentary silence they heard a siren from a television set, the thrum of the electricity substation.

Another one of those? Avery asked Tony, for want of anything else to say just then.

Tony clasped the bottle to his chest. No, this is me.

Time we were letting you get someone to B-E-D, Michele said and Ruth said bed back to her.

Sure hang on an hour or so till she's over, Avery said. We can have more of a chat.

He went back to filling the dishwasher. Frances nipped his bottom, hard, as she followed their guests outdoors, to the scent of fuchsia and barbecue sauce.

Ruth wouldn't go to bed anyway. They really didn't have a lot of people over like this. The only person who felt up to chasing her round the garden was Avery, which rather defeated the purpose of his asking Michele and Tony to stay.

It was a quarter to ten and Ruth was showing off the cardigan Avery had at least been able to coax her into when Michele produced the car keys from her bag.

Out front, beyond the hedge, a game of bicycle tig was in progress. Shouts, skids, bikes going to ground. A racer flashed by the gateway, rider standing tall on the pedals, pal leaning almost horizontal in the seat holding fistfuls of shirt-tail. Death-defying.

Pray for a girl for me, Michele said, shuddering, and kissed Avery's cheek. You come to ours next time.

Tony had started down the drive, feeling with his crutch for the shallowest gravel, waving back over his head. Yes, us next.

He had himself half into the car when he hauled his head up over the slope of the door. Avery, if you really are interested in all that stuff, give me a call. I'll see what I can find out.

Do you think I shamed him into being nice? Frances said, finger-waving, grinning at the tail-lights. Getting cross at him that time?

Avery put his arms round her shoulders, smiled. Maybe you're right. Maybe I just never gave him a chance.

3

A fortnight passed, but the season seemed stalled. The slump in Sunday-service attendance continued. The sectarian interfaces remained ugly. The flags that traditionally came down at the end of July stayed up, a disagreement, it appeared, between the loyalist terror groups over who should remove theirs first. When a feud erupted on the Shankill Road it quickly spread into neighbouring north Belfast. There were running gun-battles, cold-blooded assassinations.

Avery heard nothing more from Larry. Though he had his hand on the phone several times to do it, he didn't make the call to Tony. He was busy with the final details of a cross-community seven-a-side football tournament scheduled for the penultimate day of the school holidays. The plans had been meeting stiff resistance on both sides of the sectarian divide over the decision to allow girls' teams to compete.

In the same league as us? asked one of Avery's eleven-year-old boys. No way am I playing against wee dolls.

Scared, said Des Kehoe, on the phone to Avery. There's a team of girls over here and they'll take no prisoners.

Des's parish was deep in the heart of Protestant east Belfast, a leftover of less starkly segregated times. Many of his kids had to be driven to the church and its sister school from the enclaves into which their families had moved in the seventies and eighties. It was Des who had suggested the tournament. He had written Avery a letter of congratulation when he was first appointed to his church: You might remember we met at Sean Curran's funeral.

Sean had been a parishioner of Des's, and Avery's manager at the university branch. He had died two years before of cancer.

Cross-community initiatives of one kind or another were as old as the Troubles themselves. According to some arithmetic of deprivation, the less contact you'd had with members of the other religion, the more likely you were to be sent to the United States with them. Avery, whose early childhood at least had been spent in a relatively mixed area, had got no further than an interfaith camp in the wilds above Ballycastle on the north Antrim coast, where he went twice in his teens with a group from his local church. Midwinter both times, sleeping ten to a wooden hut (single-sex, naturally), passing the few daylight hours in table-tennis round robins with kids from a Catholic church half a mile from their own.

His first time, Avery had got drunk at every opportunity, like everybody else, Protestant and Catholic. Forget the table tennis, the greatest camaraderie was built up on the illicit runs to the nearest country bar with an off-sales. On his second visit, aged sixteen, he had met Joanna, a volunteer three years his senior. Joanna was a Christian, though she refused, as too self-satisfied, the term born-again. He chatted to her for hours, giving her a hand with her volunteer's duties, boiling sheets, mixing vats of Cadbury's Smash, and on the afternoon of his departure he sat with her in a quiet corner and asked the Lord into his life.

Not that he was all that committed to begin with. He had no desire to be an earnest do-gooder, he just wanted to do a little better by his own life. Probably he wanted to be someone Joanna could admire. Avery had been hopelessly in love from the moment he met her. Despite the age difference, the unwritten teen rule that girls did not go out with boys younger than them, the attraction was not all one-sided. One night, on their own in the kitchens, they found their faces inches apart and, hesitating a second, almost drawing back, they kissed, and kissed and knocked a chair over, and kneeling on the lino ran their hands over and under one another's clothes. And then stopped, picked up the chair. Joanna had a boyfriend at college in England. Avery at the same time didn't want her thinking he was only listening to her in order to get what he wanted. Which he wanted badly.

They exchanged letters for a month or two. Hers were full of encouragement to him to stick to the new path he had started down, in spite of all the obstacles and voices calling him back. Avery, in his, was guilty more than once of exaggerating the size of the obstacles, playing up the volume of the voices, though he valued her support all the same. They talked of meeting up, but nothing ever came of it. Joanna went to England to join her boyfriend and the letters stopped.

Avery didn't know that she had come back until he heard on the news that she had been murdered. She was found in her car one morning on a remote lane by the shores of Lough Neagh. People living a mile away had heard shots the night before. It appeared the gunman had opened up from the hedgerow. Theories were put forward – she had stumbled upon preparations for another attack; she was the victim of a mistaken identity; she was killed by someone with a murderous dislike of cross-community work – but no organization claimed responsibility and no arrests were ever made. That happened too in those days.

Avery had just turned twenty-one and was still trying in his own made-up-as-he-went-along way to be a little better.

An act as utterly senseless as Joanna's murder can make or break a person's faith. For days, weeks even, Avery vacillated, not praying so much as firing irate questions heavenward.

Then one day he woke and, as though an unseen hand had fitted the pieces together while he slept, understood that, awful though it was, her death, like her life, had to have a purpose. If it had no meaning then nothing in this world had. It was an intellectual as well as a spiritual imperative.

That, rather than the afternoon at the camp, was his moment of true conversion. That was when he first had an inkling of where the path he was walking must inevitably lead.

He was then in his third year in the bank, his second at the university branch, only months away from meeting Frances.

Decades old though the cross-community ideal was, there were still people out there to whom it appeared to be not-very-good news.

Avery was out on the main road shopping for fruit and veg the Tuesday before the football tournament when two young lads, eleven or twelve, blocked his path. Tracksuits, Nike baseball caps pushed back, one black, one buff.

Mister, said the boy in the buff cap, you running the footie competition?

Avery set down his shopping between his feet. Well, not just me.

The boy tutted. This was no time for nicety. You know what I mean.

Yes, sorry, I do.

The boy in the black cap had been regarding, with barely suppressed horror, the curly kale sticking out of Avery's bag.

His ma won't let him play, his friend said.

The boy shrugged and spat. He looked vaguely familiar.

Why not? Avery asked.

Why do you think?

Girls?

Wise up, the boys said, in unison.

Right, said Avery. Right.

A horn sounded, lightly touched, and Avery turned in time to see, through the traffic, a woman's smile and waving hand at the window of a blue car. He waved back though he had not the first idea who it was he was waving at. When he faced round again he noticed that the Pound Shop before which he was standing had a sale on: Everything 50p or Less.

So, the boy in the buff cap was running out of patience, will you come and talk to his ma some time, tell her it's OK?

Avery first asked if the boy's mother was a member of his church and then, getting only blank looks in reply, said of course he would anyway.

The house was the second last in a row awaiting demolition. For the best part of an acre round about there were not two bricks left standing one on top of the other. Footpaths ran like failed irrigation channels through the wasteland of fallen streets.

Avery sometimes imagined that it had only just sunk in in these neighbourhoods that the industries on which they depended, on which they prided themselves, were now ancient history and that the houses had simply buckled under the weight of dejection.

On another edge of this desert, behind fences mounted with CCTV cameras and hoardings highlighting proximity to the city centre, new low-density housing was beginning to grow. Who knew? When it was all finished some, maybe most, of the former residents might have moved back in. Meanwhile at any one time Avery was ministering-by-motor to several families temporarily relocated to housing estates and B-and-Bs across the east of the city.

The boy whose friend had asked for Avery's help outside the Pound Shop was called Darryl Kirkpatrick. His mother worked in a laundrette, but came home every day twelve thirty to one during the school holidays to get him and his brothers their lunch. It was ten to one when Avery knocked the door. Darryl had said that was the best time because the dishes would all be cleared away and his mother would be having a cup of tea and a smoke.

His mate had nodded sagely. It'd take a bomb to shift her when she's drinking her tea.

Avery heard a woman's voice from the back of the house shout, Will one of yous ones see who that is!

Darryl himself opened the door. He still had his baseball cap on. As he stood aside to let Avery enter, Avery caught him steal a glance across the wasteground to make sure no one had seen a minister go into the house.

Avery found himself in a room with a large television set and two small boys the image of their older brother.

Who was it? the woman called.

Darryl sat on the arm of a chair and looked at the television. Avery decided there was nothing for it but to go on alone.

He tapped on the kitchen door as he poked his head round it. Hello?

A head, bent back over a shoulder, searched him out. Found him.

Jesus!

There was the thump of a chair that had been on two legs returning to all four. The woman, Darryl's mother, sprang up, one hand to her throat, the other holding a mug at arm's length to keep the contents from spilling.

Avery brought himself fully into the kitchen the quicker to reassure her. It's all right, he said, there's nothing the matter, nobody hurt or sick. I just wanted a word about Darryl.

Darryl? the woman shouted accusingly past him.

Avery held up his palms.

No, no, I just wanted to ask if you'd let him play football.

The woman had snatched up her cigarette from the ashtray, held it poised for a fortifying gulp of smoke. And held it, and held it, her eyes seeming to swell the longer she stared at Avery. Then she burst out laughing. Do you not think you're a wee bit big? she asked.

When she had laughed herself out she got Avery a cup of tea. She could be five minutes late getting back to work for once. God knows, she said, they got their money's worth out of her.

As with her first utterance to him, she appeared entirely unconscious of the blasphemy, though if the truth were known Avery preferred this to the overplayed attempts at retrieval to which he was so often witness.

Sheila Kirkpatrick was probably of an age with him. Her face in repose bore the ravages of youthful acne, but when she smiled, and she smiled a lot, the pits and welts were recast as dimples and creases, amplifying the effect, so that within minutes of meeting her Avery had concluded she would be a lesser person without them.

The business of the football tournament was quickly settled.

Even before Avery had finished telling her about the neutral venue, at sports grounds in the south of the city, Sheila was giving in. He wasn't to get her wrong, she had nothing against her boys mixing with Catholics. (Admittedly this was not a novel construction in English as it was spoken in east Belfast.) Her Darryl was easily led. He would go along with anything if the rest of the crowd were at it and there were kids around here would start trouble in an empty room. She'd been through enough with the boys' father, thank you.

She said no more about the father and Avery didn't ask. There was not, that he could see, a trace of him about the house.

I'll be on hand throughout, he said. And there'll be other ministers and youth-club leaders there. We'll be on the lookout for any bother starting.

It was ten past one when Avery left the house with Sheila. The two smaller boys had gone into a neighbour's house. Darryl was kicking a football against the end wall of the row, which, as though in anticipation of a heavier ball to come, gave up brick- and cement-dust at every bounce.

People'll be thinking I've gone good living, Sheila said, as they came in sight of the main road. Her face pulled itself into a wide smile as though it were the funniest thing she could think of.

You should give it a go some time, Avery said. You never know, you might like it.

And she gave him a look then that was pure pantomime: *Cheeky!*

Forget Protestant and Catholic, forget high and low, *this* is the line along which today's Church divides.

The line was about ten inches long and stiff-looking. Reverend Norman Twiss held it between the pads of his index fingers, peering over the top at his new assistant seated on the far side of the table. Avery nodded, not knowing what to expect, not wanting to show that he didn't know. He was here in Holywood to assist and also to learn. Reverend Twiss raised his middle fingers, applying pressure, and the line slowly tilted into the second dimension. Sunlight on lamination. A bumper sticker? Avery squinted.

Oh, good grief.

He looked in alarm from the slogan to Reverend Twiss, hoping for a lead. Was his left eyebrow raised good-naturedly or was his right eyebrow lowered in a frown? Frown. No. Maybe. He looked at the slogan again.

Christians do it on their knees.

It's American, Reverend Twiss said, but that on its own was not enough of a clue.

Just say what you really think, Avery urged himself. And he very nearly did.

Actually, Reverend Twiss got there ahead of him, right eyebrow rising to the height of the left, I think it's pretty good. A bit of harmless fun.

Well, of course, when you looked at it like that. Avery nodded with more conviction.

And there was a serious point to Reverend Twiss's introductory joke. The religious life did not require you to be endlessly beating yourself up or, Heaven forbid, beating up other people. Avery relaxed into his assistant minister's role, relaxed into himself, losing some of the stiffness he had long mistaken for spiritual rectitude. He was well known and liked beyond his particular congregation, which he never lost an opportunity to try and increase. He had, he heard it said, a way with him and if that way was on occasion mildly flirtatious it was not as if it was his own embrace he was inviting anyone to enjoy.

He passed Sheila Kirkpatrick and a friend on the far side of the street a few days later. Sheila cupped a hand to her mouth and shouted to him, I'm still thinking over your offer, Reverend. She laughed. The friend looked pleasantly appalled.

And you know the great thing? Avery shouted back. It's always open.

4

At half past seven on the morning of the cross-community football tournament, Avery woke to torrential rain. Oh, brilliant, he said, to the bedroom window.

The phone beside the bed rang. Avery sat down to answer, still holding a corner of the curtain. Frances rolled herself on to her other side and covered her head.

It was Des.

I know, Avery said, I'm looking out at it now.

He listened.

Well, I don't know that there's anything we can do at this stage, he said. I'm not sure we'd even get our deposit back.

He remained on the edge of the bed a few moments after setting the phone down, sunk in gloom. Weeks of work they'd put into this. He imagined how disappointed the kids would be looking out of their windows, fearing the tournament would be called off, and in that moment regained his perspective on his own disappointment.

Chastened, he knelt by the bed, as he sometimes liked to do, to say his morning prayers. The bed creaked. When he opened his eyes, Frances was looking into them. You'll be drowned, she said.

Well, he pushed himself up into a crouch, at least I'll go down in a good cause.

Frances stretched out her arms to him. Do you think would they name a cup after you?

Avery lay on the bed beside his wife. Now, he said, mock stern, you know what a vanity it would be to speculate.

Their bellies touched. Behind hers the baby slumbered. On the other side of the bedroom wall, Ruth slumbered. Outside the rain came down in sheets.

An hour and a half later, and protesting to Avery every inch of the way, Ronnie the caretaker brought the minibus round to the front of the church where twenty-three kids in wet tracksuits waited to board. Eighteen boys and five girls. Ronnie counted them on with twenty-three tuts. Mind now and don't be dripping everywhere!

Beneath almost all the tracksuits, girls' and boys', could be seen the NTL sponsor's logo on one or other version of that season's Glasgow Rangers strip.

The girls were supposed to be competing in the 12–14 age group. Avery asked Karen, their team captain, what was the matter with the other two.

You really want to know? Karen asked, and behind her another girl giggled.

OK, Avery said, only a little too loud. Hands up, boys aged twelve to fourteen.

No way, said the boys, seeing what he was about.

Avery knew them by their tightly folded arms. He tapped two shoulders. Come on, he said, there's far too many of yous as it is.

One boy said he would rather get off the bus than play on the girls' team. Karen said she would rather get off the bus than have him. The bus, though, had already started, driving into the rain, away from the city. The argument carried on until the bus had turned south on the Outer Ring Road and passed the Forestside shopping centre, then silence descended.

Even for those who had been this far, here, two miles out of town from their houses, was the limit of the familiar world. Avery was reminded that for all their furious phoning and texting, his children were really only talking to themselves.

The rain had eased to merely heavy when the twenty-three kids, decidedly less boisterous, got off the bus two miles further on, outside the pavilion of the sports grounds, laid out at the top of a gentle slope down to the Lagan. (One of Avery's younger children refused to accept that this was the same river that flowed through the city centre.) Other minibuses, cars, even a couple of black taxis, were already parked, the kids who had arrived in them having wandered off – in groups, of course – to look at the football pitches, or taken cover under the overhang of the pavilion roof.

Avery spotted Des among a cluster of mainly boys in Glasgow Celtic tops. He also spotted something else. The letters on the chest of the Celtic jerseys. NTL. They were sponsored by the same company as Rangers.

Why was it so hard for people to believe that God didn't take sides either?

What do you think? he asked Des out the side of his mouth, in the sulky silence of the boys' changing rooms.

Bibs, said Des, and pointed to a large wicker basket of them beside the entrance to the showers. The brighter the better.

Bibs and welly-boots, Avery said.

Bibs and flippers.

A young Methodist couple whom Avery had last seen escorting a youth group at the Dundonald Ice Bowl proposed moving the tournament indoors. Half these kids, they said, wouldn't even have brought a towel. And half of them, said Des, wouldn't have the right shoes for indoors: they had been told they were going to be out on the grass. They could play in their sock soles, the Methodist man said. And do themselves an injury? said Des. And then, miraculously, some there were prepared to contend, the rain stopped, the day brightened.

The tournament kicked off, outdoors on four pitches simultaneously in an atmosphere of rising steam, just forty-five minutes late at eleven fifteen. The teams were organized into leagues of five or six so that each team was guaranteed at least a few matches before the winners played off. The second round of games had just started when Avery's own mobile phone rang.

Hello? he said, and the voice at the other end said, You've got to help me.

Larry? Avery walked away from the sidelines, hand to his ear. Are you all right?

I know where it happened.

Avery was looking down the valley. An ice-cream van was parked side-on to the white markings in a car-park beside a hump-backed stone bridge where the towpath began. The wet Tarmac shimmered in the sunshine. A dog coming out of the shallows fired diamonds off its pelt.

Are you there? Larry asked.

Yes. Where are you?

I'm here. I'm at the spot. I can't move.

There was a cheer at Avery's back. He turned. Karen was ruffling the hair of one of the boys assigned to her team. They were one–nil up.

Please, Larry's voice was like a child's, this is terrifying.

Avery apologized, there was just no way he could leave what he was doing. He asked Larry the name of the street; asked him wasn't there a café nearby where he could sit down, have a cup of coffee.

44

A dreadful sucking sound came out of the earpiece. At the same time another roar went up at Avery's back: two goals in a minute. The sucking sound was repeated. It was the sound of a man trying not to be overcome by tears.

Larry? What is it now?

There is a café, Larry said, but I can't go in. That's where I killed those people.

The kids were having a break between games. Platters of orange segments were passed round. The more careful bent back the skin and pulled the flesh off with their teeth. Most jammed them under their lips like gumshields, draining them of juice and flashing each other garish grins. Some of the boys had taken off their NTL shirts and went bare-chested under the coloured bibs. The girls, from whichever church or youth club they came, looked on, equally envious.

At the tea urn where the carers and coaches were gathered, Avery heard that the shop supplying the trophies and commemorative medals had messed up. Peter Lockhart from Belmont was going to have to drive into town to try and get it sorted out in time for the tournament ending this afternoon.

Avery flicked the last drops of his tea on to the grass, had a word with Ronnie, then Des. A message, he said to the first, not lying. To Des he elaborated that there was a man he needed to see who was in deep spiritual trouble. He told them both he wouldn't be long.

The kids were trooping towards the pitches again, separating according to the colour of their bibs. The young Methodist couple, sharing a bin-bag and a pair of marigolds, searched the ground for discarded orange peel, the wrappers from sweets the kids had brought themselves.

Peter Lockhart was six foot three or four. He had a little Hyundai hatchback into which he packed himself with what must have been a well-rehearsed set of movements. Avery, half a foot shorter and a good stone lighter, bumped himself off the door, the ceiling, the dashboard.

You haven't that shut right, Peter said, leaning across and opening and closing the passenger door. The window handle caught Avery's hip. There, that's better.

Peter talked most of the way into town about the loyalist feud. The Shankill Road had split in the middle. The UDA had claimed the lower end, the UVF the upper. Supporters of one or the other – their relatives, their friends, *their milkmen*, it seemed – caught on the wrong side of the divide were being encouraged to leave by having their houses wrecked, their belongings strewn about the street.

The big worry was that the feud would spread across the river to east Belfast.

There'll be mayhem, Peter Lockhart said, checking his rear-view mirror and moving out sharply to avoid a taxi parked on a double yellow line. *Idiot!*

Involuntarily, Avery remembered the phrase that was used to dismiss feud killings when he was growing up: tit-for-tit. Even now plenty of people would tell you the victims of such infighting were no great loss to anyone: a few less for the police to worry about.

Trying to ensure that every death – every life – was accorded equal significance remained one of the hardest battles to fight in this country. Never mind the country, in the clergy.

And what are you hearing yourself? he asked Peter. Will it spread?

They had arrived in the centre of town, at the lay-by in front of Principles, where Avery had asked to be dropped.

I think it would take a very little spark to make it. Peter smiled. Give it a good thump with your shoulder.

Avery looked at the door, did as he was bid and fell sideways on to the footpath.

He had half an hour. He also had half a notion that he wouldn't need anything like that long. He couldn't imagine that Larry would stand in the one spot all this time just to make his point, just on the off-chance that Avery would be able, as he said he would try, to get away.

But Larry was there. Down the narrow street he had named in the network of narrow streets behind the cathedral: the Cathedral Quarter, as no one but the developers and the council's tourism sub-committee was yet remembering to call it. He stood in the doorway of a solicitor's office, almost on top of the entry-phone, as though ready to call for sanctuary if the street threatened him any further.

Avery, coming at him from the blind side, past the street's only café ('Par, a little bit of Paris in Belfast'), said his name, and for a moment in turning Larry looked like he would faint.

Get me out of here, he said. Avery went to take his arm, but Larry shook his head firmly. Just walk beside me – on the outside of me. Not down that way, up here.

As they drew near to the end of the street Larry's shoulders hunched and his pace quickened lest the bogey overtake him. He practically ran the last few yards. He walked several streets more at speed before he would stop and talk to Avery. It was still lunchtime, not a seat to be had in any of the cafés and sandwich bars. They sat on a bench by the installation that monitored the city's air for pollutants.

I've no idea how I wound up down around there, Larry said. It's not even on my route, but something made me go that way instead. I should have known then. I thought as soon as I walked into the street – from the very first step I thought – this place is familiar.

It's a pretty well-used street these days, Avery said.

Larry was shaking his head. I was shivering.

It's shaded.

My head was burning. He tapped two fingers, hard, on his skull indicating the spot. That's always the signal, but I just kept walking, I don't think I could have turned round if I tried.

He stopped, hunching forward, brought his hands up in an awning over his eyes.

Two policemen strolled by. Pale green short-sleeved shirts, holsters on their hips. They nodded to Avery, as though in acknowledgement of an unspoken assurance that nothing was amiss here.

This maybe isn't the best place, Larry said, when they had passed.

Northern Ireland had the highest ratio of police officers to inhabitants in the entire western world. There weren't too many places where you were unlikely to bump into them.

Avery resisted the temptation to sneak a look at his watch. Larry bit his lip. His eyes shone.

All of a sudden, he said, as though there had been no interruption, I had an image of this woman. I heard her say, plain as day, Ach, now, son, don't. She was talking to me. I was outside the café. I looked in the window. There were two other women – two here-and-now women – looking back at me, wondering what I was gawping at. The woman in my head put her arms round the man she was with. His mouth was going, but he couldn't speak. There was another woman crying, Oh, Mummy, no. Oh, Mummy, no.

Oh, Mummy, no, a teenage boy coming within earshot mimicked, to the delight of his friends.

Maybe this wasn't such a good place right enough.

Everyone in the café was staring at me by this time, Larry went on regardless. The waiters and waitresses. Everyone. I must have looked a sight. His voice fell away. I must have looked like I'd seen a ghost.

Do you believe in ghosts? Spirits? It seemed to Avery as fruitful a line of inquiry as any.

No, Larry said. But I believe that memories come back to haunt you, even when someone has tried to erase them.

Some people, you know, would find that harder to believe in than ghosts, said Avery, glad to have got it out in the open. He glanced sideways at Larry to see how he reacted. Without blinking was the answer.

People don't know the half of it.

A clock bell chimed. If Avery didn't hurry he would miss his lift.

I just wonder if there's some other explanation for this, he said.

You mean you wonder whether I'm imagining things?

You don't strike me as someone who's capable of killing.

Larry was rooting in his pockets, pulling out several things that weren't before managing to locate a Kleenex. He laughed as he blew his nose. Have you watched the TV lately? Have you seen the boyos getting out of the cars up at Stormont? How many of them look like killers?

He inspected the contents of the Kleenex, folded the sides over, stood and walked the few feet to the nearest bin. He didn't sit again, but offered Avery his hand. Thank you for coming down. They might have been business colleagues parting after a productive meeting *al fresco*. It's probably best if I manage this on my own from now on.

Another bell chimed, out of time. Avery glanced down at his watch. A folded envelope, pocket-grime veining the creases, lay on the ground next to where Larry had been sitting, but in the seconds that it took Avery to bend and retrieve it Larry was already well down the street. He couldn't delay any longer. He stuffed the envelope into his pocket and ran in the opposite direction.

Peter Lockhart hadn't been waiting two minutes. He jerked a thumb over his shoulder at a cardboard box sitting on the back seat. All sorted, he said. Even threw in a player-of-the-tournament statuette by way of apology.

He asked Avery did he get what he needed done, but he was too busy watching for a break in the traffic to be really interested in his reply. When he spoke again it was to go back to their earlier conversation about the loyalist feud. Was there anything more the Church could do to wean the armed groups from violence? Or was the problem akin to the one afflicting the Northern Ireland football team: Premiership players on £30,000 a week being talked to by a manager on £30,000 a year? *What's in it for us to listen to you?*

He was still worrying over it when he turned the Hyundai into the sports grounds and passed the ambulance travelling the other way.

Before the pavilion, watching the ambulance go, Des and the rest of the adults stood like a buffer between two evenly matched groups of kids.

Something tells me we're too late for medals, Peter Lockhart said.

Avery was out of the car as soon as it stopped. Ronnie took

a step towards him and at once he knew. Was it one of our kids? What's happened?

There were voices talking all at once. He heard *wasn't him started it . . . she hardly even touched the wee fella . . . he's lucky his neck wasn't broke.*

Hold on, hold on, Avery said. Ronnie, Des, will one of yous tell me?

And Ronnie said, The wee lad Kirkpatrick.

Avery thought he was going to be sick.

They had just started the final lot of league games. A team from Avery's church was playing one of Des's. Two players went in for a ball, there was no malice, but they both went down clutching their legs.

And then, Des said, it just blew up. In twenty seconds, before any of us could get on the pitch to stop them, they were laying into each other.

Darryl Kirkpatrick wasn't even at the centre of it, but a girl who had been standing on the sidelines, supporting her boyfriend playing for the other team, pushed him – or pushed past him. He staggered back and stood on a ball.

Nearly did a somersault, said Des.

(Dislocated shoulder, said the ambulanceman.

I want to go home, said Darryl. I want to go home.)

The tournament had been abandoned. Right now there were probably people trying to work out how to segregate changing rooms. Des was driving back east, telling Avery in the passenger seat to stop torturing himself. Listen, it wouldn't have made a blind bit of difference if you had been there. There were nineteen of us and we could do nothing about it.

I said I'd look out for him. I went round to the house.

They had turned off the Outer Ring Road. They drove over a zebra crossing where one stripe in every three was red and one in every three blue, past a letterbox with a white midriff and a royal blue top.

Are you sure you don't want me to come with you and explain what happened? asked Des.

Thanks, but I'm sure.

Past the Tesco Metro, they turned off the main road, turned again into Avery's drive.

There was a note on the kitchen countertop with instructions to Avery if he got back and Frances and Ruth were not at home. Potatoes, tumble-dryer. Avery scribbled a few words of his own at the bottom. He had been, he was gone, he would return as soon as possible. Sorry about the potatoes and the tumble-dryer.

Des asked him one more time if he couldn't come with him, then reversed down the drive and sat at the side of the road until Avery had driven out.

He saw Sheila Kirkpatrick behind the counter the moment he got out of the car in one of the dried-up channels across the road from the laundrette. Her head was framed between two handwritten notices taped to the front window: Wednesday is Pensioners Day, and Band Uniforms Only £3.50. Fluorescent yellow, fluorescent orange. Waiting for the signal to cross, Avery watched her fold a duvet and force it into a blue polythene bag. She was still sorting out the duvet owner's change when Avery pushed open the door. Her eyes flicked towards him and away. Flicked back. The woman collecting her duvet asked what they charged for curtains and Sheila, with an uncertain smile over her shoulder, went in behind the flimsy partition between the counter and the dry-cleaning machines.

On a rack beside the door hung the clothes left in to be cleaned. End to end with this was a rack of clothes in transparent slips. The air was a potent mix of chemicals, sweat and cigarette smoke.

That's a better day, now, the woman said and tapped her cigarette against the rim of a pink tin ashtray.

Much better, said Avery, though it was far from what he was thinking.

Sheila reappeared. It's twelve fifty a pair up to seven foot six, fifteen pounds for anything over that.

Anything over seven foot six I'd be hanging them from the upstairs down.

The woman left her cigarette in her mouth while she took a firm hold on the bag with the duvet in it. Be a dote and get the door for me, she told Avery.

Avery was a dote. As he turned back to face the counter Sheila's smile failed her altogether. What are you doing here so early? Where's Darryl?

Avery sighed.

Oh, my God, she said.

He's had a fall, Avery said. His shoulder. They've taken him to the City.

Oh, my God.

I can drive you over there. He's going to be all right.

Avery was at the counter now. Sheila was pressing her hands on its chipped and gouged surface, perhaps to stop her doing something with them she'd regret.

When she spoke again her voice was collected. I want to know exactly what happened.

There was a scuffle, said Avery, unable to lie.

I thought you told me you'd cut anything out before it started.

Avery opened his mouth, but could find no words. His cheeks filled with air and he blew it out slowly, audibly.

Sheila Kirkpatrick made a sudden move behind the partition, returned without her overall and carrying her purse and cigarettes. She opened the till and took from it a ten-pound note. Don't bother yourself about the lift, I can take a taxi.

Look, Avery said, stepping towards her as she came out from behind the counter.

Sheila raised a hand. Look nothing. I'm perfectly all right on my own.

She had the door open.

What about here? Is there anyone I can ring to come and cover?

There's nobody, Sheila said. I'll let you stand there and explain to people why they can't leave their cleaning in this afternoon.

Guy Broudie insisted on Avery talking to the church's solicitor first thing the next morning. The wee boy's Granddad Kirkpatrick had a reputation in those parts for his cantankerousness and his choice connections. He had already been on the phone ranting and raving. Flipping outrageous that youngsters should be exposed to that kind of danger. Whose bright idea was it anyway? And where was the Reverend Avery when the *assault* occurred?

It's not a matter of if they'll sue, Guy said, but when and on what grounds.

The solicitor sat in expensive silence, turning the pages of Avery's hastily written account. Hm, he said, and was silent for several minutes more. He got up, left the room, went into another room across the corridor; returned, eventually.

OK, he said, this is the way I see it. At the lower end of the scale there's a personal-injury claim. So at the very least you could be looking at a substantially increased premium next year. At the upper end, well, the supervisor-to-child ratio may technically have been correct even without you there, but it is possible to argue that you were derelict in your duty of care for your own group. It could all depend on how they interpret your *care*taker's presence: was he acting on your behalf?

I believe at the time he was wiping the upholstery in the minibus, Avery said truthfully.

The solicitor raised his eyebrows, Guy lowered his.

That could turn out to be a very costly errand you did, he said, outside the solicitor's door, inviting an explanation Avery did not feel able to give.

Frances too was perplexed. I can't believe you going off like that.

They were lying in bed, one hundred feet from the electricity substation, nine hours from Ruth's first day at school, neither able to sleep.

I told you, it was an emergency.

It would need to be.

You said.

And you still haven't.

What?

Said. Who it was you had to see.

Avery found her hand and squeezed it. I can't.

He felt her hand grow limp.

Why?

You know. I just can't.

5

Avery batted the idea backwards and forwards for a few days then went to the library. *A* library. He decided against the one nearest his house. He wanted to be able to browse for a while uninterrupted.

In fact he found what he was looking for in next to no time.

A book had been published the previous year, a chronology, with details of all the people killed in the thirty-three years since 1966. It was a work of great integrity and restraint, entirely without sensationalism or sentimentality, a labour of the authors' true love for their fellow Northern Irish men and women. It was also one of the fastest-selling books in Belfast's history. Rumour had it that in certain parts of the city centre there were people who would steal you a copy to order, guaranteed delivery fifteen minutes maximum.

Avery wasn't sure why he hadn't bought a copy himself. He had picked it up in Waterstone's and, of course, the first entry he looked up was Joanna's. Civilian, Protestant, 24, married, youth worker. Died Armagh.

What surprised him was how outwardly calm he managed to remain as he read of her leaving home after a minor disagreement with her husband and driving to the lough shore. A couple who had been courting in the area caught her for a moment in their headlights as they drove away, leaning on the bonnet of her car. Some time later the shots were heard and the next morning her body was found.

Where the authors of the book knew the organization

responsible for a killing they named it; where the killers themselves had since died, they named them too. Sometimes they had to use best guess, based on the area, the circumstances, the methods employed. Very occasionally, though, they had to admit they had no clear idea who could have carried out a particular murder. Joanna's was one such.

Avery had closed the book to the flyleaf and stood for a moment nodding as though considering the price, then set it back on the pile and walked out of the shop. And walked. And walked.

Now in the library he took a well-thumbed copy to a table by a window and opened it at the index of place names. The street where he had met Larry merited two mentions.

The first reference, when he turned it up, was clearly not related to Larry's nightmare visions. A British soldier killed by a car bomb, spring 1972. IRA, the authors were in no doubt. All the same, Avery felt compelled to read the entry through to the end. Anything less would have been pornographic.

A call had been made, a codeword given, but the warnings were vague. The soldier had been helping clear the street and was standing beside the car when it blew apart. Eighteen, just engaged, from Solihull. Security sources indicated that the bomb-maker had killed himself later the same year lifting a device into the boot of a car.

Avery blinked, an instant prayer. Blinked a second time, frowning at the omission: two deaths to mourn. He turned back to the index. The library window was a picture of Ormeau Park: stone wall, wrought iron, leaves past their peak. There was abroad that quiet specific to the schools having just gone back. He paused with his finger under the street name. Did he really want to go on with this? He asked himself, though, what the alternative was.

An old boy in a sky-blue windcheater pulled out the chair across the table and, taking his glasses from their case, opened a copy of the *NME*. He did not look like a derelict, was definitely reading the stories on the inside cover. He stopped, dipped his chin to see Avery over his glasses.

I'm sorry, was there somebody sitting here?

Avery shook his head, turned the pages, read.

April 1976. Café Par then was a bar, Ellis's. It was half past eight on a slow Tuesday evening. There were only three customers in the bar, two women and a man, when a youth in a parka entered, hood up, woollen scarf over his mouth and nose, and, producing a gun, demanded the takings. The manager handed over the money from the till. The gunman said he wanted everything and the manager went into the back room, saying he would get more. No sooner was he out of the bar, though, than he heard one of the women say, Ach, son, don't, and then there was a shot and the other woman called for her mother and there were more shots. In the back room, the manager tried to ring 999, but his fingers felt too thick for the telephone dial. His legs were like lead. When at last he was able to drag himself back into the bar, the gunman was gone and his customers were all three dead. The money from the till was sitting where the manager had left it on the bar.

The women who died were Catholics, the man with them was Protestant. A brother of one of the women had been interned for suspected IRA membership; the man had spent some time in jail for handling stolen goods and was thought to have had links in the past with the UVF. He was having an affair with the second woman who had lived only two streets away from him before the Troubles. This was not a time for complicated relationships. They could have fallen foul of any number of organizations. Or then again, the gunman might have been intent only on robbery. (He had apparently acted alone.) The scarf might have slipped from his face when the manager was in the back room and, fearing one of the customers would recognize him, he might have fired almost without thinking, then panicked, fired again and again, and fled without the money.

The entry concluded with almost the same words as concluded Joanna's: one of the most baffling episodes in the three decades of violence.

The manager of the bar never worked again. He said he couldn't get the words of those two women out of his head.

A motorized lawnmower had started up over the road in the park. Under its noise, Avery still heard Larry's voice as he sat with him beside the pollution monitor.

Oh, Mummy, no.

He closed the book and rested his hands on the cover, uncertain what he ought to do next.

The old boy across the way was studying him again over the rims of his glasses. Everything all right? he asked. On the table in front of him, the *NME* was open at the charts pages.

I'm fine, said Avery. Just a little . . .

The old boy nodded. I know, he said. My son's in there. October the fifteenth 1974.

I'm very sorry, said Avery. For some reason he was unable to take his eyes off the sky-blue windcheater.

Long time ago now, the old boy said. There was not a trace of bitterness or self-pity in the voice. He licked a finger and turned the page of his paper. Long, long time ago, he said again, and his eyes began their slow descent of the first column of print.

Before driving away from the side-street where he had

parked, Avery phoned Tony to see was he free tomorrow for lunch. (Lunch? Tony laughed. Do they still have that out there in the real world?) Then he rang Frances and told her he'd pick Ruth up from school. She was only doing mornings for the first month, though it seemed to be enough for her. So far when she got home she would talk all through lunch, eating only when she was reminded to, then fall asleep for half the afternoon. She might have slept the other half too if they hadn't woken her to keep her from ruining her night's sleep.

There were no other fathers waiting outside the school. The mothers all seemed to know each other. They clammed up at Avery's approach. One woman from his church cupped in her hand the cigarette she had been about to light. Avery wanted to tell her to stop being ridiculous. Instead he smiled, said, Lovely day, asked had the bell already gone, which was the precise moment that the bell did go. The parents turned as one to face the railings. Soon the playground to the side of the main building began to fill with children so excited at being let out they didn't know which way to run first. They darted here, they darted there. Two girls stood before one another and bounced. Through this mêlée, Miss Peters, newly graduated from Stranmillis College, dressed in carpenter's trousers and a pink T-shirt, led a line of infants, who held on tight to each other's hands and looked with awe at the seven- and eight-year-olds roaring around them.

Ruth was third from the last in the line arriving at the gate, her schoolbag sticking out on either side of her, like a suitcase strapped to a grown-up's back. She had on her serious face, which grew more serious still when she picked out Avery.

What have you got there? he asked, bending to her head height.

60

She handed him a paper plate painted blue and stuck haphazardly with cotton wool.

Did you do this all yourself? Isn't that great, the clouds and everything?

Ruth nodded as well as a child could whose chin was resting all this time on her chest.

Avery brushed strands of hair from her face, touched her forehead with the back of his hand. Are you OK, sweetheart?

Again the constrained nod.

Miss Peters was holding the hand of a child whose parent had not yet arrived. She called across to Avery. Not quite herself today. Think she misses you-know-who.

Will we go and see Mummy, then? Avery asked, to no response.

He strapped his daughter into the booster seat for the short drive home. She sat with her head pressed against the padded side, hands flat on her lap. Despite all his attempts to draw her out, she didn't utter a word until they were stopped in the driveway. Daddy, she said then, did you hurt a wee boy's arm?

Avery spun round in his seat. Ruth was squinting out the side window. A cold wave washed over him as he thought she might be frightened.

Did I hurt a what? Who said that to you?

Ruth shrugged. Just people.

Avery took his time undoing his seat-belt and going round to Ruth's door to help her out. He wanted to get his answer right for her. He crouched on the gravel.

A boy fell when Daddy was supposed to be looking after him. It was an accident. He managed at last to catch his daughter's eye. And if people say anything like that to you again you tell your teacher. OK?

Still the serious face but, OK, she said.

She was walking ahead of him to the front door when she turned. As well, they called you a bad word, she said, and ran inside.

At a rough guess, I would say it was supposed to be Fenian, Avery said.

Ronnie had been waiting for him when he arrived at the church for a meeting of the finance committee. Avery followed his caretaker up the north side of the church to the back of the Robinson Hall (the Big Hall, as it was more often known), where there was a three-foot space between the wall and the thick privet separating the church grounds from the street. The graffiti had been painted so recently it was still wet to the touch: Feenin love.

Feenin love *squiggle*, to be precise.

They must have heard me coming and run before they could finish putting the *r* on the end, Ronnie said.

Or *rs*, said Avery. I mean, usually if it was singular they would write, So-and-so is a. Wouldn't they?

My specialist subject, Magnus, the syntax of sectarianism.

Youngsters, said Ronnie, making it sound like the diminutive of gangsters. He pushed aside the foliage at random, searching for breaks in the hedge. We should have barbed wire in this. We used to have barbed wire.

It was not Avery but his predecessor who, on chancing to discover this fact, had determined that barbed wire and churches did not sit well together. They should be concentrating their energies on getting people in, he said, rather than keeping them out. Avery had had to do no more than agree to carry on the policy.

Do you think we should phone the police? he asked.

No point, said Ronnie flatly. It'll only be harder to clean if we wait on them coming. Which was Ronnie's way of saying that these days there was too little of the barbed wire in the police force as well.

Avery usually looked forward to finance-committee meetings. The church was in difficulties, of course. It went with the territory. What Luther had begun, television and the internet had completed. Christianity was the most deregulated of industries. Only cults made money any more. There was, though, a comfort in pages of figures. No matter how great the challenge before you it was at least measurable. Who knows? Even solvable.

Tonight, however, the faces round the table in the committee room were more than usually grim.

The freewill offering is slightly up on the same time last year, Avery remarked at one stage.

Last year's was the lowest ever August total, Guy Broudie said.

Still, we've stopped going *backwards*.

Mervyn Armstrong, the youngest member of the committee, cleared his throat, the better to strike a positive note. If you look year-on-year we're actually up four months in the last five.

Guy Broudie shook his head. We have to face facts. You should know it better than anyone, Minister, we're looking very vulnerable to contingency.

Ah, yes, Avery thought, watching the frown return to young Mervyn's face, contingency. Instructions had come from the solicitors acting for Sheila Kirkpatrick, or her father-in-law, that Avery was not to attempt to visit the boy in hospital.

Has there been any more word on that front? he asked.

The wee fella will miss the first two weeks of school. Disruption to his education, they'll say. It all mounts up.

Over the silence that followed, Avery heard the rhythmic sound of scrubbing out the back of the Big Hall. Ronnie still going at the wall.

Come in!

Tony was standing over by the window, weight thrown forward on to his crutch, but when he saw Avery he cast the crutch aside and came staggering across the room to meet him. It's a miracle! It's a miracle!

Better, is it? said Avery.

Tony stopped in his tracks, hoisted a trouser leg, showed Avery what looked like a grey nylon sock. Just got to wear this thing for another week or two.

They sat. Avery set a bag next to a Meccano helicopter on the table between them. I brought you a sandwich.

Not from over east, I hope.

Did you not know? We've restaurants now and everything.

Tony whistled, looked inside the bag. His expression said whatever it was wouldn't kill him. He asked how Frances was.

Frances was remarkable, considering. And Michele?

Michele, considering how long she still had ahead of her, was almost constantly out of sorts. Michele, Tony was afraid to have to say, was not one of nature's stoics.

Ah, now, said Avery, if it was us . . .

If it was us we'd have made good and sure we could grow them in laboratories by now. Tony dragged his leather swivel chair round to the side of his desk. Don't tell me, bad taste.

Avery rolled his eyes. For dear sake, Tony, how long have you known me?

Tony brought the Meccano helicopter towards him and inspected it for a moment or two as though he had never

64

before set eyes on it. What he was doing, Avery knew, was trying not to smile at his own mischievousness. He batted a propeller blade with the flat of one finger. The propeller barely budged. He batted again. It didn't move at all. He pushed the helicopter away.

Avery remembered walking into the manager's office at the university branch and handing him Tony's file. Remembered, as he turned to leave, Tony's winking at him, as for some reason now he winked at Tony, who laughed, seemed to let go a little tension.

So you're still working on your sermon? he said.

My what?

Your memory sermon. Or don't tell me you forgot.

No, said Avery, I'll tell you what it is.

He stopped. Tony had picked up a Dictaphone and was turning it over in his hands. Avery thought for a moment he saw a red light.

You'll tell me what it is? Tony said, then when Avery still didn't continue, Hello?

Sorry, busy morning.

Tony set the Dictaphone on the desk – it was, of course, switched off – and took a sandwich from the bag. You want half of this?

Avery shook his head. I've had something, thanks.

Tony nodded, took a bite out of the sandwich.

So, about a month ago a certain person came to see me, Avery said. A bit distraught. Very distraught. Claimed he was having problems remembering things.

Tony swallowed. Elderly? He took another bite.

Middle-aged. Forty-fiveish.

Forgetting things?

No, remembering. Well, both.

Avery stopped. He wasn't making a very good job of this. Some part of him was still trying to avoid using Larry's words for fear of how he might look simply for repeating them. Clearly, though, they were the only words adequate.

This person, to cut a long story short, believes his memory was wiped, deliberately.

Tony let his mouth fall open in an exaggerated, sandwich-flecked show of incomprehension.

I'm only saying what he said, Avery went on. His brain was operated on.

Tony tossed the sandwich on to the bag. How?

He didn't say.

Well, there'd be scarring for a start.

Avery drew a line with his finger: *I saw it there*. Tony said nothing.

But, whatever happened, Avery said, some of the memory started coming back.

None of it good, I'm guessing, said Tony.

No.

No. People never come to see you with happy memories. These are particularly bad.

Things done to him?

Things he did.

Ah.

A shooting, in the seventies.

Even without the detail, Tony was grimacing. The Northern Irish seventies were one long horror movie. It had been the business of many of Tony's generation to grow as far away from them as they could manage. His hand drifted back towards the helicopter. He flicked the side with his nail, patience wearing thin.

Sounds like head injury to me. A tumour, even. Any trauma

at all to the brain can cause problems: amnesia, schizophrenia, fantasy . . . He was telling them off on lazy fingers.

Avery halted the list. Some of what he told me about the shooting tallies.

With what?

That book that came out last year, you remember.

All the deaths? Again, the slight grimace.

Yes.

Tony sat forward. And the things he told you are written up in there?

Avery could see where this would lead. He wondered at his stupidity in not getting there by himself before dialling Tony's number yesterday.

Are you sure, Tony said, bank manager to Avery's student, tallies is the word you're looking for?

Tony hauled himself out of his chair and stumped round behind the desk, where he pulled open a drawer, then closed it, not finding whatever he was looking for. There are a lot of damaged people walking about this city, he said. The ones who don't choose us to talk to choose you.

Avery too got up. He hadn't in truth expected to hear anything different, still less wanted to. He thanked Tony for his time, asked for his love to be given to Michele, as Tony's was to be given to Frances and to Ruth.

He turned at the door. I'm sure this looks a bit foolish, he said.

Not at all, said Tony. I mean theoretically it would be possible to tamper. It's Cold War stuff, isn't it? But you'd have to ask yourself why, even if it could be done, it would be done to some bozo here.

Which was really not the note that Avery needed to conclude on.

Besides, Tony said – Avery had one foot in the corridor – I'm pretty sure that's the wrong place for a scar.

That was a bit better. More than a bit.

Thanks, he said.

Des it was had told Avery the story of the best man's brother at a wedding he had conducted. The reception was in one of those places, whose names Avery always confused, out the road to the international airport: motoring lodges once upon a time, extended and extended through the fifties and sixties and, in nearly every case, bombed in the seventies and eighties and more or less substantially rebuilt since. Whichever of these the reception was in, Des had not been there for some years. He knew the bride's father fairly well. He let himself be persuaded to stay on a while after the meal. Quite a while, in fact. At some stage he was making his way through the foyer from the toilets when he came across the best man and the best man's brother smoking side by side on the rim of a blue-lit fountain. Des asked could he join them. He hadn't congratulated the best man properly on his speech, which had been funny without being near the bone as so many best-man speeches seemed to be these days. Anyway they chatted, Des at first standing and then sitting down. He accepted a cigarette: My one for the year, he told them, told Avery.

He watched with the brothers the people, dressed for a Saturday night, come out of the dark to the yellow light before the automatic doors. Inside there were lights tucked into the plaster on the walls as well as in the ceiling, lights in the floor beneath their feet. Stars, Des thought, and not just of the lights. He had a memory of sitting out here once on a greasy maroon and blue striped sofa, of a revolving door that grated on the ground.

Some changes here all the same, he said, and the best man said, Talk to the brother here.

Why? said Des, leaning out. Did you do the building work?

The brother looked the other way.

No, said the best man, it was him that bombed it. Did five years, didn't you, our kid?

Five and a half, the brother said.

They smoked their cigarettes. The best man exhaled a mirthless laugh. Dough bag, he said.

The brother shrugged off the ribbing, went back to watching the people coming and going through the constellation of lights.

And the thing about it is, said Des to Avery, prison had been the making of the fella. GCSEs, A levels, Open University. I'm looking at him wondering is this guy a bad example or a good example of a bad one reformed. It's a test of vocabulary half the time as much as morality. You never know to look at anybody the things they might have done.

It had been in Avery's mind to give Des a call after he had been to see Tony, but it *had* been a busy morning – it was a busy time of the year all round. He would leave it for another day.

Lou Reed was in the Ulster Hall that Sunday night. Avery was a big – if nowadays a somewhat closet – fan. There was, of course, no question of him and Frances going, though even if he had been given special Sunday-night dispensation Avery, after two services and an afternoon of visits to the housebound, was far too tired. He dozed off on the settee listening to the Velvet Underground, third album. 'Jesus', 'Beginning to See the Light', 'I'm Set Free'. Music to nourish any soul. He woke at half one. The house was silent, even the substation seemed to be generating a brand of night-time electricity, noise-free. He stood on the back step, trying to detect the change of season in the air; he walked in bare feet from room to room, downstairs and up-, a pilgrimage of thanksgiving for this house, this unlooked-for life.

On Monday morning he went to put on the trousers he had been wearing the day of the football tournament. Something fell from one of the pockets, a piece of paper, *an envelope*, folded in three. He opened it out as he walked to the wastepaper bin. Then stopped. This wasn't his. The name meant nothing to him, in fact he wasn't sure he could even read the forename properly, but he knew the street all right. The stamp was unfranked. He hesitated a moment before he looked inside. Nothing.

It was some moments more before he remembered where it had come from. In the panic over Darryl Kirkpatrick it had completely slipped his mind.

Two more steps and he would be at the bin.

He took one of them.

I'm *pretty* sure, Tony had said.

He took the other step.

Pretty.

PART TWO

I

Before Belfast rediscovered its river and, alongside it, the pleasures of inner-city apartment dwelling (or at least of dwelling in inner-city apartments where damp, crap workmanship and vandalism did not come fitted as standard), the roads radiating southwards from the university had offered those of its citizens who could afford it the closest approximation to the modern urban-village experience. Even now when the hunger for hi-spec flats was so great developers were beginning to eyeball city-centre car-parks, the two- and three-bedroom Victorian terraces off the Stranmillis and Lisburn Roads changed hands for the price of a profitable farm west of the Bann, of an entire row east of the Lagan, and located their owners within a stone's throw of some of the city's best all-day-and-nightlife.

Or, in the case of the house that Avery was currently watching from the window-seat of a coffee place on the Stranmillis Road, within spitting distance.

The Place, the place was called, a rival back formation from the *ur*-Belfast café-diner the Other Place, of which (so successful was the original) there were now several around this part of the city. The Place was fitted out entirely in unadorned MDF and smelt strongly of something Avery finally worked out, as the umpteenth glass of frothing tea wafted past him, was cardamom.

Avery sipped his sparkling water and turned the pages of the *Daily Mail*. He had already turned the pages of the *Guardian* and the *Irish Times* and the two local morning papers. He had already sat here once before, the Wednesday of the previous week, turning pages, sipping water, wondering what exactly that smell was. In all that time he had seen no one come or go from the fourth house in the street that opened on the other side of the road.

He had knocked first, of course, the previous time and today. He had stepped back from the door and looked at the upstairs windows, which showed him both times bits and bobs of early-autumn sky. He was not skulking, not spying. (He was not wearing his clerical collar, it's true, but that was not *so* unusual.) If the curtains hadn't been drawn downstairs he would have walked right up and peered in.

Is that empty? A waitress lifted his glass and shook the waterlogged lemon. Can I get you another?

Avery looked at his watch. Almost five o'clock. No, I'm all right, he said.

The woman sitting next to him at the window-seat asked him was he finished with the *Mail*.

Sorry, he said, looking at her, looking at the paper, surprised by the presence of both. Take it.

Can I ask you something else? she said then. Why are you so interested in my house?

He told her he was a minister. He added what it seemed he was fated always to have to add, that she wasn't to worry, there was nothing wrong. The moment he spoke Larry's name, though, she was rummaging in her bag for her purse. If you don't mind, I'd rather not have this conversation here.

Where did you see him? she asked, in the hallway of the house.

They were the first words she had spoken since they left the café.

At my church, Avery said. He came and talked to me a couple of times.

The woman glanced at the letters she had picked up from the tiled floor, put one in her coat pocket and ripped another in two, in four. Avery had stepped aside to let her close the door after him so was further down the hall than she was.

Your church? she said, as though only just hearing.

Across the river, Avery said, east Belfast. I thought maybe he had people over that way.

She looked at him a few seconds longer, then pointed to the front room. Go on in.

The room was a knock-through, thrice as long as it was broad, a settee to the left of the door facing a fire surround of cobalt blue and a settee to the right along the end wall, beyond a second fireplace with ruby-coloured tiles. There was a piano on this side of the room, dust on its lid and no stool before it. Avery sat on the side with the blue fire, where the wide-screen TV and hi-fi were. Two separate luminous displays reminded him how late he was already.

The woman drew up an upholstered wicker chair between the fireplaces. She had unbuttoned her coat but not removed it. She wore a skinny-ribbed jumper underneath. Teacher, Avery would have said, without so much as a book in sight to support it.

I suppose he's been filling your head with stuff about me, she said.

No, said Avery, then thought better for the moment of explaining how he had come by her address. Nothing bad, anyway.

I had to ask him to leave, she said. Did he tell you that? Her chin was tilted up, like she was daring Avery to have a go at her.

Really, he said and glanced down at his hands crossed between his knees, he told me very, very little.

She looked down at her own lap, transferred the unopened letter from one pocket to the other. No, she said, as though he had tried to contradict her. It was getting too scary.

I understand, Avery said, and her chin came up again, a smile balanced precariously on top, and he wasn't sure that he did understand after all.

She got up and went into the kitchen. The fridge door opened and closed; a cutlery drawer. A cork was pulled. She appeared in the doorway, with a bottle of white wine and two glasses, asked was he a drinking or a non-drinking minister.

Non- today, he said, and she said she was sorry she'd nothing else but tap water.

Avery's kidneys couldn't have coped. I'm fine, he said.

She poured herself a glass and walked down the room to the window. She opened the curtains, then, clearly unimpressed by what she saw, closed them again.

Avery didn't know how to frame the necessary questions. *Do you believe your former partner is guilty of multiple murder? How did you react the first time he told you someone had been meddling with his memory?*

Instead he said, This is very rude of me, I haven't really . . . Ken Avery's my name.

Elspet Grey, she said.

Elspet? (So that was the name on the envelope.)

Yes, she said wearily. Elspet. Bane of my life. Everyone I'm ever introduced to, the same expression: Else-*what*? Mind you, I got off lightly. I've a sister called Morag and a brother Hamish.

Family Scottish? asked Avery.

My father wished. He packed us off there at every opportunity when we were kids to hang around with the Alisons and Johns and all the other Scottish people with normal names.

She sat down again, sipped her wine, smiled thinly. It's funny. One of the things Larry and I had in common: wannabe fathers. Mine was obsessed with Scotland, Larry's was obsessed with the Wild West. Liked his friends to call him Duke – you know, like John Wayne? And the worst of it was when Larry was small he thought his father really was a duke. Well, of course, when you're that age . . .

There was more warmth now in the smile.

Avery struggled to imagine Larry the boy falling prey to so innocuous a misapprehension.

How was he looking when you saw him? Elspet asked.

Avery had nothing against which to measure the Larry he had seen.

A bit – he laid especial emphasis on the word – *haunted*.

Elspet didn't pick up on it. And did he say where he was living?

No, but he must still be working somewhere in town, because . . .

Elspet laughed.

What's wrong?

Work? Larry? Larry hasn't had a job in all the years I've known him.

Avery glanced round the room.

I don't know what you're looking at, said Elspet. There's not a stick in this house he paid for.

Avery asked if he might have a small drop of wine after all.

Of course, when he had had a moment or two to gather his

thoughts he couldn't point to anything Larry had said or done that day in town to mislead him into thinking he was working. He just didn't look like – whatever else he looked like – a man who wasn't.

He has a PO box I send cheques to, Elspet said. I put an envelope in with each one, stamped and all. It can be two or three weeks before it comes back, or it can be a couple of months. I don't even look inside, I know there won't be anything there. The envelope is the message. He needs money.

They were sitting now on the settee at the end of the room with the ruby-tiled fireplace, next to the kitchen.

I don't feel good about it, Elspet said, but he was getting more and more unpredictable. I just couldn't cope.

He certainly says some extraordinary things, Avery said.

The operations on the brain?

Avery nodded, relieved of sole ownership of the story.

It's not entirely invented. He came off a motorbike one night, a lot of years ago. He'd been at a party, he'd no helmet on. They'd to put a steel plate in his skull. He was in a terrible state apparently.

Apparently? said Avery.

What?

Did you not see him after the accident?

I didn't even know him then, not for another eighteen months. He was still having treatment, but. That's how we met. I was taking a year out. My father had fixed me up with voluntary work in a convalescence home just outside Edinburgh. He was an awful nice big fella, Larry, quiet. You'd never have dreamt any of this.

Avery raised the glass to his lips. Held it there.

Is there something the matter? she asked.

He sipped. Just thinking.

And?

Well, you didn't know him when he was supposed to have had the crash.

What do you mean, supposed to? I saw him in the home.

Eighteen months later.

Oh! Elspet stood up, struck her thigh with her right fist. I can't believe I've let you get me into talking like this.

I didn't mean . . . said Avery, but she had left the room.

He heard her upstairs. He heard something being dragged, perhaps from under a bed. A minute later she swung round the door with a Linn hi-fi box. She thumped it down on the floor in front of him and began sorting through. He saw bank statements, used chequebooks, letters bundled together with elastic bands.

Here. She reached out an A4 envelope, read the contents pencilled on the front – No, that's not it – put it back and pulled out an identical envelope: Here. Every letter he ever got from the hospital, every doctor's appointment, every blood test, urine test, every damned thing.

Avery looked into the envelope's open mouth. Listen, he said.

She shook her end of the envelope. Take it!

Avery sat forward in his seat and she started to cry.

He saw himself out. It was a quarter past six when he got into the car, parked on the Stranmillis Road. He turned the key in the ignition then turned it back again. She had said for him to go, but even so he wondered about leaving her on her own like that. He closed his eyes a few moments, felt his decision being made. He got out of the car and ran back down to the house, nearly tripping over the lead of a dog crouched with its behind off the kerb at the corner of the street. The dog yelped, its concentration broken. The owner, an elderly woman in a felt hat, carried a nappy sack with the handle of a blue plastic spade sticking out the top.

He stood on the doorstep for close on five minutes waiting for Elspet to answer. He thought toilet, he thought bath, but it was the thought of something worse that kept him there, knocking.

The windows now offered him a purplish-tinted version of the sky.

She's away on out, said a voice behind him.

Avery turned. The old woman in the felt hat stood at the gate. The bag looked fuller, the dog emptier, happier.

Oh, said Avery. He checked his watch again. He couldn't have been gone more than two or three minutes before making up his mind to come back. She would have to have left practically on his heels.

I'm glad I saw her, said the woman, chivvying the dog, turning from the gate. I was starting to wonder was there anyone living there at all.

I'm sorry, Frances said, her hand stroking her neck as she peered at him beneath the kitchen light, do I know you?

Avery rubbed his own neck. Come on, I don't *always* wear it out.

Oh, is this one of those days doesn't end in a *y*?

Avery took her in his arms and bent his face to hers. The baby kicked him to the left of his groin. He flinched. Frances stopped kissing him. You've been drinking, she said. The discovery clearly amused her. Now I have a husband just like the other women's. Dressing oddly, coming in late, stinking of drink.

I had half a glass of wine, Avery said.

That's half a glass more than you've ever had with me in the daytime. Who's the lucky girl, then?

I'm a lucky girl! Ruth said.

She was sitting at the kitchen table where she had just finished, an hour after starting, a tea of sausages, waffles and broccoli. The sausages and waffles were essentially decoys for the broccoli, the strawberry and vanilla Petit Filou, whose pot she was now inspecting for remnants, her reward. She knew, because she prayed to God before every meal that she might never forget them, that there were everywhere little girls and boys not lucky enough to have sausages and waffles and Petit Filou, even broccoli.

Avery kissed her forehead. What all did they teach you today?

It was what his own father had asked him every day when he came in from work. Avery was in his teens before he realized his father was joking: he wasn't really expected to recite it all.

Ruth frowned to remember. Already school was an age away. We had a song, she said.

A song!

Ruth sang. Frog went a-courting he did ride, crambo.

What *is* crambo? she asked.

Nothing, said Avery, a song word.

Frances passing behind him whispered in his ear: I'm waiting, you know. Don't think I've forgotten.

Frances forgot. There were high winds that night. The old house creaked and sighed. Ruth was hard to settle. She wanted stories, company. Frances's mother phoned. Michele phoned. Avery went to his study and didn't come out till near eleven. No need to commit or omit. Frances was already asleep.

The following morning Avery and his collar went with her

to the Royal for her monthly check. With having to leave Ruth to school and drive half-way across the city the earliest appointment they could make was ten o'clock. They had been warned at their first, nine a.m., appointment (how long ago that seemed) to avoid if they could ten o'clock. The waiting room was chock-a-block. The waiting room was a head-on collision between chance and planning. There were pregnant school-age girls with their mothers, there were women who looked like they could already be grandmothers, there were women with toddlers, women with friends, there were couples embracing front to back in the queue before the desk, there were couples looking tired, bored, irascible, couples, like them, just looking for somewhere to sit.

The mother of one of the schoolgirls gave up a seat for Frances beneath a warning about smoking in pregnancy. I won't say no, Frances said.

I remember what it was like myself, the woman said, with a nod to her daughter, and walked off to search through the magazines on the central table.

When are you due? Frances asked the girl.

New Year's Eve, she said, with just a touch of my-rotten-luck, her gaze drifting towards Avery.

Avery was used to being stared at in these situations. Sometimes he turned it to his advantage, engaging the starers in conversation. *What was it exactly they found hard to imagine? Would it surprise them to know that a healthy sex life was not the opposite of the religious life but its perfect complement?* Other times, like this time, standing by Frances's shoulder, he did nothing but keep his half-smile fixed.

The names of mothers-to-be were called, seats were vacated and occupied the next second by whoever was at the head of the queue at Reception. A man and a woman and their pre-school daughter joined the far end. The child spoke French to her mother, English to her father. The mother and father didn't exchange a single word. A woman left a side room wiping her eyes. Avery's eyes and dozens of others followed her to the door. A midwife swung herself round the frame of another door reading aloud from a chart. Frances Avery? And someone somewhere in the room said, Tweet-tweet.

The baby was lying slightly lateral, its bottom almost directly under the right side of Frances's ribcage.

Still plenty of time. Still plenty of room to turn, the midwife said, kneading the bump. She looked at Frances's file. You were over with your first?

Ten days, Frances said. I'm really hoping I don't go that long again.

The midwife smiled. They all come in their own sweet time, don't they? This'll be cold.

She squirted gel on Frances's tummy.

Does Dad – I'd better watch I don't say Father – Dad want to come a bit closer?

They held hands, watching together the brain's convolutions, the anemone-puff of the heart beating, and looked away at the same time when the baby kicked, twisting round at the hips.

You're OK, the midwife said. Too quick to see anything.

Frances was convinced that she had spotted Ruth for a girl from as early as the eighteenth week.

I told you, I *told* you, were the first words she said after the delivery, sounding, Avery thought, like a child at Christmas peeved to have finally got what it had spent the fifty-five days since Hallowe'en owning in its head. Weeks passed before she was able to take pleasure in the baby, though a fierce kind of pleasure it was then. Neither of them had any wish for that to happen second time round. Avery kept to himself the suspicion that he might – just – have glimpsed something other than cord on their previous visit.

They stopped on their way from the hospital for coffee and cake at the in-house café of a newly opened furniture store. From the first-floor window they looked across the lots of car showrooms and the MI beyond to the lower slopes of the Belfast hills, housing estates spotted with sunlight where the cloud cover broke. Looking inwards, they saw people testing sofas – back, buttocks, hands pressed flat; a woman bending to see the price on a tag turned the wrong way behind glass; a man attempting to measure a dining-table on a biblical gauge of spans and cubits.

Frances stirred the strata out of her latte. I really do hope I don't go over with this one, she said. I don't know if she ever had to go through it, but there's nothing sweet after forty weeks.

Avery remembered the days before Ruth was born. Frances's tears, her stinging rebukes to his every effort to comfort her. To him – he had thought till now to Frances – those days had represented only a fraction of the otherwise copybook pregnancy.

He dragged his fork across the plate, chewed a thin-filled segment of *tarte au citron*.

The man at the dining-tables turned for assistance, his two arms different lengths.

But anyway, said Frances, and found a smile.

2

Eddie Izzard could have given you a good one. Bob Monk-house could not. Ken Dodd on his day, Lenny Bruce, when he didn't try too hard. Billy Connolly practically did every time he walked on stage. Avery never watched a comic in action (and he had a stack of videotapes of stand-ups living and dead) without wondering how they would handle a sermon. For the majority of churchgoers, a minister was only as good as the sermons he gave; when the search committees and interview panels had concluded their work, congregations still voted for new ministers on the strength of them. They had to contain the right mixture of instruction and diversion. They had to be brought in for preference at under half an hour and jokes, in fact, did not go entirely amiss, so long as the congregation actually recognized them as jokes. Avery's own first sermon had contained two, neither of which, he felt, had raised even half a smile. Frances confirmed, reluctantly, what he had not seen.

That was your problem, you were looking down the whole time.

He had more or less read it from start to finish, though in his defence he hadn't had a lot of time to prepare. Reverend Twiss had been laid low with a nasty bug doing the rounds.

It's the full works, said Mrs Twiss, when she phoned on Friday night with the bad news. Vomiting and diarrhoea.

It was touch and go, she was still telling him on Saturday

morning. Avery heard the toilet flushing in the background.

Reverend Twiss himself rang an hour later. I'm sorry, son, he said. All the same, there are worse Sundays for your début than the first Sunday of Advent. It's pretty dot-to-dot.

Of this dot-to-dot, Avery made an impenetrable abstract.

It all just got out of control, he explained to Twiss at the earliest vomit-and-diarrhoea-free opportunity.

Mrs Twiss said it was a wee bit tricky all right. Reverend Twiss took a long drink from a tall glass of water, wiped his mouth with the back of his hand then spoke behind it. I'll tell you what my own minister told me when I was assistant. Trade secret. Watch Tommy Cooper.

Avery laughed.

It's no laughing matter, said Twiss, though his eyes said otherwise. I watched him and the old man was right, he never, ever lost the thread.

So Avery watched too, on UK Gold, the Paramount Channel, starting with Cooper, working forward and back.

(George Burns could have, Jack Benny could have, Bob Hope couldn't to save his life. Arthur Askey could have made converts.)

He experimented with coloured pens and flow-diagrams and found in the end that if he wrote the first line of a new section in capitals at the top of an index card even his memory could retain the gist of six inches by four's worth of words. He still wrote the full text out, but in ever-smaller script. It was the opposite of distance-swimming: how long could you go without letting your head dip down?

He carried the cards blindside of the Bible when he processed to the pulpit at the start of each service. He became adept at shifting them one-handed (one-fingered, one-thumbed) as he preached, using the left hand as a baton with which to measure the beat of his words, to keep from running away with himself or descending into drone.

Realism as much as humility kept him from thinking he would ever be a memorable preacher, but there was no doubt he had come on leagues from that first Advent Sunday in Holywood. Far enough to know that the success or failure of any sermon could sometimes be taken divinely out of your hands.

Sunday was the annual Boys' Brigade enrolment service. The members of the company marched up the aisle two abreast behind their gold-fringed standards, which Avery, in full ministerial regalia, accepted, fitting the poles into a V-shaped holder set on the floor before the communion table. The boys shuffled into the first three pews to his right. They fitted with comfort. This was the first year that there had been no Guide troop to be enrolled. Of last year's remaining half-dozen, three were sisters, whose family had since moved out of town. The Guides had always struggled for numbers, but the BB, Guy Broudie told Avery, had once boasted a company of a hundred and twenty. What Guy didn't tell him and Avery hadn't been able to verify was that the company had supplied half the officers for the UDA when it formed in the area: teenage boys with drill experience.

Avery remained before the communion table for his address. He asked the boys to consider their motto. Sure and Steadfast. How many times in their BB careers had they heard those words? Sure and Steadfast. He wasn't going to patronize them by asking them to put their hands up if they knew what they meant. He *knew* they knew. (Wasn't that like an entry requirement?) But had they, he wondered, stopped to think how those words had come down to us? Sure, from the Latin *securus*, by way of Old French. Steadfast, from the Old English *stede*, place, and *faeste*, like the German *fest*, fixed. These were not words that were born to be together. For years and years – centuries – their families weren't even on speaking terms. (Smiles from some in the congregation.) When people talked about the language of accommodation, the boys were to remember that language itself was the greatest accommodation. We could not string together two sentences without giving voice to the many influences that had made us who we were.

The boys in the front three rows kept their eyes on him. Some of them had taken part in the cross-community football competition. All of them undoubtedly knew about Darryl Kirkpatrick. One of them perhaps was responsible for the misspelt graffiti at the back of the church. None of them showed any emotion. Nor would they. This was their end of the bargain for a week's camp next July in the Isle of Man.

They were, Avery told them anyway, and meant it, a credit in their turnout to their company and to the church. He trusted that in the year ahead, in all that they did and all that they said, they would be a credit to themselves and the community.

Watch your words and let your motto, Sure and Steadfast, be your *watchwords*.

The boys in the front row grinned as one – relieved, maybe, that he meant it when he said there would be no hands-up participation – then there was a general commotion far beyond what Avery associated with the end of sermons. Michael Simpson was struggling to stand. Guy Broudie said, Minister! Avery instinctively hunched his shoulders as he turned towards the communion table. A V of flagpoles still in their holder fell past him brushing his upper arms. His hands shot out and caught them before they hit the floor. The BB leaders rushed forward to help. The rest of the congregation gasped, then broke into unprecedented applause as he jerked the poles back and the flags unfurled. All that was missing was the marching band rising from a trap behind the choir, fireworks.

At the end of the service some of the boys gave him the thumbs-up as they passed him on the front step.

That was class, one of them said.

Avery couldn't recall seeing a congregation in better heart.

He woke in the middle of the night to a space in the bed where Frances should have been. He found her sitting on the side of the bath inspecting her pants. Not already? he said.

She shook her head. Just a twinge.

She was not entirely awake. He helped her get the pants back on, stand. She went to the sink and ran the hot tap.

That's a relief anyway, he said, and her head drooped forward and snapped back again in the mirror. Yes.

Two nights later, dreaming her waters had broken, she wet the bed. She lay curled on the floor and cried as Avery stripped the mattress. I'm sick of this, she said, between sobs.

In the morning Avery bundled the duvet into the boot of the car and drove Ruth to school. He paid a home visit, a Mr Booth, whose daughter had contacted him the week before. The man was dying. He hadn't set foot in a church in years. He was scared, but stubborn.

He won't actually come right out and ask for it, his daughter had said, but I know it would be a comfort to him to talk.

He said next to nothing while Avery was there. Hello, goodbye, can I have another bit of sugar in my tea? The house had the air that the houses of widowers often had of a museum to the departed wife. It was kept meticulous by the old man's daughter who lived a few doors up and came in three or four times a day to do for him.

Mr Booth sat tight against the right arm of the settee, taking up half of a cushion Avery could imagine him once having filled with ease. It didn't take much to imagine him gone altogether.

The daughter told Avery her father had worked in the ropeworks. Or maybe Avery was too young to remember them?

East Bread Street, Avery said. The biggest in the world.

The old man looked at the floor, like children Avery had seen in the presence of prospective foster-parents.

Oh, it's all changed round there, said the daughter. Who'd have thought, a golf shop? That right, Daddy? It's like that big thing they're building now in the middle of the shipyard. – That big thing was the Odyssey: cinemas, restaurants, and a home for the city's instant ice-hockey team. – How many people do you think's going to get work out of that?

Daddy kept his thoughts on the matter to himself.

Avery joined in a few more attempts to draw him out then said he had best be going. He would call again next week. He left a question mark at the end.

Grand, the daughter said. Avery stood his ground.

The old man at last looked up, nodded.

Grand, the daughter said again.

There was a note on the door of the laundrette: Back in five minutes. Avery waited fifteen before starting the engine. As he was moving away from the kerb he saw Sheila coming across the cleared ground on the far side of the main road. He made an immediate right turn and another right and another on the flattened streets. From above, the car must have looked like a piece on a giant Monopoly board. He pulled in just ahead of Sheila and got out of the car, trying to make it look like chance. She hesitated, drew heavily on her cigarette, put her head down and made to walk past him. He kept step beside her. Please, Sheila.

I'm not supposed to talk to you, she said.

I had some dry-cleaning.

So. She stopped a few yards short of the main road. There's plenty of other places you could take it.

A flatbed lorry loaded with scaffolding poles turned into the street. Someone inside wolf-whistled. Sheila threw him the fingers and, with their opposite numbers, brought the cigarette to her mouth. She breathed in, stoking up.

Well, said Avery, and I wanted to ask how Darryl was.

Raging, thanks.

I'm sorry to hear that.

What did you expect? He goes out to play football and winds up strapped to a bed in the hospital and no one says boo to the ones that hurt him.

I'm sure you're wrong there. I'm sure there was plenty said.

Sheila was not prepared to be impressed: Plenty said but nothing done. If it had been one of ours done it to one of them they'd have an inquiry and all set up by now.

Well, I hardly think . . . I mean I'm not saying it isn't serious . . . It is, I know, for you, for Darryl.

He was getting tangled, but it didn't matter, she wasn't listening.

Look at Derry, she said. Them ones only have to ask and they get.

As with *I have nothing against my kids playing with Catholics, but* . . . this was not a novel sentence in Protestant east Belfast. What it meant was that after almost three decades of campaigning a new judicial inquiry had opened earlier that year into the killing in Derry of thirteen civilians in January 1972: Bloody Sunday.

Avery could have hoped for a better time and place, but he couldn't just let this go unchallenged: The other way of looking at it is that these inquiries are for all of us, he said. If the security forces have done something wrong, we have a right to know, for our own protection if nothing else.

So it's all right, is it, for them ones to bomb and shoot us for thirty years, but not for anyone to do a thing back?

Across the wasteground scaffolding poles were being unloaded, which is to say, chucked on the ground.

See, you're saying them ones, Avery said, but it wasn't *them ones* were shot in Derry, that's the whole point.

The point, he knew, was that even if it had been, with or without due process, it was still wrong, but that was an argument likely to meet with more resistance than he felt up to. He reminded himself that he had only come here to ask after the boy's arm.

They were out on the streets, Sheila said.

The state is supposed to protect us even when it doesn't agree with what we are doing, said Avery, even when we're criticizing it. It's supposed to be better than us, not just no worse. You'd want an inquiry yourself if it was someone you loved.

He realized too late he had come full circle. Sheila's smile did not extend beyond the rim of her lips. Her face looked pained from long years back. She took the few steps to the pedestrian crossing. I might want it, but I wouldn't get it.

Avery shook his head. You can't believe that.

I thought that was what we all voted for the other year in the referendum. We can believe whatever we want.

The green man was flashing. She threw down her cigarette. Now, she said. I've my work to go to.

She half walked across the road, half ran. If she had turned before going into the laundrette she would have seen Avery kneeling by his car. In his agitation he had dropped the keys opening the door. They had caught between the bars of a grating behind the offside front wheel. The danger, of course, was that in trying to retrieve them he would only succeed in knocking them right down the drain.

Gently did it. Gently.

He wasn't aware of the lorry's return until the engine was revved needlessly as it passed too close behind him.

Yo! came the voice from inside. Bin hoker!

Avery swung round, arm raised, hand closed in a fist about the keys.

Someone phoned for you, Frances said. It was eleven thirty and she was still not dressed. Didn't leave his name.

Did you ask?

Oh, gosh, no. Is that what you're meant to do, ask? Of course, I asked. I always ask. I can't make people.

There's no need to be sarcastic.

And there's no need to treat me like an idiot.

Nor was there a good way, Avery decided, to tell her she wasn't to feel bad about last night. He was in the hall flicking through the message pad, as though in hope that some trace of the call had been left, when the phone rang again.

Approximately five per cent of all memory is confabulation, Tony said, the instant after Avery's hello. That's your memory and my memory. Stories produced unconsciously to fill the holes left by the passage of time. But there are also Fantastic

Confabulators, people who, for one reason or another, go way beyond compensation or even over-compensation. They can experience memories, some of them, completely unconnected to anything in their past lives. A very few epileptics, for instance, are subject to particularly strong *déjà vu*, particularly *unlikely*. An entry in a book could quite easily trigger it.

Were you ringing earlier? Avery asked.

Really, Tony? Tony said. That's very interesting, Tony.

Sorry, said Avery; of course it couldn't have been Tony called, Frances would have known without asking. It *is* interesting to know. Thanks for going and finding that all out.

I didn't go and find anything out, Tony said. It just landed on my desk. Transcript of a radio discussion in one of the journals we get here. Gives all sorts of examples of the lengths the unconscious will go to to justify these impossible memories. Your man seems to me to fit the bill perfectly.

Yes, Avery said, his concentration slipping again. For some reason he kept thinking about the envelope full of letters Elspet had shown him. He hadn't looked inside.

Damn, said Tony.

What?

I'm sorry now I told you I got it all out of a magazine. I could have hit you for a consultation fee.

I'll pay you back in kind, if ever there's anything you need from me.

I doubt it very much, the line of work you're in now, Tony said, and before Avery could come back: I've been looking through baby catalogues this last while with Michele. He whistled. How do people afford it?

A question Avery had never heard posed by anyone with a joint income of less than £50,000 a year.

Michele would only want the very best, Frances said when

Avery reported this bit of the conversation. We won't be bumping into them at Primark, that's for sure.

Avery was making coffee.

Frances stood behind him, slipping her arms under his. See what fatherhood does, she said. She seemed a little recovered from her earlier mood. Imagine Tony phoning you to talk about baby stuff.

Yeah, Avery said. Imagine.

A few days later he parked the car outside the house off the Stranmillis Road and knocked the door. When there was no reply he took out his card and wrote on the back. Any time you feel like a chat . . .

He pushed back the letterbox far enough to see that the mail mustn't have been collected for a week.

You ask me she has a man somewhere, said a voice behind him.

He turned to see the old woman with the dog and DIY poop-a-scoop.

Avery dropped the card inside. I don't suppose that's any of our business, he said, walking down the path and getting into his car.

3

That weekend there was a renewed bout of loyalist feuding across the river. Attempted murders, pipe-bombings, ransacking of homes. In east Belfast there were reports of brawls in bars, stand-offs on street corners, but no more. On this side of the river there was little to distract the self-styled punishment squad that forced its way into a terraced house on Sunday night and beat a young father about the arms and head with a baseball bat and wheel brace. Avery, called away from the breakfast table to the hospital, had trouble recognizing him as the youth who had presented his son Marshall for baptism back in August. The eyes were swollen, the lips were swollen, the nose and cheekbones broken. One side of the goatee had been shaved off to allow the surgeons to work on the jaw and there was stitching running in a jagged diagonal across the scalp, to which, here and there, tufts of dyed orange hair still adhered.

Nor was it easy to associate the pale and drawn girl by his bedside, whose own face seemed held together by studs and pins, with the mother of that day.

She cradled the baby in one arm. The little finger of the other hand was wet at the tip where the baby had been sucking.

Dee was holding Marshall just like this when they came through the door, she told Avery, giving him his bedtime bottle.

(Marshall, the only one of the three changed for the better, was dressed head to toe in Baby Gap. His hair was black and glossy, his cheeks shone. He might have been inflated by foot pump.)

There was that many of them they were getting jammed in the doorway. I was shrieking at them to get out, and all Dee was saying was right, right, yous can have me, but mind the child, yous Bs, mind the child.

Her boyfriend's head moved from side to side on the pillow. She chuffed a laugh, her eyes brightening. He's saying he called them a lot worse than Bs.

Avery couldn't say he blamed him.

A nurse came in to check on the drips and monitors. Now, she said, after each completed action. It sounded to Avery like the very distillation of compassion. She rearranged the sheets and for a moment he glimpsed the boy's midriff where the girl's name was tattooed. Wendy. It had quite escaped him.

Now.

Wendy waited till the nurse was gone.

They took me and the wee one up to the bathroom and locked the door on us. I can't tell you what it was like listening. By the time they let us out they had Dee beat senseless. You'd have swore he was dead to look at him. There was blood all up the walls.

The baby stirred. She stroked its cheek with her finger.

An ambulance had arrived within minutes. She didn't know who had called it, unless maybe it was one of the ones who'd given Dee the beating.

They made a friend of my sister's phone 999 on his own mobile before they done him, she said. Then they smashed up his phone and all.

Avery asked in parting if they would like him to say a prayer with them. Wendy reached for Dee's fingers, protruding from the end of a splint. They attempted to close over hers. Aye, she said.

Out in the corridor he talked to the policeman who had arrived at the house as the ambulance was leaving. Rossborough, you called him. His parents were members of Avery's congregation. He didn't hold out a lot of hope of anyone being brought to book for the beating. The perpetrators rarely were in these cases.

It's hard to say, he said, but my guess is the wee lad stole from them. They didn't touch the lower body, all concentrated on the arms and head. Maybe a car. The wheel brace is certainly a new one on me.

They wouldn't be that precise, would they? Avery was reminded of the perversely literal mutilations he had heard reported from inside Afghanistan.

Oh, you'd be surprised, the policeman said. Or then again maybe a wheel brace was the first thing that came to hand.

Further along the corridor a priest was deep in conversation with a doctor in a saffron headscarf. Without seeming to take his eyes from the doctor, he raised an index finger as Avery approached, signalling to him to wait.

The doctor made a note left-handed on the top page of her clipboard. I'll look in again in an hour, she said.

The priest shook her hand then turned to shake Avery's. Bernard Moody, he said. You know a friend of mine, Des Kehoe.

Of course, yes, Des, Avery said, returning the shake with vigour. Ken Avery.

Father Moody nodded back the way Avery had come. Sorry to hear about your young fella. I've one of my own was admitted Saturday night. Hands, feet and knees.

Avery winced: a crucifixion, they called it.

It's his second time being done, Father Moody said. They told him when they came for him he obviously hadn't learnt his lesson the first time. Fifteen and a half. They pinned a note to him: crimes against the community. The left kneecap's non-existent.

Avery let out a moan.

Judge not, that ye be not judged, Father Moody said, shaking his head in sympathy with Avery's distress.

The doctor in the saffron headscarf passed again, smiling, bowing her head.

All the same, said Father Moody in an undertone, I hope the ones that did the like of that to a fifteen-and-a-half-year-old boy get what's due to them.

And Avery said, Amen.

He rang Des from the car park, but got only the BT answer-service. It had been such a dispiriting start to the day, though, that he decided to drive over there anyway on spec and arrived, a quarter of an hour later, as Des jogged down the street of villas-become-insurers to the parochial house. His wine-coloured sweat top had a breastplate of deepest burgundy. His calves were livid.

Punctured, was as much as he could say when he saw Avery get out of the car. He pressed his hands beneath his ribs. Pure, pure, punctured.

It never looks to me like it can be good for you, Avery said.

Do you want to know what's worse? Des had recovered a little. I've gone and entered myself for next year's marathon.

I'm impressed.

I'm scared out of my wits.

He showed Avery into a dining room where unmatching armchairs flanked a picture window overlooking a garden with plum trees and quince. On the table behind the arm-chairs was a single place mat, an *Irish News* before it open at the arts page.

I'll not be a minute.

While Des was gone Avery sat by the window contemplating a print of the Blessed Virgin, palms outstretched, robed in radiant white and blue. To some on the wilder fringes of his Church, this Mary was at best a rival twin of theirs, smuggled away at birth and favoured with a more gilded upbringing. At worst she was a blasphemous pretender. Queen of Heaven, indeed. No doubt the same people would have been appalled by Reverend Twiss's glossing of their two-in-oneness as Dress-up and Dress-down Mary.

He became aware of a scratching in the room and, getting up from the armchair, tracked the sound to a corner by the fireplace where a pied hamster was sitting in its cage – its food dish – preening.

The eejit, Des said, coming in the door, changed into the work clothes and carrying mugs on a tray. He tapped the cage with the side of his foot to chivvy the hamster to somewhere a bit more hygienic.

He wouldn't normally keep pets as a rule, but he'd inherited it from a parishioner whose children had lost interest. I don't know what they'd expected it to *do*, she said. She'd told them when they got it she hadn't the time herself, that it would have to be taken away and destroyed if they didn't look after it properly.

Actually, it was watching yon thing in its exercise ball started me thinking about the marathon, he said.

He took the hamster, bottom end swinging, from the cage, stroking its stomach with his little finger. The ball was a murky Perspex with a sliding hatch to let the hamster in and out. The hamster's legs were going before Des had set the ball on the ground. It ran straight into the skirting-board. Des bent down to turn it round and it ran into the table leg, then a chair leg, then the table leg again.

The virtue of perseverance? Avery said, making an essay at its homiletic usefulness, its prompting to marathon running.

Des lifted his mug, holding back a smile. I just started thinking what could be the opposite of such *pointless* exertion.

Avery said, I met a friend of yours at the hospital, Bernard Moody.

Barney? How's he keeping?

Well enough, in the circumstances.

Avery told him about the boys they had each been visiting.

He's in a rough spot, Barney, Des said. I mean, we think we're bad. You've never seen so many young lads on crutches. It's like that film. What do you call it? You know, with your man – what's this you call it? – he's lost his legs. Tom Hanks.

Not *Born on the Fourth of July*?

That the one? Has the parade of Vietnam vets in their wheelchairs? That's what it's like where he is. I'm not joking.

You must, said Avery, though he might as truthfully have said *I*, feel powerless to help.

Des tore the wrapper off a Nutri-grain bar – I didn't get shopping at the weekend, he said – and broke the bar in two. The wee lads will know exactly who it was did it to them, he told Avery, but they won't let on to the police or anyone. And who can blame them? They're too young, the half of them, to have any choice but to go on living where they are. And it's not like their neighbours are clamouring to have it stopped.

There had been a case in Newry a few years back where three teenagers had sought refuge in the priest's house in defiance of an IRA expulsion order. Avery had a vivid memory of the fear in the voices from the blacked-out faces on the television news, an equally clear recollection of the muted response to the priest's pleas for community support. He tried to imagine taking one of these young fellas into his own house and hoped if ever he was faced with it he would have the strength to overcome the sudden doubt the attempt gave rise to.

Was it not Tom Cruise? he said.

What did I say?

Hanks.

Sorry. Tom Cruise.

The hamster ball thudded against the wall beneath the window.

Des asked him about the business with the wee boy with the arm.

Darryl?

They had stepped out into the garden, to the edge at any rate. The grass was long and dew-laden. On the shrubs spider-webs looked like they had been hung out to drip-dry.

It's hard to know, Avery said. There's talk he needs physio-therapy. I only get what comes through the solicitor. Tell you the truth, I'm more worried half the time about the mother. You wouldn't think to look at her, but she's so full of bitterness and anger.

Des took his mug from him, launched the dregs of the two teas towards the long grass. There was a bit of fallout here too. There's a few in the diocese would prefer our kids-coming-together efforts to be a bit less head to head for the time being.

What does that mean?

Cyber meeting has been suggested.

Seriously?

Who knows?

The phone rang.

Excuse me, Des said.

I'd better be going anyway, Avery called behind him, but by the time Des came off the phone five minutes later he had made it no further than the chair by the picture window again.

Was there something else you wanted to talk about? Des asked.

I don't know.

Between you and me and these four walls? he prompted.

A female blackbird dropped into the garden, checked left, checked right, then bounced to within pecking distance of a tan squelch of windfall. Checked left and right again. Pecked. The hamster ball had come to rest under the table. Avery moved his shoulders trying to slip out of the hold the tension had on him. He drew a long slow breath, let it out through his nose.

Imagine, he said and stopped till he found another way in. Just suppose.

No sin in supposition, Mrs Heaney, said Des, in a north Dublin accent. Sorry.

Avery shook his head, though the words had scarcely registered as a distraction. Suppose someone told you they killed some people. A long time ago.

Des nodded, supposing.

The police or the army, they knew about it at the time, but they didn't do anything. At least, they did, they tried to hide it, to make him forget. I mean like permanently forget.

Des's nod was slower – the skin around his eyes tighter – as though he was steeling himself for more.

Avery stopped. He had been prepared for scepticism, rank

disbelief. You wouldn't find that a bit, I don't know, far-fetched?

Des's nod turned to a shake, the shake to a shrug of the sort that says sorry if I'm letting you down. Some of the things you hear starting to come out, he said.

Some of the things that you heard starting to come out, frankly, Avery considered mischievous. Yes, but messing about with people's memories, he said. It's like something out of John Le Carré.

People would probably say the same thing about fake laundries and secret agents running massage parlours.

Avery had got up from his seat. He walked to the table.

The hamster, said Des. Mind.

The ball trundled out from under the table.

Maybe I didn't spell it out, Avery said. I'm talking about *surgery*. Do you seriously think that the security forces would do something like that?

Well, why were you asking me to suppose it if you didn't think it yourself?

Avery opened the dining-room door. Forget I ever mentioned it, he said.

I can if you can, said Des.

It took Avery an afternoon of ferocious DIY to get over his annoyance.

4

Frances said it was no good, she just couldn't sleep with him any longer. Every time she closed her eyes she was heart-scared she was going to wet again. She'd hardly had a wink in days. This was about one a.m. Avery asked could they not talk about it in the morning. But, no, Frances said, she was too exhausted, she was going to the guest room.

The guest room hadn't had a radiator on in it since last winter.

Indeed you're not, Avery said, and took himself off to sleep there instead.

It wasn't until he opened the door that he remembered the broken curtain rail. The hot press was back along the landing, right outside Ruth's door. He didn't want to risk waking her hunting for a sheet, let alone tacking it up.

The mattress was tense with cold. He lay beneath the unfamiliar duvet, feeling the heat flow out of him then little by little flow back in, looking across the dark pool of garden into the stairwell of the maisonette block, pink in the emergency night-lights. Once, working into the small hours in the study next door, he had seen an old man in a baseball cap come out on to the top-floor landing with a bag of garbage and make his slow descent. Twenty minutes it took him to the ground floor and back. Twenty minutes in which Avery was always just a second away from running out to help him.

All the summer's flags had come down, bar one, ragged as a hermit, atop a concrete lamp standard to the left of the stairwell. From that distance, in that light, it was next to impossible to identify, though that didn't stop his exhausted brain trying. When, some time after three, the wind began to pick up, the rags wrapped themselves round the light fitting and Avery finally slept.

By the middle of the next week the guest room had become the rule for him rather than the exception, though even with the curtain rail fixed Avery found it hard to get over. He read his Bible, he read his committee papers; he read a paperback on army undercover operations in Northern Ireland he had picked up in a bundle of ten for a pound in a car-boot sale at his last church. It was poorly written – a quick newspaper cut-and-paste job to cash in on the appetite whetted by similar books about the Gulf War.

The same handful of incidents cropped up in every book he had ever looked at on the subject. The fake laundry, the massage parlour Des had spoken of, the brave – or foolhardy – SAS captain, captured deep in enemy territory and buried somewhere so deep that to this day no trace of him had ever been found; his earlier alleged involvement in the Dublin and Monaghan car bombings.

Not only was there no mention in this book of the killings Larry was claiming, they didn't fit any pattern that Avery could discern. Two women and a man on a Tuesday night in a Belfast bar, minding their own only slightly more than normally complicated business.

He was not altogether immune to the weary distaste that Tony evinced when obliged to contemplate such matters. Dark deeds were a drain on the soul. So it was a relief in more ways than one when the night after he finished reading the book Frances turned to him in the bathroom as they cleaned their teeth and burrowed into his outstretched arms. Could you bear to spend a night next to this? she said, shrugging her shoulders, like quotation marks about herself.

Nothing in the world could give me more pleasure, he said, from the bottom of his heart.

Avery dreamt he was in a bus station waiting for Joanna. He knew in the dream that she was dead, but thanks to negotiations, which he understood without having to articulate, the Troubles' dead were being allowed home for the weekend. Temporary release. The station was full of people clutching photographs, bits of old clothing, soft toys, letters, newspaper cuttings.

A bus pulled in with no one on board. Limited Stop, said a handwritten placard leaning against the windscreen before the steering-wheel. The doors opened and the people in the waiting room moved forward, waving, calling names, holding their photographs and mementoes above their heads.

It's the wrong bus, Avery shouted to them, but he couldn't be heard above the sounds, all around him, of tearful reunion.

The dead were materializing as though from contact with the bus-station air. They looked like they had been on a particularly hectic holiday, weary, but full of stories. Avery tried asking those closest to him had they seen Joanna, but everyone was too busy talking. He tried pushing through to the bus doors. The crowd was moving in the opposite direction, bearing him back. He heard the hiss of brakes being released, the *gronk* of a gearbox thrown into reverse. Then suddenly where there had been resistance there was none; the crowd melted away and he was slapping the flat of his hand on the bus door.

Ronnie was driving. He shook his head at Avery and carried on manoeuvring the bus through a 180-degree turn.

An unfamiliar woman's voice behind Avery said, You obviously didn't want badly enough, but when he turned no one was there.

At lunchtime the following day (Avery was glad his faith precluded a belief in premonition) Larry rang.

I'm sorry, Avery said. I meant to call you before now.

No, said Larry. I changed the number. Anyway, I'm the one should apologize. I said I wouldn't bother you again, but something's happened, I thought it was better to tell you.

They met an hour later in a café next to the Habitat customer-collection door and dominated by a clock face projected back to front on the rear wall. They would be safer somewhere like that, Larry had said, ominously enough for Avery not to think twice about cancelling an afternoon appointment. Somewhere busy.

The café was so busy that Avery had difficulty picking Larry out, at a table for two half-way down on the left-hand side, though his eye had already passed over him once before coming back to rest.

You didn't tell me you'd grown a moustache, he said as he sat.

Larry touched it with his fingertips. It's coming off tomorrow.

It suits you.

Suits isn't the point, believe me, said Larry.

At the next table a boy and girl in grammar-school uniform held hands. A second girl sat facing them, striking one after the other the matches in their complimentary matchbox, talking non-stop, always one decibel above the café's sound system: I was just, like, who do you think you are? And here's her, I *know* who I am, sweetie, and I'm, like, don't you fucking sweetie me, wee doll.

Avery was out again without his fifteen-inch swear-word filter. Larry had asked him – advised, actually – to come in civvies, so as not to draw too much attention to them both. He had also advised him to show no sign of alarm at anything Larry might say.

Anything like *I think they might be on to me*.

Who might be? Avery asked, face all unalarmed.

The people who did this thing, Larry said, turning his eyes towards his own hairline. Plus some other ones. A crowd I used to run about with.

She's a complete fucking bike, said the match-girl. Marnie says to her, have they not got you in the tourist guide yet, love?

She threw the matchbox on the table, wafted the smoke away with the other hand.

Coffee? Larry asked, and Avery, looking round, saw a waiter at his shoulder.

Ah, yes. Black.

Two black coffees, said Larry.

Two Americanos, said the waiter and swept up the rest of the cutlery, keeping an eye on the next table, beneath which the handholding couple had now locked feet. He lifted the ashtray and what remained of the box of matches.

Huh! said the second girl, and folded her arms.

Larry leant in towards Avery. Somebody had a pop at me last night.

A pop?

A pop.

Like a . . .

Pop. Yes.

Avery drew a deep breath – *don't be alarmed, don't be alarmed* – made a wet pop sound of his own with his lips. There had been nothing on the news this morning about pops. Why would they do that?

Why do you think? They want me dead.

The music on the café's sound system came to an end a crucial fraction before Larry's sentence. The boy at the next table jerked as though slapped.

You OK? his girlfriend asked. The boy frowned and shook his head. It was a useful survival strategy for a male of his age, pretending not to have heard sentences with the word dead in them. The next track started brassily.

They know about the memory coming back, said Larry beneath it. They must have been tipped off somehow.

Avery had the by now familiar feeling of being hustled on to Z when he was still trying to find his feet at A. Never mind the how, or even the who, he remained to be convinced of the if. If any of this. Again he thought of Elspet with the envelope she said was full of letters from the hospital. She really couldn't have guaranteed that her tears would dissuade him from looking inside. Why would she take such a gamble if she was lying?

Because the prize was so worth the winning. The prize was Avery walking away without asking any more questions, letting the matter drop.

And then he had another thought. He hadn't told Tony or Des Larry's name. Elspet was the only person who could connect them. Elspet, who had disappeared the minute he left her door.

Chairs scraped on the floor. The young people had vacated their table leaving a 30p tip.

The coffees arrived.

Americano, said the waiter. Americano.

Avery shook a sugar stick he had no intention of using. Did

he tell Larry he had been to Elspet's house? Doing what exactly? Looking for proof that Larry was imagining all of this, was unwell?

No.

I really think if you're in so much trouble you'd be better talking to someone else, he said.

Larry started to laugh. Right, like the police?

Avery set the sugar on the lip of his saucer; it drooped, broken-backed. What will you do?

Make sure they can't find me before the memory comes back more clearly.

Then?

I'll see.

Avery couldn't help himself. Will you promise you'll call me before you do anything?

I'll see.

On his way out of town Avery stopped at a filling station and bought an early edition of the *Belfast Telegraph*. The news in brief was on the second page. Pensioner robbed, student lauded, disabled athlete hailed. Then this. Police are investigating a reported shooting incident late last night close to the city centre. A spokesman said they had so far been unable to determine whether anyone had been injured or who the intended target had been. He appealed for any-one with information to contact Musgrave Street RUC station.

Avery closed the paper and caught sight of his hands. They were damp with sweat, ink-sponges. He wiped them on his thighs and remembered too late he had changed before leaving the house into honey-coloured cords.

★

Someone had once quipped to Avery that Northern Ireland divided into two camps, those who believed conspiracy theories and those who thought they were being put around to make us all paranoid.

Twiss maybe? Whoever it was, the quip had been made, he was fairly certain, in the touch-and-go year before the signing of the Belfast Agreement. One early-summer night he and Frances were at the Lyric Theatre (they had talked to Michele in the lobby: we *really* must meet up) when, twenty minutes into the second half of the play – it was Friedrich Dürrenmatt's *The Visit* – the lights went out. For five minutes more the audience sat looking silently, respectfully, towards the stage. You sensed a few of them were preparing to applaud, until the noises off could not be confused with anything scripted or directed and they began at last to murmur among themselves. A cone of torchlight leapt from the wings, bringing a hand, an arm behind. It stopped centre stage and turned through ninety degrees into a spotlight on the director's face. He explained that the lights would not be coming on for the – excuse the pun – foreseeable future, in the theatre or anywhere else in the city. Belfast was blacked out.

By *happy* coincidence this particular production of the play called for the use of torches. (*Ooos* from the audience: aren't you smart?) So, the director said, recovering from his bow, if no one was planning on going anywhere . . . (General laughter.) The actors reappeared holding torches beneath their chins. More torches were handed to audience members in the second row. (The show was playing to around eighty per cent capacity that night.) At the end, with the lights still out, audience and actors stood and applauded one another, exhilarated alike.

The front-of-house staff had been busy all the while lighting candles on the tables and countertops of the lobby bar. There were gasps of appreciation and enchantment as the audience emerged from the auditorium. Frances squeezed Avery's arm.

The bar was doing brisk cash-only trade, though the majority of people had gone straight out on to the street before the theatre to take in the strangeness of nothing seen clearly, not the river off to the right, or the edge of the Botanic Gardens ahead, or the houses ascending on the left to meet the Stranmillis Road.

People were making calls to family and friends, offering their phones to those without, plotting the extent of the power-cut: Glengormley's out, one shouted. Mallusk, called another, Dunmurry, Ballygowan.

Frances spoke to her parents. Ruthie's fine, she told Avery. Dead to the world. Her parents were fine too. Just like old times, in fact. They had dug out the candles they always kept as a precaution under the sink and were listening to the emergency services on short-wave radio.

It was the first time since the lights went out that Avery had heard the word emergency. Shortly afterwards he heard a siren.

With no street-lights or traffic-lights there was no question of anyone trying to drive home. Those who lived close enough walked, those who remained swapped stories of power-cuts past: the Three Day Week; May '74 – the Loyalist Workers' Strike. LA came up and the rioting and looting that had followed the blackouts there. The question was asked how long it would take for the same thing to happen in Belfast. There was, Avery thought, a change in the atmosphere, although it might have been no more than the chill that pervades any building with doors open on to the street, with no electricity for the best part of an hour, and candles here and there starting to gutter. Still, it felt a lot like the presence of fear.

(What is it that we are most afraid of when the lights go out? Other people? Ourselves? Avery tested the words to see would they take the weight of extended argument.)

He heard the first theory before the supply was restored. The power station workers, whose withdrawal of labour had been crucial in '74, were reminding the New Labour government what they could do in the event of further concessions to Sinn Fein.

On Sunday he was told, with absolute assurance, by three separate members of the congregation, that the blackout had been a dry run for the security forces, testing their responses to a breakdown in public order. They all pooh-poohed the power-workers theory. Almost no one Avery spoke to believed there had been a simple mechanical failure. Over an entire city? For more than an hour and a half? Catch yourself on.

Standing in the forecourt of the filling station, hands and trouser-legs streaked with ink, Avery found himself in possession of a growing number of facts, all of which on their own had the status of mechanical failure. There was a scar across Larry's head. Elspet had burst into tears before he was able to look inside the envelope she said would explain it. There had been unconfirmed shots on the edge of town on a night when Larry said (or did he actually say?) an attempt had been made on his life.

He wondered when you reached critical mass, when the urge to combine into theory became impossible to resist, and suspected that by wondering he was still some way off.

Anyone could report shots being fired. Avery could. Larry could.

5

In the third week of October the Dalai Lama came to Belfast. Avery was one of several hundred members of clergy, laity and fourth estate who, with one hundred and nineteen uniformed officers and twelve plain-clothes, joined the Buddhist leader on the short walk through a gate opened as a rule only three times a year, from one side of the Springfield Road peace line to the other. Every step was caught on camera. Avery's face, a pale moon in partial eclipse behind the Dalai Lama's sunburst of a smile, was bounced from high in the heavens to homes on the other side of the globe, and was snapped a second later, fully emerged from the eclipse, by a freelance photographer whose work was regularly syndicated to the city's free newspapers.

Why me? he asked, as the photographer pushed past, trying to keep up with the Dalai Lama.

Why any of us? said the photographer over his shoulder, catching the mood of the day.

Avery had managed at the last minute to get a ticket for a lecture that evening in the Ulster Hall organized by Amnesty International. Frances's legs were bothering her – she'd spent nearly the entire day on the settee – and only for her parents offering to take Ruth for a couple of hours he wouldn't have been able to make it.

Des had got a ticket too. Avery had bumped into him at the peace line. Neither of them mentioned their last conversation in Des's dining room, though Des must have felt it as keenly as Avery: that brief bad-tempered exchange had pulled back the rug on a rift in their beliefs deeper than any liturgy could open up.

They talked about trying to meet that evening and left it in the end as maybe see you there. Avery, though, discovered when he arrived at the hall that his ticket was for the second last row of the balcony from where he had to strain his eyes just to see the figures on the stage clearly.

A man from Amnesty was outlining the evening's events. The lecture would be preceded by a celebration of Northern Ireland's cultural diversity. The woman in front of Avery leant in and said something to her neighbour, who smirked, nodding. In fact, when the Amnesty man had handed over to the MC, a well-known broadcaster, who had begun introducing the acts, it was the colour white that most impressed itself on Avery: the white dress of the Nicaraguan woman who danced, barefoot, two dances of unaffected beauty to a musical accompaniment that suggested to Avery's ears that her homeland was not on the far side of the ocean, but closer to the end of the pier; the white robes of the Nigerian man who followed her, carrying his own guitar case, and who sat patiently on a stool, centre-stage, while a technician searched for the correct amp to plug his lead into. For a moment Avery wondered uncharitably – for the man had the eyes of hundreds upon him – whether this search for the amp was the act. Then the man sang: 'Biko', 'Stand By Me', his voice tremulous with nerves or emotion. When he sang 'Nkosi Sikelel' iAfrika', however, his voice simply soared. Some in the audience stood and swayed. The woman in front of Avery looked at her neighbour who nodded again, smiling now, fingers flexing.

(Avery had a flashback: November 1990. Thatcher's resignation. Billy Bragg in this very hall leading the audience in one last rendition of 'Stand Down Margaret' and the 'Internationale'. Himself and two colleagues from the bank clenching their fists like veteran fist-clenchers.)

A giant of a poet came up from the front row, white-haired, white-bearded. He read a poem Avery remembered being in the papers at the time of the IRA ceasefire: old Priam kissing the hand of Achilles, killer of Hector, his son.

There was more music, a group – from the Indian subcontinent, the MC announced, reading from his script, and wondering perhaps with Avery at the percussionist with the long blond hair – and then the Dalai Lama himself was on stage, making an adjustment to his red robe as he walked, crouching every second step, gesturing to the audience, who had risen in ovation, to take their seats, and looking, Avery noted, first with alarm then with an almost overwhelming desire to cheer, like Frankie Howerd in *Up Pompeii!*. Desist, *desist*.

Reverend Twiss would have loved this.

The audience at last desisted. The Dalai Lama sat.

His English was broken, he said. And he was old. But he would try to manage without an interpreter. He laughed. Broken English. Saves time, but you may get wrong meaning.

This was the Ulster Hall, where generations of Unionist Party leaders had been elected, where Lord Randolph Churchill had once proclaimed, *Ulster will fight and Ulster will be right!* Not many people who had taken the stage down the years could have been quite so relaxed about being misinterpreted. Certainly not Lou Reed.

This topic – the Dalai Lama paused, looked to his right, and an aide supplied it: What is Justice?

What is justice? he repeated, and for a moment said nothing more. Something true. Something positive.

Avery had once been cold-called at home and asked by the

voice at the other end of the line to answer a general-knowledge question. Correct, the caller said, and said he would call again the following night with another question. After four nights of correct answers Avery was told he had won a major prize and should attend a ceremony to collect it. His parents warned him it sounded like a scam (Frances then was still in the future), but he knew the venue: certainly it was capable of hosting an awards' ceremony. So he went along and found himself in a hall with four hundred other people who had answered questions correctly, who had ignored the doubts of friends and family, of their own more rational selves.

There was a rustling in the seats that night – or a sound that was the beginning of not not-rustling – the instant before time-share was first mentioned that Avery heard again in the long pause after the Dalai Lama made halting mention of *basic human value*.

He wasn't winging it, was he?

The Dalai Lama adjusted his robe, his glasses, smiled. Of course, Avery should have understood, the killer line would come when least expected.

Justice, he said, is all individuals looking after others' rights.

It sounded like the answer to a problem more mathematical than moral, a simple formula that cut through the reams of cant and equivocation. Justice was a thing you did, not demanded. QED.

It should have stopped mouths; it should have stopped hands; it should have stopped buses and cars. It should have reset the clocks.

Avery was propelled back to the morning, six weeks after Joanna's death, when he woke and felt that all the jagged pieces of his life had been slotted into place. He remembered the stretching-out of the moment into absolute contentment, absolute certainty.

So, that's about my talk, the Dalai Lama was saying. He asked something of the aide standing in the wings and turned back to face the audience.

Still ten minutes, he said. Who wants to ask a question?

People laughed out loud, so delighted were they by this novelty added to novelty. Ask a religious leader a question? Hands went up: why not?

The first question was about patience, the second about grace. Patience was the awareness that enlightenment is a long, long pursuit. Actually, and again these words might never before have been spoken from the Ulster Hall stage, the Dalai Lama wasn't sure he did know the meaning of patience. Grace it was, though, that made us accept we were who we were because of previous lives.

When asked what could be done for Tibetan political prisoners he said, Keep trying. When asked about the possibility of establishing a just society he said it was easier to talk about than to do and that the masses must improve. And then the ten minutes were up and the Dalai Lama was bobbing to wave and shake hands as he left the stage.

The MC returned saying that it wasn't over yet, folks, but the event had already run on longer than Avery had expected. He didn't want to impose any more on Frances's parents, didn't want to be whisking Ruth home and putting her straight to bed. He joined that portion of the audience heading for the balcony doors as a tall young woman in a vest top wandered centre stage with an acoustic guitar. The wee girl from the Omagh bomb thing, he heard someone say.

There was a spot of confusion on the stairs, with those

leaving meeting those returning from the toilets, from a short reflective smoke. There were sorrys, excuse-mes; there were a few less gracious comments. As Avery made room for a woman to pass him on the second last step someone clattered into him from behind. He lurched forward and was immediately reined in by a hand on his collar. His head snapped back against a burning bar of jarred nerve ends.

Sorry, sorry, sorry, a man's voice said.

They had stumbled together into the foyer.

Avery tried to turn, but the pain flared further up his head. He hunched his shoulders, as though trying to duck out of it. His eyes swam.

The man moved round in front of him, took hold of him by the upper arms.

Are you OK? Do you want to sit down? I'm really, really sorry.

Ow, said Avery, and half laughed. He knew there was no damage done.

Is it that thing you get up the back of your head? Rotten, isn't it?

Avery was able to look up, focus. He blinked. Refocused. If it hadn't felt like it would lift right off he would have given his head a good shake.

Are you sure you're OK? said the man.

Even the voice, now he heard it again, had a familiar quality.

He knew it wasn't even as he was forming the name, but his shook-up brain still let it out: Larry?

The man let go his arms.

Avery straightened, offered an apology of his own. Is there something the matter?

Larry's my brother's name, the man said.

★

Ruth was asleep when Avery arrived at Frances's parents' house.

Frances has called us twice, Mr Burns said.

Mrs Burns stood on the stairs. I lay her down, she said. It'd be a sin to wake her.

She has school in the morning, said Avery.

Well, Jim or I can drive her over.

I told Frances that thing would run on, her father said, shaking his head.

Mr Burns was a retired newsagent and Rotarian. Frances claimed to have been well trained by the example of his absences in what to expect when she married a minister.

A pity I didn't have the example of a minister's salary to pass on to you, her father said.

Avery didn't know from one meeting to the next whether he would be received with empathy or with the amused disdain of the Gentleman for the better-paid Player.

Thanks, said Avery, bending to see up the stairs to his mother-in-law, but I think all the same I should take her on home.

It would be a break for Frances, she persisted, her voice exaggeratedly low.

Avery began to think that she had positioned herself on the stairs as a guard. Maybe at the weekend, he said.

Mrs Burns looked at her husband, who turned and walked into the living room.

All right, then, she said, in a tone that asked what did she know about anything who'd only had three of her own. I'll get her.

Avery stood in the doorway. Mr Burns was reading the City news on Teletext.

How are they doing today? Avery asked.

Well, I don't think we'll be jetting off to Florida just yet.

Frances's parents, Frances maintained, could jet off to Florida tomorrow and not miss a penny. There was, though, Avery well remembered, no more tenacious saver than the newly retired saver. Who knew how long you'd need to make the money hold out?

He heard a heavier tread coming down the stairs than had gone up, so that it ought to have been possible to calculate from it the precise extra weight of his daughter in her grandmother's arms. Ruth rubbed her eyes with the backs of her hands in the bright hall light.

There now, there now, Mrs Burns said, and kissed her cheek. Poor sleepy girl. Poor, poor sleepy girl.

It was almost an invitation to her to cry, but one, fortunately, that Ruth passed up. She buried her face in Avery's shoulder and was asleep again before he had her strapped into the car.

He waved to his parents-in-law as he pulled away from in front of the house, then stopped out of sight of the street to check for the third time since leaving the Ulster Hall that he did have the flyer with the telephone number Larry's brother had written on it.

His name was Blain. He hadn't been in touch with Larry for the longest time. Larry was the elder by five years, they were never what you would call close. From ever Blain could remember there had been difficulties at home. Their father was a drinker. He fought with their mother, who fought with Larry, who fought with their father, until one day in his teens he decided, stuff this, he'd had enough.

Sorry, Blain said to Avery. Other people's families. It's all a bit convoluted.

They were sitting in a side corridor of the Ulster Hall. The occasional opening of a door from the auditorium was like the clearing of a waterlogged ear. The young woman in the vest was still singing. Something about a black suit.

Anyway, off he went, said Blain. Didn't ring, didn't write. He could have been anywhere. He could have been lying dead in a ditch, my mum used to say, more to get at my dad I always thought. Then, just like that, he turned up again on the doorstep asking could he come home. He'd been in a house somewhere about the Cliftonville Road. I think this time he stuck it a month before he took off. My dad died a couple of years later. Drink, what else? Larry came for the funeral and left before the coffin was even in the ground, and that was him again, disappeared without trace, until he had his accident.

His accident, right, Avery said, like this much he knew.

From another part of the backstage came the sound of a large drum being tightened and tested.

He must have been in a bad way, Avery said.

Blain brought his bottom lip tight across the top, nodded. I was off on my travels myself then, he said. A bit farther afield. India, Pakistan, Afghanistan. It took weeks for the letters to catch up with me and then, I thought, well, what could I actually *do*?

He glanced at Avery.

It was a very selfish time, looking back on it. He raised the first and second fingers of his right hand to his mouth to suggest smoking. A bracelet of jade beads slid the length of his wrist. By the time I got my head together and came back Larry was away in the convalescence home.

Applause swelled in the auditorium then burst out through the doors as the corridor began to fill with people. In the background the MC was saying there was still more to come.

Blain and Avery instinctively stood, went with the flow.

Do you mind me asking, Avery said close to Blain's ear, is your mother still alive?

She is, more's the pity, said Blain, then added a quick God forgive me. Alzheimer's, he explained. And after the life she had with my dad. It'd break your heart sometimes to see her. Doesn't know me from Adam.

They were through the foyer and on to the street. It was late-night shopping, the start of the weekend. A blackboard before a neighbouring café-bar said, Every Hour is Happy Hour, above a clock with no hands. Buses and cars sped people to their nights on the town.

Two youths moved among the departing lecture audience with newspapers and flyers. *Socialist Worker*, they shouted. End oppression home and abroad.

I think your brother might be in need of help, Avery said.

Listen, said Blain, scribbling on a flyer, this is my number, if he ever gets in touch again.

Ruth roused being carried into the house. Seeing Frances, she started to sob, reaching out her arms.

I don't believe you, Frances said, over the child's shoulder. The one night I ask you to try and be on time.

As soon as she had Ruth settled again she had a bath and got ready for bed. Avery said he would sit another half-hour. Take as long as you like, said Frances, in such a way that she didn't have to add, you always do.

6

My brother has been got at too, Larry said.

He had phoned again asking to meet, at the taxi rank outside Central Station as the lunchtime train from Dublin arrived. The moustache was gone and there were red marks either side of his nose suggesting he had recently been wearing glasses. Even with the glasses, though, Avery would have recognized him straight off. He had on what Avery realized this fifth time of seeing it was the same sports jacket he always had on, a blue-grey tweed of a style so unremarkable that it lent shape to whatever version of himself, real or feigned, he wanted to project: Sunday-morning drunk, man-about-town on business, cross-border day-tripper.

It was a Tuesday. The season seemed decisively to have turned since the day before. They had walked – or been pressed by the wind into walking – riverwards, past the Maysfield leisure centre, and along the Laganside path as far as the gasworks before Avery mentioned Blain.

Larry had stopped, holding on to the guardrail, listening while Avery recounted all that had passed between the two of them in the corridor of the Ulster Hall. A rowing eight of foundered-looking teenage girls drifted in an arc before the old lock-house. On the far bank, a man riding what appeared from the wayward front wheel to be a trick cycle shouted instructions, which did not carry the distance. Larry pitched in his opinion that his brother had been got at.

Avery, beside him, said nothing.

Larry slapped the guardrail. Oh, come on, you must see that. They're paying him. Or just keeping him out of prison. He has a drugs conviction. Did he tell you that?

No.

No, I bet he didn't.

Rain had started to fall. The man on the trick cycle dismounted and pulled a nylon anorak from a pouch at his waist. The girls gathered themselves, leant forward into the wind, leant back almost flat, and the boat arrowed out of sight beyond the lock-house before he could get back in the saddle.

It's the way they work, said Larry. You not think it's a bit strange my brother just bumping into you like that? Him and you, out of a whole city of people?

Not a whole city. We had narrowed down the chances. We were a self-selecting group. I have a professional interest in the Dalai Lama. And your brother *did* go travelling in that part of the world.

When I had my accident.

Avery had decided on the drive down to meet him to omit nothing. I'm only telling you what he told me.

Avery didn't tell Larry that it was also what Elspet had told him, having no fortuitous meeting to explain his talking to her.

A blue-liveried commuter train came from the direction the schoolgirl rowers had just gone and from the other side of the lock-house, winding down as it rolled between the riverside walk and the gasworks on its way to Central.

You think I might just remember myself having this accident.

Avery said nothing.

Larry laughed. So that's their insurance policy. If I start to remember what really happened they just say I fell off a motorbike, there's something the matter with my head. The more I remember, the more they say it, and the less anyone believes me.

It was a pretty good policy, Avery thought, if policy was what it was.

The commuter train had stopped behind them, its carriages, as Avery glanced back, sitting high on their wheels, the passengers at the windows for a moment as two-dimensional as targets in a fairground rifle range. He thought of the odd discontinuities of his conversations with Larry. Today it was as though the pops of their previous meeting had never been mentioned. There was a tremendous silence, ended the second after it became apparent by the boom of a goods train breaking cover for the border, rust-red wagons jolting.

Larry looked at his watch. The rain was getting heavier. We should head back, he said, but didn't move. His eyes closed. They were a long time opening again.

I feel I'm failing you, Avery wanted to say.

Larry put his hand into his jacket pocket. He turned something over – a coin, maybe – between his fingers.

I remembered last night, he said, as clear as if I was there again, pushing a bar table over with my foot. One of the women had slumped to the side and I wanted to be able to get at her, you know, to make absolutely sure.

He coughed, took the hand from his pocket in a fist.

But you only had to look at her, she was dead all right. There was no way she couldn't be. Whatever way she'd fallen, her neck was twisted, and the chain she had on her had broken. I mean it was a cheap-looking thing, a wee gold locket on the end of it.

He opened his fist.

Avery gasped.

Larry jogged his hand, demonstrating the want of weight. The chain swirled and then drained down without sound to the locket in the well of his palm.

Avery resisted, as instinctively wrong, an urge to touch it with his own fingertips.

All these years I've had this in a box, trying to work out whose it was. I was thinking maybe a gift to some old girlfriend. Tore it off and flung it back at me in a row.

(The chain was clearly snapped above the clasp.)

And then last night it finally came back to me, holding out my hand as it slipped off the woman's neck. And I remembered panicking. Worse than panicking. I totally flipped. That's why they opened my head up. They were looking for the off switch.

Why'd they not take the necklace away from you?

Larry looked at it, then at Avery, eyes pained that there were still gaps he couldn't fill, for both of them. He shrugged. Maybe I didn't let on to them I had it. Maybe I'd an idea what they were going to do to me and hung on to it to remind myself.

Twenty-odd years later, Avery said.

Larry shrugged again. Better than never, isn't it?

His hand was feeling for the pocket when Avery asked him was there anything inside the locket.

He used his thumb-pads, having no nails to speak of. So great was the pressure, so flimsy was the locket, that at the moment the lid lifted, Avery thought the thing was broken. Larry's touch was gentle as he nudged the lid back far enough for Avery to see inside. A wizened stem of small bluish flowers.

Forget-me-nots, Avery said.

They parted in the station concourse where the black-taxi drivers plied their rival and unregulated trade. Taxi? they'd ask, appearing at your shoulder, then keep you standing after you'd said yes while they found four more fares to fill their cab. Taxi? Avery, distracted by one of these, didn't see where Larry went, though there were as many sideways-talking black-taxi drivers as there were passengers in the station at that hour of the afternoon. One moment he was there the next he wasn't. Avery wasn't surprised. He wouldn't have been entirely surprised if he had caught sight of him in his sports jacket herding five bewildered passengers towards a waiting cab.

There was no arrangement to talk again soon, but equally no doubt in Avery's mind that they would.

He still had another call to make before going home – the taciturn Mr Booth and his daughter. The daughter talked for the three of them today. *This used to be a great area for shopping, now it's all mobile phones and tat.* Avery had to struggle the whole time he was there to keep his mind from wandering to the Laganside walkway and the locket in Larry's hand.

It was closer to half five than five when he let himself in the front door. Ruth was watching TV unsupervised in the family room. Avery called out to Frances that he was home as he sat down on the floor beside his daughter.

What's this? he asked her.

Em.

She had been told that she wasn't just to sit in front of the TV looking at it, but only watch what she wanted to see. He could tell she knew she should know and that this was making it harder.

These boys, she said. Em. And there's a lady in a thing.

A castle? he asked, seeing a woman just then descend into a children's television idea of a dungeon.

A hat, said Ruth.

Avery's knee cricked as he got to his feet.

Switch it off when that's done, now, won't you?

Ruth relaxed, relieved.

Frances was sitting sideways at the kitchen table, feet up on another chair, spooning mash from a pot on to a bed of mince. Close the door over, she said.

Ruth's in there on her own.

I know, she'll be OK for a minute. Close the door over.

Avery pushed it almost to.

Turn on the radio.

What's this all about? Avery asked.

Tony's having an affair.

What?

An affair. I've had Michele round, she's in bits.

Tony?

I know, isn't it awful?

Did he say something? I mean, is she sure?

That's what I asked her. She says she knows the signs. Apparently it's not the first time. You'd have thought, like, with the baby and everything. Well, clearly, *Michele* thought with the baby and everything.

Avery walked to the sink, ran the tap too hard, turned it till the gush had reduced to a fluid rope. He inserted his fingertips, shook them free of drips and kneaded the hand towel. What's she going to do?

Frances was ploughing furrows in the mash with the back of a fork. Top to bottom, side to side, criss-cross, criss-cross.

I said if it was me I wouldn't even stop to think, I'd send him packing.

You didn't say that?

I did. And I would.

It was said without challenge or threat. She was still imagining herself in her friend's shoes.

There's no use preaching the sanctity of marriage to the wife who's having to put up with the like of that, baby or no baby.

Avery didn't reply.

Well, is there? Frances asked, levering herself out of her seat.

She must have known it was an unfair question.

You'd want to be good and certain before you went and did anything you'd regret, he said.

How much more certain does she need to be? She's seen it all before, the creeping around, the *sneakiness*.

Has she talked to him?

And what's he going to say to her? Funny you should ask, I am actually having an affair? He's a sneak, there's no point talking to him.

I'm only thinking there might be some other explanation.

What? Like being a minister?

What does that mean?

It means it's just as well I know I can trust you.

For the first time in the conversation he thought he detected a note of warning. Do you think we could slow down here, take a couple of steps back? he said.

Frances slumped against the fridge. Oh, listen, I don't know what I'm saying. I'm just upset for her. It's rotten and she's pregnant and it's just not fair.

Avery took his wife in his arms. No, you're right, it's not fair. Not fair at all.

He left four messages next day before Tony finally rang back, barely able to contain himself. Avery, I don't know if you're aware how things work here. It's a hospital, you know, sick people, dying people. We're not supposed to jam the lines with social calls.

It isn't something I could ring you about at home, said Avery. Michele's been round.

There was a pause. He thought he heard the blades of the Meccano helicopter being struck. The sigh that followed sounded forced.

I'm telling you this in strictest secrecy, Avery said. She seems to think there's something going on. I just wanted you to know that I'm here to talk to, as a friend.

The next sigh lacked all conviction. Don't flatter yourself, Tony said and put the phone down.

He rang again an hour later. I'm sorry, that was uncalled-for. You're right, I'm in a bit of a spot.

Do you want to talk about it?

Maybe another time.

Now it was Avery who was exasperated. Tony, he said, Michele . . .

And the baby, you don't have to tell me, it's all I'm thinking about, trying to sort this out.

That was genuine enough, Avery decided. He didn't press the point. If there's anything I can do.

I will, I'll let you know. Thanks.

Avery cleared his throat. Listen, while I have you on.

Oh, no, here we go, Tony said, much more like himself. You need me to check something. What is it this time?

A medical record.

Tony emitted a sharp *ha*, in the key of B for biscuit-taking. You have got to be joking. Tell me you're joking.

Of course I am.

Bad joke, Tony said. Very bad joke.

★

The following day, Thursday, the *East Belfast Community News* appeared. Avery was on page three, looking just a little cross in the crowd gathered round the Dalai Lama. The caption explained that the picture had been taken at the Springfield Road peace line, but the main story, immediately to the right, focused on protests, staged elsewhere in the city on the day of the visit, by fundamentalist Protestant clerics.

It was anyone's guess what meaning the casual reader would have assembled from this smorgasbord of image and words. Avery looked to have a foot – a face – in both camps.

7

North Belfast was not so much another country as another continent. In comparison with its myriad internal borders the sectarian divides in the east and west were as clear-cut as the 38TH Parallel. While he was still assistant in Holywood Avery had been asked to entertain a colleague from England, in town for the General Assembly and requesting a tour of the city. Avery, coming in by bypass and motorway, started in the north at the sectarian roulette wheel that was Carlisle Circus. Twenty-five minutes later – the Crumlin Road later, Ardoyne, Ligoniel, Oldpark, Limestone Road, Tiger's Bay, North Queen Street, enclave within enclave later – he was approaching the junction again, intending to take the turn for the Shankill and all points west, when his passenger asked could he be dropped off in the city centre. He had a bit of shopping to do. Avery apologized for not fitting more in, he hadn't realized they were so pressed for time.

I didn't say, said the Englishman. But don't worry, you showed me plenty. He touched Avery's hand, like sorry for your troubles. Really, he said, I've seen enough.

North Belfast had peace lines in public parks. When political storm clouds gathered, it was a fair bet they would empty first over north Belfast. Even before the millennium, even before the peace process, north Belfast now and again seemed like another century.

Avery closed his glove compartment and stepped out into a tree-lined avenue off the Cavehill Road. It was a glorious morning, the last of the leaves turning lazy circles in the pale November sunshine as the branches let go their grip. Traffic was muffled. A dog – perhaps the one Avery had seen just now, with a stick in its mouth, on the rising bank of the waterworks, as he waited to make a right turn – yapped distantly, ecstatically.

That was the other thing about north Belfast, there were few parts of the city – of any city Avery could think of on the island – more beautiful.

He rang the bell of a three-storey Victorian townhouse. The door was opened by a man in his later sixties, heavyset, carrying a copy of the *Irish Independent*.

You found us all right, he said, offering Avery his hand. Leo.

They walked down a long hallway to the back sitting room. The windows looked on to a yard with an archway through to the narrow garden, a green oil tank at the end of it raised on a bed of concrete. A bird-feeder hung from a bracket on the yard wall. A woman came through from the kitchen. She had a hearing-aid, so diminutive as to be decorative, in each ear.

Patricia, said the man by way of introduction.

Ken Avery, Avery said and shook her hand too.

Is it maybe too soon for tea? she asked.

Avery wasn't long finished breakfast. I'm fine for the moment, but you go ahead.

Oh, we're all right a while, aren't we, Leo?

Yes, yes.

Birthday cards lined the mantelpiece. Wife, Mum, Grandma, Sister.

It's not today, is it? Avery asked apologetically.

Yesterday, said Patricia.

Seventy-one years young, said her husband, and she laughed, Avery laughed.

They all stood looking at the cards.

Will you? Patricia pointed to an armchair.

Sorry. Leo moved the television remote from an arm of the settee, turned another chair to face into the room more. Sit anywhere.

He waited for Avery to choose then sat himself. His wife continued standing. I hope you don't mind me asking, she said. Was that you on the radio a while back?

Why, yes, it was. But how did you know? I mean, Avery went on, not wanting her to think he was thinking of her double hearing-aid, well, that was the middle of the summer.

It was Leo remembered your name, she said.

You were repeated on the *Best of* on the Saturday morning, said Leo. I tape them and send them to the brother in California the odd time. I thought when I was talking to you on the phone the name was familiar. Avery. I was able to phone him and ask him to look the tape out.

You went to a lot of trouble.

It was no trouble to me, said Leo. It was the brother listened back to them all until he heard you.

You were very good, said Patricia. I normally can't be in the same room as that programme.

A clock in the hallway struck the quarter-hour.

I'll just fill the kettle anyway, she said. Have it all ready.

She eased the kitchen door closed behind her. Avery read it as his signal to start. I really appreciate you agreeing to talk to me like this. I'm sure it can't be easy.

Leo rearranged the folded paper on his lap. Actually there are days I can hardly call her to mind at all, he said. The physical fact of her, I'm talking, not the photos, the same lot of stories you repeat about her.

He nodded towards the cards on the mantelpiece: Like we always say, she was hopeless about birthdays. Always something going on made them slip her mind. You'd get a call from her two or three days later, all apologies, or she'd turn up with something, buns in a box. Or maybe she only ever did that the once. And maybe it was only a handful of birthdays she missed, all told.

He stopped, seemed to review what he had just said then shook his head as though dismissing it. But it's like that with everybody, isn't it? Doesn't matter how they died or how you try to keep their memory alive. They sort of get boiled down. They lose their – well, like I say – their physical substance.

Avery nodded through the substantial memory of Joanna's body and his knocking over chairs.

So something as small as the necklace you were telling me about on the phone, Leo said, I could say yes or I could say no. I could imagine just from you mentioning it I remember Mairead having one like it, or I could swear I'd never clapped eyes on it, forgetting she wore it every single day. You see what I'm saying?

Avery nodded again. Was this the house the police had brought the news to that night? (Police? Police and half a battalion of soldiers, more like, the ambushes and all that there were.) Was this the brother who was interned back then, or the brother in California? It was Des's mate Bernard Moody had helped trace this one. Ask around enough and you were almost guaranteed to find someone who had known, or knew someone else who had known, any victim's family. Des, to his credit, hadn't asked Avery why he was so interested.

I've been on the phone to Clare, Leo said, Roisin's daughter.

Roisin was the other woman in the bar, the woman having the affair. Her daughter by a previous marriage was twelve when her mother was murdered.

She's in England. She doesn't really come back now. Anyway. She says it doesn't ring any bells with her either, the necklace. But then again, she was more or less living at her granny's the last lot of months, after Roisin took up with your man Davy. It's always possible. Anything is.

The kitchen door opened a couple of feet and Patricia returned and sat in the nearest armchair, looking out the window as if that denoted an added, voluntary deafness.

Roisin and my sister, Leo went on, had, well, a reputation I suppose you'd call it. They were both a bit on the reckless side. Careless, at least.

Out the corner of his eye Avery saw a soft smile surface on Patricia's lips. A cat was patrolling the yard wall above the bird-feeder.

What age would you be yourself? Leo asked, out of the blue.

Me? Avery blinked. Thirty-four.

Leo nodded. People had their own ways of coping with what was happening in those days, he said. It's easy to be critical now.

Nothing could be further from my mind, Avery said. I hope you didn't think . . .

No, said Leo. No.

He looked down at the paper, appeared for a few moments to become absorbed in a column.

Patricia stood. Tea now, I think.

Yes, said Avery. Please.

Leo set the paper aside. Do you think it's him? he asked. Patricia sat again.

I don't know, Avery said.

When – after talking to Des, who talked to Bernard, who talked to whoever had given him the number that came back via Des to Avery – he had first phoned Leo he had said he had come into possession of certain information that might, just might, relate to his sister's murder. It wasn't the cleverest of approaches. Leo kept asking him the obvious and reasonable questions and Avery, try as he might to put off answering till they met face to face, did not say a categorical no when asked had he spoken to someone who had been involved.

And if it is him, Leo said now, then changed tack. I mean, whatever about the necklace, you wouldn't make it up, would you?

You wouldn't think so, thought Avery.

Funny, Patricia said.

The two men looked at her. She shook her head as though at a thought inadvertently given voice. Conscience, she said. Her tone was still apologetic, but Avery guessed there was nothing accidental about the intervention. The way it only gets too much to live with once they know that no one can touch them for what they did.

Her understanding of the legal status of offences committed before the ceasefires was as wide of the mark as it was widely subscribed to.

Patricia and I disagree on this, Leo said simply.

Patricia turned her attention once more to the window. The cat had gone. An unseasonably plump sparrow sat on the wall in its place. I just think it's funny, that's all.

And I just think it would be good to know, said Leo to Avery. To look someone in the eye and ask them how she died. Ask them why.

They were silent for a moment then Leo sprang up. Sit where you are, he told Patricia. I'll get the tea.

In the hallway, half an hour later, he opened his wallet and showed Avery a photograph. A studio passport shot, the dimensions on their own dating it. The face was all drawn in towards the mouth, a study in not smiling. The hair looked like it had been lifted off a props shelf – *early sixties perm* – and balanced on top of her head; the eyes turned slightly upwards, like she was pleasantly surprised by how light it was. There was mischief there, all right.

How old is she in that? Avery asked.

Twenty-five? said Leo, thinking. Round about. She's carrying a bit of weight there, like. It's really not that good of her.

He turned the wallet away from Avery, peered into its slowly closing V. Actually, it's not like her at all.

Avery put a hand on the doorknob. I'll call you straight away I have anything more definite.

Leo made a clucking sound. I've waited this long. To tell you the truth I'd pretty much given up hope.

They were on the doorstep when Patricia called out.

What? Leo had to walk back down the hall. He leant in the sitting-room door, leant out. She says she'll listen out for you on the radio.

Oh, I think I've had my fifteen minutes, I can't see them asking me back.

Leo relayed this into the sitting room: He says he doesn't think they'll have him back.

And Patricia said – Avery heard it before Leo bounced it on – Tell him he should make them put him on.

Avery was over the river and half-way up the road to his church, wipers still working to clear the north Belfast leaves from the windscreen, before her words revealed their kernel of rebuke.

★

He put his head round the door of the Wee – that is the Hatton Memorial – Hall where the Old Wives' coffee morning was drawing to a close.

Morning, ladies.

Typical man, an Old Wife (it was Dorothy Moore) said, with an Old Wife's licence and daring. Just in time to be too late for the washing-up.

Never listen to her, said another, taking another Old Wife tack. Come on ahead in, Reverend.

Many years ago, before Avery was even a twinkle, before PC was more than a polite term for peeler, the Old Wives had been the Young Wives, until the church, wanting to move with the times, rechristened them the Wives' Fellowship and then the Women's Fellowship Group, the name by which they were still listed in the weekly announcements and annual accounts. But the eight remaining Old Wives didn't care any more what the church thought they should be. They weren't kidding themselves or anyone else: they were old. Say it loud. They had survived.

A gang of four crowded round Avery. A Tupperware box of homemade buns was waved under his nose.

Pineapple delight?

Thanks, I won't.

Take one home. Take a couple. Take a few, one for each of you.

Not be long now till you'll need an extra one.

How is Mrs Avery?

Great. She's her bag and all packed.

I'll bet.

Where's she having it, the Royal? Dundonald?

The Royal.

Oh, the Royal's great.

Our Karen's youngest had hers in Dundonald, now, and she hadn't a bad word to say.

Oh, Dundonald has a great name.

They both have.

They do.

So had the City.

Oh, yes, the City.

(Turning their attention again, now that was all settled, to Avery.) That wee one won't know herself.

What age is she now? Six?

Just coming up to five.

Five?

The size of her.

Dear, dear, it doesn't be long.

I'm sure she'll be as good as gold for yous.

Here – the pineapple delights were wafted again – there's no tinfoil left, take the lot of them. You can give me the Tupperware back some other time.

It was like a mugging in reverse. They dispersed towards their coats and bags, leaving him holding more than he had come in with.

On the far side of the room Lorna Simpson, the youngest of the Old Wives, was turning a table on its side.

Leave that, Avery called.

I will not, said Lorna. We always put the hall back exactly as we found it.

On the wall, over her shoulder, was a sign requesting that groups do just that, if you could call something punctuated with three red exclamation marks a request.

Well, let me, then.

Avery set down the box of buns.

It's no trouble, Lorna said. I do it every month. There's a knack.

She hit a hinge with the heel of her hand. Hit it again. The table's legs folded in as if in self-defence. She allowed Avery to turn it on its end and walk it to the store cupboard.

Ronnie would have done this, he said.

Ronnie has enough to do.

And he's paid enough to do it, Avery didn't say. Rather, he asked after Michael.

Sure I hardly see him he's out that much. And then, of course, this time of the year . . . Avery held her coat for her to put on. Well, it's – thank you – all gearing up to Sunday.

She smoothed her collar, looking down the length of her face to make sure the leaf on her poppy was straight. Avery turned to find the other women had put on their coats too: fleecy, tweedy, and quilted; this year's, last year's, no year's you could put a number to, made uniform by the poppy at the breast.

I thought for a moment there you'd forgotten, said Lorna Simpson by his ear.

No.

What Avery had forgotten was that the poppy he had been wearing when he left the house, and which, switching off the engine twenty minutes later in that avenue of falling leaves, he had thought it diplomatic to remove, was still lying in his glove compartment.

Sorry. A lot on my mind, he said.

Of course you have, said one of the gang. Away you on home. Put those buns in the fridge now, they've fresh cream in them. Tell Mrs Avery I was asking after her.

And me.

And me.

And me.

And me, said Lorna Simpson. Look forward to hearing you in church on Sunday.

Frances ate four pineapple delights, one after the other. She groaned. Oh, those are just . . . *Unhh!* I'm a terrible mother. Take that last one away before I eat that on Ruthie too.

Half an hour later she ate the last one too.

Take her out on to the road after school and get her a wee treat, she said.

Avery had a full afternoon. The treat had to keep to Saturday morning. He went with Ruth to the pet store and looked at the rabbits and goldfish. He went with her to Buy Rite, a local cinema become local department store, where Ruth spent a long time wandering the aisles before deciding on a transparent purse and a ruler. They stopped at the door to let Ruth put a pound in a poppy-seller's tin and had just stepped on to the street when Avery was hailed from under the awning of Granny Knows Best by a teenage girl with hair in beaded blonde braids all the way to her scalp.

He smiled his playing-for-time smile.

It's Wendy, the girl said, her own smile turning uncertain, Marshall's mummy?

Wendy, he said, I'm sorry. Your hair.

She raised a hand to it. Had it done the other day. You know, try and give myself a wee lift.

She'd succeeded. She looked transformed – again – from the girl he had last seen keeping vigil by her boyfriend's hospital bed. The resilience of youth was not an empty phrase.

My mummy's minding the baby, she said. Let me get

out on my own a while. Tell you the truth, but, I'm just wandering around here killing time till I can go and collect him again.

Granny Knows Best had its awning opened whatever the weather. Beneath it were to be found rails of kiddie-sized T-shirts, which changed not with the season but with the rise and fall of the child-friendly chart acts whose faces were printed on them; a wire bin of socks; another of underwear; and a third, which in the marching season held plastic Union Jacks and at Hallowe'en witches' masks, though it was anybody's guess what you would find there at other times of the year, on one occasion tobacco tins decorated with marijuana leaves: *Only £2.99!*

(The tins were shrinkwrapped with a pack of Rizlas, a novelty lighter and, Granny alone knows why, a chunky LCD watch. Avery had picked up one of the packages. The lighter was a lipstick, the tobacco tin had a slogan below the leaf, Love It Like It Is.)

I wouldn't normally shop here for him, Wendy said, as if it was something she had to apologize for.

Avery said it was a great place for a bargain, then he apologized he hadn't been back in to see Dee.

Wendy told him there was nothing to be sorry about, she and Dee just thought it was sound he'd come when he did.

Dee and me weren't the kind to get on with teachers or nothing, she said, know when we were at school. And, like, we never went back to church after Marshall was christened.

I sometimes wonder that parents can even make it along for that, Avery said. The first lot of weeks especially, you're lucky if you can get out the front door.

Wendy said, Door? I thought I was never going to get out of *bed*. I'd Dee running around like two men and a wee lad.

When she laughed her head flicked back and the braids trembled so that the beads clicked. Ruth was mesmerized.

This here your wee one? Wendy asked, settling her hair with her hand. She's lovely. That's what I was hoping for, a wee girl. Like, I'm not disappointed or nothing, don't get me wrong. I wouldn't change our Marshall for the world, but at first, you know, I was certain I was having a girl.

I'm going to have a baby brother, Ruth said.

Brother or sister, Avery corrected her.

Brotherorsister.

Won't that be great? said Wendy, and Ruth, who had not always or even often been persuaded of this, nodded enthusiastically.

How much longer does your wife have to go? Wendy asked Avery.

Not long now. And what about Dee? he asked. When do you think he'll be out?

Could be the end of next week, they've him moved on to the main ward. He's able to hold his own knife and fork and, ah, everything.

Her face flared in a sudden blush.

Oh, right enough, Avery said, as his own face came out in sympathy.

Frances was where they had left her an hour before, where she would, if let, have been all the hours of these last long days, in the bath. Avery asked at the bathroom door was it OK if they came in. Ruth went ahead with a bunch of yellow Bonnie Jeans.

Are these for me? Frances took the flowers, pulling Ruth down for a kiss.

We met a beautiful lady, Ruth said, and Daddy went all red.

146

Frances raised her head from the blooms. The bath plug was old and pitted, the water had been leaking slowly from its pink high-tide mark around her navel.

Oh, aye? she said.

It was just Wendy, said Avery. You know, the wee girl whose boyfriend was beaten up. I went to see him in the hospital. Remember, they had the baby?

Frances handed him the Bonnie Jeans. Why'd you go red?

I can't tell you now, he said, and made a face at Ruth's back.

Frances paid it no heed. You can't tell me much these days. Why'd you go red?

I didn't, really, not like that.

Like what? Like you are now?

I'm not.

But he could feel it, he was. I'll go and put these in water.

You might want to put your head in too.

Beam, beam, said Ruth, who was, of course, learning as much in the playground as she was in the classroom. Her hands were little flashing headlights. Beam, beam.

It was not the start he wanted to the day before tomorrow. He went to the study after lunch to prepare his service, but couldn't concentrate. He went there again when Ruth was in bed and there was less traffic on the maisonettes' staircase. Still his attention strayed. He wandered downstairs, watched a bit of the Festival of Remembrance on TV, returned to the study. He brooded. He fretted. He turned to the *Lectionary*. Year B, the Year of Mark, suggested readings for Remembrance Sunday. Deuteronomy four, commencing at verse nine: Only take heed to thyself, and keep thy soul diligently, lest thou forget the things which thine eyes have seen, and lest they depart from thy heart all the days of thy life.

He didn't read on to verse ten. Frances came to tell him to

go to bed. (He was back in the guest room these nights.) I'm going, he said and sat on till Saturday ticked down into Sunday, waiting for the uplift. He sat some more. He looked at his stack of six-by-fours and saw the top one was filled with doodles. Elaborately linked chains, clusters of tiny flowers. He tore the card in two and put his head down on his desk.

8

Avery knelt in the Minister's Room and prayed. A prayer almost free of structure, free beyond the springboard *dearfatherinheaven* of words. More an opening up, too visceral to style the outpouring of the heart alone. He felt drained.

It was eleven minutes past the eleventh hour and in the moment before the words went he had been wondering how he was going to put from his mind for the next ninety minutes the things he had lately seen and the accusations he had heard made in this room against the descendants of the servicemen whose sacrifice he was tasked publicly to remember.

Tomorrow, the thirteenth day of the eleventh month, the inquiry was due to resume in Derry into the events of Bloody Sunday, as far in one direction from the last war as they were in the other from today. Avery had no difficulty accepting that the army had been culpable there, though he didn't believe you needed to see premeditation in its murderous actions. Young men trained for combat – for airborne assault! – hyped-up and sent into a residential area? Recklessness was what it was.

He was still on his knees when Joel Prentice knocked to let him know there were five minutes until service began. Avery picked himself up, like a man who had taken an accidental tumble, checking the knees of his trousers, the toes of his shoes, and used up half the time that remained ensuring that his robe, his hood and his bands were just so. Lifting his Bible, six-by-four cards clasped blindside, he took one step out the door and another, the next instant, back. The choir, robed in Presbyterian blue, passed at a clip. Up the line to sing. He counted eleven of them, a full company. When the last member had disappeared round the corner he listened for the momentary swell of congregational chatter as Joel opened the door into the sanctuary, the almost immediate hush, and the first notes of the organ, before the door swung shut again, leaving him alone in the corridor. He stood a moment at the vertex of the L and the thought – it was no more than a pulse – passed through his mind that he could turn and go the other way, but already his feet were moving. They felt far, far away from his trunk. He paused again at the door, giving Joel time to open the pulpit Bible, fold back the blue silk bookmarks to hang down over the fall, their gold tassels mingling with the flames of its ever-burning bush. *Ardens sed virens.*

He pushed the door. In the second before he averted his eyes, he gauged that there was barely a seat free downstairs. His feet carried him the length of the two front pews, a single woman, with a single medal, among the two lines of veterans, and officers and NCOs of the Boys' Brigade, rising to attention; the organ first ahead, then alongside and finally behind him, giving him the extra push that took him up the carpeted steps of the chancel to the foot of the pulpit stairs. His prayer at the top was a gulp as of oxygen. Help.

The organ stopped. He raised his head and held out his hands. Let us . . .

He swallowed. In the front left pew Michael Simpson's service medals tilted to the right.

Let us, he began again, and in his head the words were forming, *I'm sorry, I don't think I can*, when help arrived. A sneeze, directly in front of him, eight rows back. A woman's face, beetroot.

Bless you, he said, and suddenly there seemed more air in the church, as though everyone had decided to let go a little of the breath they were holding. Avery got his line out.

Let us join together as a congregation in prayer.

A service is a sermon squared. Rhythm is all. (Patter, from – whisper it – paternoster: it was *us* invented stand-up. Twiss again.) Avery found the rhythm he had despaired of finding yesterday. The rise and fall of the voice, the announcement of hymns and psalms, all stand, all sit, the opening and closing of the Bible, the pregnant pause, the pregnant pause, the pregnant pause, the release of Let us pray.

Sometimes when it was over he would wonder where the time had gone.

The service was reaching its climax. The woman with the single medal (her name was Deborah Magill and she had sailed with the Falklands armada) stood side-on to the pulpit with two captains, Davidson formerly of the Royal Artillery, and Rogers currently of the Boys' Brigade. On the wall before them, where they had just laid wreaths, was a simple bronze plaque. To the glorious memory of the members of this congregation who gave their lives in the service of their country. Their names were repeated in black biro on a card beneath the lectern light. Avery scarcely needed to glance down to read them.

Robert Benson, Michael Harbison, Matthew Herbert, Alexander 'Sandy' Hope, St John Hope, William Hope, William McElvey, George McIlhenny, Terence McMaster, Oliver Owens, James Ross, John Ross, Norman Stewart . . . always there was a moment, it came back to him from his own childhood, listening, when it seemed they would go on and on and on, just before – Ashley Thompson – they ended.

For two minutes afterwards, utter silence. Then a note ballooned, crimson from brass, filled the sanctuary and yielded a second note, stretched thinner, higher, disappearing; then, one-two, there they were again; gone again; a fading – though Avery could see through the doors thrown open at the end of the central aisle the living, breathing bugler's shoes and trouser-legs – like a battery running down. But already the first note was ballooning again and the second this time broke into a loping run of seven notes. The trouser-legs rose on the toes of the shoes.

(The bugler was thirteen. The first decent bugler the BB had had in over twenty years.)

In the foreground Avery saw grown-old men and women fill up, remembering. Robert. Michael. Matthew. Alexander-who-got-Sandy. St John, who no doubt got all sorts. The two Williams. George. Terence. Oliver. James. John. Norman. Ashley. Friends, some of them, though you didn't need to have known them personally to be caught up in the emotion of the moment; the emotion and, yes, the beauty. Like the soft rain of leaves at the end of the televised service. Tens and tens of thousands. He raised a thumb to an itch on his face. It came away wet.

Not leaves. Poppy petals.

The other side of his face itched. He went at it with the heel of his hand.

He didn't know how he made it through to the benediction.

Minister?

Guy Broudie, breaking his own after-service rule, was calling from the other side of the Minister's Room door.

Avery had been expecting him.

Come in.

It wasn't Guy came in first, but Eleanor Todd followed by Gregory Martin: a fellow elder and the church organist. Guy, bringing up the rear, stopped one step ahead of them, or they allowed themselves to fall one step behind.

Avery held up a hand. Before you start, I know what you're thinking. I was just a little overcome by the occasion.

Minister, said Guy without preamble, there was no national anthem.

Avery's hand dropped. It was not what he had thought they were thinking at all. He said the only word that was left to him. What?

Gregory says you were to give him the nod –

You were to give me the nod, Gregory said, like a man who could easily persuade himself otherwise. That's what I thought we'd agreed –

And by the time he thought about starting without you, you were already half-way down the stairs from the pulpit.

I was afraid it would look . . . Well, I didn't know how it would look, said Gregory.

Avery remembered the arrangement all right. But, it was true, he couldn't remember the anthem being sung. He hadn't given the nod.

If you recall, that was my objection to moving it in the first place, said Guy.

The national anthem had used to be sung, like any other hymn, in the course of the Remembrance Sunday service. Last year Avery had moved it to after the benediction. Guy's weren't the only concerns he had had to contend with at the next meeting of the Kirk Session.

I promise you, he'd said, it won't just drop off the end, as you put it. (Though he knew plenty of churches who had dropped it altogether. None of them had collapsed yet.)

Look what happened in the picture-houses, Michael Simpson had said.

Well, I hardly think picture-houses are a good comparison, said Avery. This is our church, we need answer to no one but ourselves.

And now, at the very first time of being put to the test, he had failed to deliver on his promise.

He addressed Gregory: I can't apologize enough.

It's not just the anthem, said Guy. He looked over his shoulder. Gregory and Eleanor looked at the floor. People are starting to worry. You've been under a lot of stress: the baby, this whole business with the Kirkpatricks. There has been some discussion – it's only fair to tell you – there has been talk of going to the Presbytery.

No we, no they, no people even this time. There has been. It was hard to appeal to There Has Been.

Is this an official complaint? Avery asked.

Guy's gaze had strayed to the calendar on the wall. Avery didn't need to turn round to know it was probably displaying the wrong date. He didn't have to think too hard how in the circumstances that might look.

An expression of concern, Guy said.

I'm OK.

Guy shrugged: that was a matter of opinion, and that in any case was not what he was concerned about.

Between the three of us, he said, and indicated Gregory and Eleanor, we've given a hundred and fifty years to this church. We have to think of the congregation.

Guy Broudie did not talk much about his career in the civil service. He volunteered even less. When Paddy Devlin died the previous year, Avery asked had Guy ever come into contact with him.

Guy nodded. He was my minister for a time. Health and Social Services.

Paddy Devlin was a socialist and a Catholic. The time Guy so matter-of-factly referred to was precisely 148 days. January to May 1974. The first, doomed attempt at power-sharing. History.

I read somewhere he would only eat in the staff canteen, Avery said.

Guy pursed his lips, nodded more slowly. I enjoyed working with him. A good minister in the making.

You must have seen a few.

More than I care to remember. The seventies especially. It was like a revolving door up there.

And that was all he would say. Personal feelings, good or bad, didn't come into it, Avery realized. Guy's allegiance was to the office of minister, not the person. Ultimately they were both servants of the people who put them there, and when change had to come, change had to come.

Reverend Jebb would be prepared to come in for a week or two if need be, Guy said now.

You know this?

I had to phone him, discuss some details.

Jebb was on standby in case Frances went into labour on a weekend. Avery nodded. There was more to come.

Say you needed some time after the baby was born. Or there's always Dr Talbot.

Talbot had been minister to the church for a brief spell in the 1960s on his way to the moderatorship: the only Moderator ever associated with the church. He had also spent a week in prison for non-payment of fines arising from an anti-Civil Rights protest. (Anti-*Republican* Rights, he would have contended then.) Now that he was retired even his former adversaries – Twiss was one – conceded that he was one of the Church's great entertainers.

Well, I hope there wouldn't be any need for either of them, Avery said.

No, said Guy, and Eleanor and Gregory shook their heads, I would hope there wouldn't be.

So you're still thinking of taking this to the Presbytery?

We'll not rule it out altogether for the moment.

Just in case?

Just in case.

Frances was arriving with Ruth as elders and organist left. She looked to be in discomfort. Avery summoned the will to stand, but Frances preferred to lean against the wall. Ruth clambered into the vacated chair and swivelled it squeakily.

I think I might just have been threatened by my own Clerk of Session, Avery said.

Frances stroked his ear, her expression tilting into pain on his behalf. I'm sure that's not the way it was meant, she said.

Avery rested his head on her shoulder. Lifted it.

What do you mean the way *it* was meant? Did you know about this?

Frances sighed and went to the cupboard for her husband's jacket. I knew they were worried about you.

You might have told me.

Frances gave him the amused look of the seriously unamused. So you're allowed to keep secrets and I'm not?

I don't keep secrets. I have a duty of confidentiality, it's part of my job.

The chair had stopped squeaking. Ruth slipped from the seat, chin dimpling, bottom lip trembling.

What's the matter? Avery asked her.

You're shouting, she said.

I'm not.

You are, said Frances, and Avery was about to say they were doing it again, ganging up on him, when Ruth pressed her head to her mother's side.

Avery dropped back into the chair. Oh, God, he said. What's happening to me?

He had been wrong to raise his voice.

He had been wrong even to think of accusing his wife and not-yet-five-year-old daughter of ganging up on him.

He had been wrong to allow himself to become so remote from them this past lot of weeks, so preoccupied.

He had been wrong to let his preoccupations, almost from day one, affect his responsibilities as minister.

He had been wrong not to insist to Larry that he was unable to help him on his own. Despite all the anxieties he had brought, Larry had appealed to his vanity in seeking him out. And he had been wrong to let that happen.

He had been *so* wrong, whatever the truth of Larry's story, to put Leo and Patricia through this, though putting them through wouldn't have been half as bad as leading them into something that he had no idea how to lead them out of.

There was only one way he could see to begin to put things right.

Towards that long day's end he sat at his study desk with the mobile phone, searching through the stored numbers. He didn't know that he had the strength to talk, or at least the strength if pushed to it to keep saying, No, I'm sorry, I've made my mind up; but it was imperative he got the message through without further delay.

He had never texted in his life. He started, as he had started long ago on his first portable typewriter, picking out the letters one-fingered. It had taken him years to become any way fluent in QWERTY. Now he had a single night to master the Nokia keypad.

Fifteen minutes passed before he figured out E. He tried to type in A and the display suggested B. He tried again, and again: B, and B. When he tried to erase he simply added more letters. Dear became DEBACA question mark. In the top right-hand corner the number 160 he remembered having seen when he switched on was now 153. It was counting down the characters. Even if he could have salvaged it from DEBACA question mark, Dear was an unaffordable politeness. Larry on its own. He supposed it conveyed a sense of urgency. It took him another twenty minutes to write. He persevered. Everything was in capitals and then suddenly nothing was. What had he pressed? He tried a couple of likely-looking keys and then tried keys at random and in combination. The capitals came back and wouldn't go away again. It wasn't working with just the index finger. He cradled the handset on the upper joints of all eight fingers, gave his itching thumbs free rein. (Timpanists, he thought, seizing their moment, turning evolution into revolution, blazing the trail for a future of timpani concerti.) At the end of two hours he had ten words: LARRY I SHOULD HAVE INSISTED on this from THE START

His shoulders and neck muscles ached. Still he persevered. I AM NOT THE MAN FOR THIS YOU NEED A MAN WITH COURAGE ALL IS AT RISK FOR ME

Thirty-three characters remaining. He could see now the impulse to abbreviate. His watch read eleven twenty-two. Almost twelve hours since he had risen at the sound of Joel Prentice's knock.

He looked at the truncated form of his name, worried it might be mistaken for its Latin double, erased it, then reinstated it. It was late. He needed this concluded before the day was out. He left the phone on the desk while he went to the bathroom. As a rule he avoided looking at himself in the mirror above the sink. Something to do with the light. Even a healthy person looked unwell. Tonight, though, lest there be any question in his mind as to motive, he stared himself straight in the eye. He looked unwell. His hair was straw, his face was putty, smudged and roughly handled. When he had finished he walked back to the study and OKd the message with the same decisiveness with which he reached for the switch of the reading lamp.

That was that.

9

It should have been the worst thing that could have happened. He was just back from leaving Ruth to school on Monday morning and was in the garden, picking wind-blown bags (mostly off-licence blue) and cigarette cartons (mostly Mayfair) out of the hedge when Frances called him from the back door.

A Mrs Press on the phone.

Press? he asked himself all the way up the garden through into the hall. Press?

Reverend Avery? It's my daddy, she said, and then Avery had her: Mr Booth's daughter. I found him this morning when I came in to check on him. Her voice broke briefly; she gasped it back together. He's dead.

I'm terribly sorry. That must have been an awful shock for you.

It was, awful, but you know at first I just stood in the bedroom doorway looking at him. I mean, I knew, but I was still thinking if I made a noise he'd wake and he didn't look like he wanted to wake. It was just like they say in all the cards, Gone to sleep.

Avery was already feeling under the stairs for the cloakroom light.

(He had added more shelves for his videos in recent weeks. There was room for only one coat per family member at any one time.)

Where are you now? he asked.

I'm sitting here on the bed, she said, her mouth turning away from the phone. Beside him.

Avery checked with her that the doctor had been called, asked was there a neighbour she could phone to come in and sit with her until he arrived.

June's already here, she said, and a voice that could only have come from inside the bedroom called, I'm looking after her!

Frances came to lean against the frame of the sitting-room door to watch him put on his coat. Her arms were a tight link below her breasts. A death?

He nodded. Father.

The poor woman, she said flatly.

Even her voice was holding him at bay. He stood before her and placed a kiss, inquiringly, on her forehead. He felt a bit of the resoluteness go, flowing down from where his lips had touched: head to neck to shoulders. She tightened the link of her arms, pulling herself back, stood straight. Too soon for that.

I'll go ahead and have lunch if you're not back.

I'll do my best. It just depends.

Frances withdrew to the sitting room. As he settled into the driver's seat, though, Avery saw her at the window. She kissed her fingertips, turned them slowly and touched them to the glass. He received the blessing with a smile, which held as far down the main road as the post office with its habitual first-thing-Monday-morning queue stretching out into the street. Those for whom the weekend's end couldn't come soon enough. The old, the unwaged, the only just coping, the man who appeared wherever there was a queue to have a yarn with whoever was in it whatever the weather.

★

An ambulance had arrived – much good it could do – and was parked half on the footpath, three feet from the front gate, to allow traffic to pass along the narrow street. Two primary-school boys, as essential to a parked ambulance as a man spinning yarns was to a post-office queue, clambered on the wheel arches trying to see inside.

They spotted Avery getting out of his car and slunk off down the street a way.

No school, boys? he called after them.

No church, mate? one of them called back, and they loved that, so much that the other one repeated it. No church, *mate*? No?

The front door was three feet in the other direction from the gate. Avery knocked, even though the door was ajar. A woman he didn't know looked round it and disappeared again. Alberta!

Avery was still waiting for the shout to be acknowledged when the door was thrown open. Alberta Press grabbed him by the arm. I have to show you.

She was excited, close to smiling, Avery would have said.

An ambulancewoman crouched near the top of the stairs, talking to a colleague on the landing. Avery was dragged into the front room. The woman who had looked round the door at him and who Avery guessed was June stood at the far side of the fireplace. Alberta took up position at the near side. Between them were her father's reading glasses, the television remote (for it was his museum now too) and bang in the centre of the mantelpiece, propped against the wall, a copy of the New Testament and Psalms: a Half Bible as some wags in theological college called it; and, judging by the numbered code Sellotaped to the spine, a library edition.

Alberta did smile now, satisfied that he had noticed. There

were heavy footfalls in the room above. A piece of furniture was shifted.

She lifted the Testament down carefully. What do you think? she said. This was under the bedclothes when the doctor pulled them back. I brought him it home one day after you'd been, to see would he read it. There were maps and all in it as well. He liked maps.

Loved them, June said. If you were ever going anywhere, England or that . . .

Alberta nodded, her focus gone. Avery had a vision of Ruth, once when she lost sight of him in a supermarket, and thought this was a being that lived within all of us, the child separated from the parent. The book weighed suddenly heavy on Alberta's wrist. It snapped her back. The smile resurfaced.

I thought even if he started looking at the maps, you know, it'd be a break from the television, but it just sat where I left it on the arm of the settee and then, to be honest with you, it went right out of my head. It could have been – she searched for somewhere particularly unlikely – up the chimney for all the thought I gave it. You wouldn't know with my daddy half the time what way his mind worked.

Very quiet, said June.

But look, Alberta opened the cover, pointed to the returns page. Avery's eyes, not knowing what they were looking for, could fix on nothing. Dates spilled out of their columns, blue ran into black, there were smudges, biro where date stamps had been misplaced or the pad had run out of ink.

Do you not see it? Alberta underlined the point with a nail. *There.*

And there indeed it was, today's date: 13 Nov 00.

Due For Return. June capitalized each word, then for good measure translated: Called Home.

Like it says in the cards.

They don't write them like that for nothing, June said, as solemnly as if she had been asked in a court of law to back up the word of her friend.

Alberta sat on the two-seater settee, on the cushion next to her father's, thumbs stroking the Testament's covers. When I was leaving last night he said, 'Bye, love. Not, See you in the morning, like he normally did, but 'Bye, love. I think this here Bible had let him know it was time to go. I think he was ready.

Avery sat beside her and put his hand on hers. It certainly looks that way.

He picked a psalm – even the word soothed – from the borrowed Bible. Number thirty-nine, verse four: Lord make me to know mine end and the measure of my days.

The ambulance workers and the doctor crowded in the doorway while he said a prayer.

Amen, said June at the end of it.

Frances was so delighted to see him back before afternoon that she practically turned him round and sent him out again. Are you sure they don't need you? You didn't rush home because of me, did you?

He didn't wait for her say-so. He put his arms round her. Held on tight.

Texts breed texts, or that at least was the nature of the medium as Avery understood it. He had deliberately left his phone off that morning, wanting to retain some control over what was otherwise out of his hands. He would read when he was ready to read. But though he checked half a dozen times (three in the course of the evening alone) there was not a word of any kind. No word either when he looked again at the first opportunity next morning. It was after lunch before he found something. To his own carefully measured message (measured to the last character) about what God had chosen, Larry had replied with the cheapest, most childish of shots: And if God said stick yr head in fire?

He texted back, faster than before. ID DO IT. The reply this time was as close as texting got to instantaneous. Keep listening, it said.

It was all a bit unseemly, but maybe that was in the nature of the medium, too. It generated heat. And, anyway, what had needed to be done was done and would not be undone, he suspected, without the application of more than thumbs.

He and Frances had been at the hospital that morning. The baby's head was perfectly engaged, snug as a plug in her pelvis.

Clever baby, said Frances. Clever little Yogi. And she was right, there was something mystic-like in holding the one pose from now until the onset of labour. Even the way the back was turned seemed to speak of an intense concentration. Nothing was going to stop this baby getting itself born.

I'm putting you down for another appointment in a fortnight, but I don't think we'll be seeing you back here, the midwife said.

They went from the hospital to the café they always went to after check-ups, in the furniture store on the Boucher Road. The Christmas displays had just gone up, red beginning to make a comeback amid all the blues and whites and silvers. Across the road, to the right of their window-seat, the courtyard of a garden centre was being cleared for temporary forestation in cypress and firs and spruce and pine. All far too early, it went without saying, though Avery would probably say it anyway on Sunday. Could he risk a joke? Imagine if Our

Lord had been born in Belfast instead of Bethlehem, there'd have been no need for a star: the Wise Men would have had leaflets delivered to them in the middle of November advertising his Coming.

Penny for them? Frances asked.

He shook his head. Writing my script.

You will tell me one day, won't you? she said.

What?

What you haven't told me. What's been going on. Not today or tomorrow. One day.

He thought about tomorrow, or even today – right now – and thought, just a little longer, till he was clear in his own head. One day, he said. Soon.

Frances took his hand and placed it on her stomach. Feel.

I can't feel anything.

Not even like a buzz? She moved his hand around. No? I could swear this baby's humming.

As was to be expected Wednesday, being the funeral, it emptied out of the heavens. A day for short dashes, not slow walks. It didn't dampen Alberta's spirits.

My daddy was an Orangeman, she said as she stood with Avery on the steps of the church, watching the most senior male relatives dispute among them who should have first lift of the coffin. He was well used with processing through the rain.

I thought the saying was the sun always shone on the Twelfth?

That was only ever said by those who never walked it, said June, who had materialized at Avery's other shoulder.

You got me there, then, said Avery. I've never walked it.

Of course you haven't, you've more sense, said Alberta.

She still had the library Half Bible. Avery didn't like to ask had she remembered to renew it.

Later, walking away from the grave, practically the only hole in the entire cemetery not brimming with tea-coloured water, she slipped Avery a twenty-pound note: A wee thank-you.

Sssh, she said, before he could tell her he couldn't possibly accept it. Do whatever makes you happiest. Get yourself something, or put it in the charity box. You came back when many's another one wouldn't have. You made a difference right at the end.

On Thursday morning he had a primary-school assembly. The children sat cross-legged on the floor of the dinner hall, which was also the gym and the music room. They looked, as children at these assemblies often did, as though they'd been summoned for final judgement. A few of the faces he recognized from his own congregation, but they, if anything, were more unnerved than the rest: *how did he find us here?* A teacher pointed to the words of the hymn projected on to a screen above Avery's right shoulder. They sang like their lives depended on it and only relaxed when he began his object lesson.

Can anyone tell me what this is? he asked, holding a spool of audiotape above his head. There were whispers behind hands, but no offers. No? Shall I tell you? This is what they used when I was a wee boy to record music and voices on. And one day somebody came and recorded one of *our* assemblies. Would you like to hear it? Hear what me and my schoolfriends sounded like singing?

They nodded. They would like it very much.

He turned to the head teacher and asked her did she have a reel-to-reel tape-player he could play it on. She didn't. They didn't use tape-players like that any more; they were becoming obsolete.

Oh dear. Avery's hand went to his mouth. *Obsolete?* You know what that means? Unless I can find a way to record this on to something else – producing a MiniDisc from his jacket pocket – say, one of these, nobody will ever again hear me and my schoolfriends singing.

He raised an eyebrow to let them know this might be no great loss to the world. Some were disappointed, most got the joke.

But you know, boys and girls, there is one person who always hears us, no matter what new inventions there are, no matter how we speak to him.

The hands were going up in anticipation of a question he hadn't intended asking. One boy couldn't contain himself: It's Jesus.

The head teacher, out the corner of Avery's eye, looked peeved, but Avery addressed the boy directly. That's right, it's hard to keep it in sometimes, isn't it? And he invited all the children to say it together.

Jesus! they yelled.

He watched them as they readied themselves for the closing prayer, hands flat together, wedged beneath their noses, backs straight: wholehearted now.

Afterwards he drove into town and, finding no change in his pockets, left the car for five minutes without paying and displaying while he ran into Family Books. He crossed back over the river again and pulled in at Alberta's local library. The place was practically empty. Thursday. Pension day. The library's usual morning constituency was in the supermarket.

The librarian wore a Velvet Underground T-shirt so tight that it kinked at the hem, revealing spider-legs of navel hair crawling across his shorts' white waistband. Avery explained the circumstances of the overdue New Testament and Psalms, how hard it might be for the borrower to let it go.

I know there's probably a lot of paperwork involved, but if you could accept this one as a replacement.

It was still in its white presentation box. The librarian turned the box round on the counter as though it might contain a nasty surprise. Avery had some sympathy. More than a Belfast person, the librarian was a Velvets fan, he knew to be wary of unexpected packages: how could he forget the pop of the metal cutters at the end of 'The Gift', piercing Waldo Jeffers's skull?

It is kind of unusual, said the librarian.

Mailing yourself to your girlfriend in Wisconsin is *unusual*, said Avery.

Hm? The librarian had eased the lid off. He looked at Avery, uncomprehending. So he wore the T-shirt, didn't mean he wore out the records.

It's the same as the other one, just newer, said Avery.

Yes, but everything's computerized. I'd have to . . . The librarian started keying something into the computer. He read the code on the bottom of the box, blew through loose lips, hit the space bar four or five times.

It would mean so much.

I suppose, the librarian said.

Thank you.

Avery stepped out on to the street and gave vent to the song that had been whistling round his head as he walked from the desk, its scary movie cadences following, like a groove in the memory, as inevitably as they did on disc from 'The Gift'. 'Lady Godiva's Operation'. Sex-change, Avery had long assumed (wasn't the Lady she and he in the course of the song?), until one day, catching the words *growth* and *cabbage*, he listened more closely and realized – 'Now comes the moment of great, great decision, / the doctor is making his first incision' – it was the brain.

He stopped whistling, turned abruptly into a newsagent's.

The local papers were full of Bill Clinton. The American president had confirmed that he would be visiting Belfast next month. The farewell tour. *Clinton's Christmas Odyssey*, said one headline, a reference to the address he was to give, free to whoever could scramble a ticket, at the city's new ice-hockey arena. Avery had decided before he had even paid for the paper that he would move heaven and earth to be there. Take Ruth out of school early, bring her with him. A real live American president in her own backyard. *A brand spanking new arena.* She would love it.

He risked his Wise Men joke on Sunday. It got a laugh. Wondered aloud whether he shouldn't have advertised this as a Grand Pre-*pre*-Advent Sermon! Which got another. The numbers were well down on the previous week. It happened anyway after Remembrance sunday, but he wasn't going to fool himself: he had much ground to make up. And, joking aside, he wasn't going to make the mistake of rebuking the ones who did come for the ones who didn't. He made sure and shook the hand of every person leaving. Thank you, he said. Thank you for coming. He felt like a man who had been given a second chance, again.

At lunchtime the next day the phone rang out in the hall. Avery stood up from his soup.

Don't answer, Frances said.

What if it is someone? Remember last Monday.

I do. At least eat your lunch first.

I should get it.

When you've finished your soup.

He sat.

The answer-machine picked up. The volume was set on low, the kitchen door was closed, the spoons skreighed on the bottom of their bowls. And, of course, they weren't listening.

They both recognized the voice at the same moment. Guy Broudie.

Frances gave him a weak smile. Finish your soup, she said.

He swallowed another two or three spoonfuls, but his appetite was gone. Guy had barely said a word to him since Remembrance Sunday. Even catching the peaks of his words now was enough to raise the spectre of a journey through the Church courts, from Presbytery to General Assembly.

He allowed another ten minutes to pass, taking only sips of his tea, before he went out to the hall.

Frances reached over her shoulder for his hand as he passed behind her. I'm sure it's nothing.

Which was precisely what Guy's voice gave away when Avery played back his message: I'd be grateful if you could call me. The civil servant's ingrained reticence on the record.

The phone sat like a demonstration of his Clerk of Session's reach. One of these days Avery wouldn't give in to it. He gave in, dialled.

Guy, it's Avery, and Guy said, I have some good news.

Well?

Frances was still at the table. He could tell from her expression that she had heard half the conversation. The missing fifty per cent was killing her. Was it about the insurance claim?

He nodded. It's been – the word teetered for a moment – dropped.

Dropped? Frances got up as fast as the table and meditating baby would allow. But that's brilliant.

I know, said Avery, and couldn't work out why he didn't feel it more.

Guy had said it was too complicated to start going into on the phone. He would have driven up to Belfast, only he was waiting on a man coming about the satellite. It would keep, of course, but if Avery wanted to drive down to him . . .

Go, Frances said. *Go.*

Guy's house was at the end of an S-shaped driveway on a hill above the road between Belfast and Portaferry. The front, which was angled inland, was no-nonsense eighteenth-century County Down farmhouse, big but not grand, whitewashed. The back, overlooking the neck of Strangford Lough, was dominated by a 1970s glass gallery and managed against all the odds to look like the logical, evolutionary extension. The furniture too here (Avery had never been in any other part of the house) had a seventies feel: deep carpet, brown leather sofa and chairs strewn with cushions, beige, more brown, and orange. There was a large television set – definitely nineties – and a portable CD-player jacked into the expensive but superannuated hi-fi system. (An object lesson in itself.) A pair of binoculars rested on a table next to the sofa, a guide to the seabirds of Europe and North America face down beside it. And everywhere there were photographs. Hockey teams and rugby teams, children in graduation gowns, Guy at the Palace, holding his medal, his late wife's face in the shadow of a terrific hat.

I'm still not sure I understand this, Avery said.

He had collected Ruth from school and driven her and Frances to Frances's parents, before doubling back and taking the road way-out east to Guy's. There was only so fast a man with a Primary One child and a wife in her fortieth week could go, *go*.

I mean, why their sudden change of heart?

Guy had just come back into the room with two glasses of squash. (That was what he had offered: Glass of squash, Minister?) He wore a bottle-green fleece, open at the neck, over his habitual striped shirt and tie. His leather slippers were backless and to keep them from slapping when he walked he had perfected a sort of glide across the carpet, imprinting it with a map of his favourite routes.

He handed Avery one glass then glided to the sofa, nudging the bird book aside to make room for the other.

Well, he said, I was wondering after our last conversation – delicately put, Guy – why we hadn't heard anything from Thompsons.

Thompson and Thompson were the church's solicitors.

So, I rang Tom – Robert and *Thomas* Thompson – and he said he had been waiting till he heard from the Kirkpatricks' man, McKenzie, but yes, now that I mentioned it, it had gone a bit quiet. So he rang McKenzie's and then he rang me. Well, *that*'s interesting, he said. I was all around the houses and still didn't get talking to McKenzie. I think they're stalling. And I think I know why. And he said to leave it with him for a bit.

Ensconced in his brown leather sofa, cushions to his left and right and rear, Guy was more than usually expansive. And of course, as he'd said on the phone, this was good news, it was worth stringing out a little.

He rang me again this morning. First thing he said: I was right! McKenzie was stalling. More than stalling, panicking. His client had missed two appointments with the specialist who was to write the medical report. And when he spoke to

Mrs Kirkpatrick himself she told him she didn't want the boy examined.

She must have known there would have to be an examination, said Avery.

Maybe she just wasn't prepared for it being so thorough.

Avery shook his head. It still wasn't making sense. But he had the X-ray on the day of the accident. His shoulder *was* dislocated. She can hardly have been worried that anyone would dispute it.

She might have been more concerned about what would show up than what wouldn't.

Avery pondered for a moment what this might mean. He went in the end for the slightly less distressing option. Other injuries, you mean?

Guy nodded. Historical injuries. Unreported injuries.

Avery closed his eyes and there was Sheila Kirkpatrick's face when he walked into the laundrette that afternoon in August: before the anger, the horror at the thought of *any* hurt. Some things there was just no feigning. He opened his eyes. I know there isn't a *type*, he said, but she really didn't seem to me like she was capable of it.

It doesn't have to be her.

The father? I can't see her covering for him, said Avery.

Again, it doesn't have to be her. Who is it has been driving this along up to now?

You think her father-in-law leant on her to protect his son?

We can but surmise. The circles these men move in, beating up a child is likely to lose you a lot more than friends. The only thing we know for sure is that Mrs Kirkpatrick won't agree to an examination and the claim is dead in the water.

Avery was silent a long time. Guy spread his hands. We

weren't fighting this. We were trying to speed things along. I don't think we have anything to reproach ourselves with.

It's the wee lad, Avery said. It's appalling to think.

It is, Minister, appalling, said Guy. We're both parents. But if there *is* a problem there then all of this has helped bring it to light.

Should we contact the police, then, do you think?

No, Guy said, a little sadly. I don't think we should. I don't think we can. And I wouldn't be too quick either to go making calls on the family, no matter how well intentioned.

It was already getting dark outside the big windows.

I just hate to think that our good fortune is at someone else's expense. A child's expense.

Guy walked round the room turning on lamps. With each one the world beyond the window dimmed a little more. We could always ask Session if they would approve the buying of a gift for him, once this has all settled down, he said. A football kit or something.

A football kit? Avery looked at him, disbelieving.

Or something.

A white van appeared from the murk down below on the driveway, disappeared, appeared again.

That looks like your satellite man, said Avery as the van passed out of sight round the front of the house. I should probably be going anyway.

Guy dipped his head, too deep for a nod, too shallow for a bow. I know it's a long way to come, but I thought in the circumstances, well, it would be a weight off your mind.

And although, as Avery drove back along the road from Portaferry, leaving the lough and its seabirds behind him, he tried his best to be offended by the sentiment; though he resolved to dig his heels in about the size of the gift to Darryl

Kirkpatrick when the time came, and resolved – breasting a rise in the carriageway, Belfast a surprise party of lights below – that he would be the best judge of when was soon enough to call at the house, Guy was right. It was a weight lifted.

10

When he worked at the university branch Avery would often take his lunch in the cafeteria of the Ulster Museum, across the road from the bank, in the grounds of the Botanic Gardens. He would always bring a book, though if there was a table free by the cafeteria's window he would spend more time looking out over the perimeter wall into the old Friar's Bush cemetery – for the friar's bush itself – where legend had it mass was celebrated in penal law times. There was a plague pit in there too. It bent the mind to comprehend what those two words contained. Plague pit.

On warm days he wouldn't bother with the museum, but would buy a sandwich and find a spot on the grass to spread his jacket among the snoggers, the sun-worshippers, the full-time cider drinkers and lunchtime soccer stars. Once he fell asleep with a book over his face and was woken by the sound of laughter to find his legs had been buried in cut grass. An (almost) empty beer can angled on a stick was his headstone. It was three o'clock. He ran back to work, pursued by hoots and whistles and, more closely, by a persistent smell of beer, spreading grass seed and clover far and wide. He burst through the bank's revolving door. All the counter staff were busy with customers. No one looked up as he let himself in the security door to the back office. Inside, Stu and Eilís were having a heated, whispered discussion. They parted to let him pass, then leant in to make their vehement points. Avery hung his jacket (a daisy dropped into the well of the umbrella stand) and went and sat at his desk.

At the desk opposite, Marcus bit his nail and frowned at the point where his pencil had come to rest at the bottom of a column of figures. He drummed the first two fingers of his other hand, dragged the pencil to the top again. Gail passed, floated a sheet into Avery's in-tray. No hurry with that, she said. The phone was ringing. Avery looked round the room. Were they huffing? Bluffing? Had they really not noticed he was an hour and a half late getting back from lunch? Was the smell of beer really in his head and not, as he had worried, all through his hair?

Marcus glanced up. Can you get that? he said.

Avery lifted the receiver, pressed the button for his line. Good afternoon, University Branch.

They *hadn't* noticed.

A freak occurrence, maybe – going to the toilet too often or for too long was normally enough to draw scowls and fits of watch-tapping – but one that Avery felt had granted him a glimpse of how little, ultimately, he would be missed, how impermanent was his presence here on earth. He was, true enough, on the lookout for big signs in those days. Still, it was all he could do to stop himself shouting with joy.

Hold on, please, he said, and covered the mouthpiece with the heel of his hand. Marcus, we charge for Midland cheques now, don't we?

The following morning Sean called him into his office. You're allowed one of those lunches in a working lifetime in my bank, he said, and made a gesture towards his mouth like hoisting a pint.

No, you don't understand, Avery said then stopped. Sean had sat back in his seat, as though staggered that his generosity was being refused.

Avery was faced with the choice of accepting blame for

something he hadn't done or aggravating Sean further. Nothing like that will happen again, he said.

That was the month before Joanna was murdered when all manner of things happened for a while before the true blessed meaning of impermanence reasserted itself, by which stage Avery – having weighed in late half a dozen times, performed so badly half the rest of the time he might not have bothered weighing in at all – had been let know he was lucky to still have a job.

A good man, Sean, when all was said and done. He had turned up at Avery's service of licensing, however he had heard about it, looking badly failed. He made light of his illness, but the signs were there, he wouldn't get better. When he died later that year he left word with his parish priest that Avery be let say a prayer at the graveside. That was how he first met Des, never suspecting that they would soon be near neighbours.

Marcus was at the funeral, and Gail and Stu and Eilís and all the rest. They shook Avery's hand without warmth. He might have been contagious.

We never thought you were so serious about being good-living, Gail said. When I think about all those nights out and Christmas parties.

What it was, Avery decided, they were afraid that he'd been a spy among them, cataloguing sins that would otherwise have passed unnoticed.

Avery recognized no one now when he went into the university branch. He barely recognized the branch itself since they'd got rid of the security screens, which in his day had made every customer a potential villain and rendered every transaction as guarded as a prison visit.

He stepped in to pay his Visa bill on Thursday lunchtime

on his way back from the City Hospital. (Mervyn Armstrong, emergency appendectomy.) As he queued he tried to locate, in the new open-plan area behind the counter, where his desk had been and tried too to guess where all the middle-aged bank workers had gone.

With its discreet terminals and youthful staff, it had the air back there of a casual debate about the movement of money.

The day was cold, but bright and windless. Avery had nowhere to be for another hour. He toyed with driving the short distance to the dealership where he had bought the car and booking it in for a service – the 90,000 miles was about to come up – but in the end decided to leave the car in the layby before the bank and crossed over to the Botanic Gardens.

It was too late in the year for sitting on the grass and all the benches were already taken. The usual off-season mix of trysting sixth-formers, mothers with pre-school children, cider drinkers putting in their hours. He kept going, taking the fork in the path away from the museum, past the Palm House and Tropical Ravine, and had just formed the notion to walk as far as the Chinese bakery on Agincourt for dim-sum-to-go when he saw up ahead a woman's face he knew coming from the direction of the university's gym and swimming-pool. Her hair was wet and combed to the contours of her head. It threw him. Not Gail, not Eilís. No, he was in the wrong area altogether. He ran through a few of the other possibilities as the woman strode straight on, across his path, towards the fine parade of houses overlooking the Gardens and opening on to the streets up to Stranmillis.

Of course: the quick disappearance the evening she invited him into her house.

His mouth opened, but before he could get her name out a man running from the same direction called it for him: Elspet.

She carried on walking, faster now. The man shouted again: Elspet!

Avery, though he did a quick double-take, had no trouble putting a name to his face. It was Larry's brother Blain.

They were both some way off, Blain gaining on Elspet with every step, by the time Avery decided (if you could call feet leading head decided) to go after them. Instinct told him not to get any closer. They had been too preoccupied to notice him so far, but a dog collar did catch the eye, were one of them suddenly to look round. And though instinct also told him that something here was not right, was badly wrong, he didn't fear for Elspet's safety, or Blain's. No, the only person in the park he feared for was himself. Maybe it was the siren he could hear cutting in and out of the city lunchtime soundtrack that made him think there was a fire and he was about to stick his head in it.

Elspet passed through the side gate a bare two seconds before Blain. They had both slowed their pace. She was talking to him, was Avery's impression, over her shoulder. Her hand held tight to the strap of her bag. Blain's hands were in his pockets, like he didn't trust them not to reach out for her. Avery arrived at the gate a quarter of a minute later. He gave them an extra fifteen seconds, just to be sure, then stepped out of the Gardens after them. He looked up the slope of the street to where Elspet lived, but they were nowhere to be seen. Even at the lick they had been going when he first spotted them, half a minute was nowhere near long enough for them already to be inside.

A car door slammed to his left. He heard an engine start and before he had time to react a car pulled out and passed right in front of him, turning up Elspet's street. Blain was driving. Elspet sat, arms folded over her bag, in the passenger seat. The car stopped almost level with her door. Elspet got out, but instead of going up the path she looked back down the street. Looked straight at Avery. Then she got into the car again and it took off, indicating left for the Stranmillis Road out of town.

He drove home in a fog of his own mind's making, unable to get hold of a single thought. Lights, red triangles, white arrows on blue. He stopped when the cars in front stopped, started when they started. One minute he was behind the wheel, the next he was in his study with the phone in his hand. For the first time since he had managed to tear his feet from the pavement outside the Botanic Gardens he asked himself what he was doing. He had pressed all but one digit of the number when he put his finger on the cut-off button, then dialled the number again . . . almost. He set the phone on the cradle, looked at it, snatched it up, dialled too fast and got the woman telling him the number he had dialled had not been recognized. He had to dial again just to make sure he *had* made a mistake the time before.

Tony answered on the second ring. Avery? I don't believe this. I was just psyching myself up to call you.

That doesn't sound good, psyching.

I need your help, Tony said, as though he had been handed Avery's script by mistake. I need you to ring me.

I just did.

No, at home, this Saturday, say five o'clock.

Five o'clock.

Five. I'll make sure Michele answers. I'll be upstairs, I'll shout down to her to get it. Tell her you need to speak to me. You can say what you like once I pick up. You can read me the football scores. I'll tell her when I come off the phone it's something to do with one of your congregation. I'll tell her you couldn't go into details. Sanctity of the confessional.

Wrong crowd, said Avery.

I'm not that much of a heathen. Anyway, what do you say? He didn't leave Avery time to say anything. I can't think how else to do it. She's been watching me like a hawk. I *have* to get away for a few hours. I think I can get everything sorted out.

Avery got his word of objection in: You're asking me to lie?

I'm asking you to save my skin.

Avery didn't want to imagine how Tony had got his skin into a position where it needed his salvation. All right, then, he said.

You mean it?

Yes.

Brilliant.

On one condition.

Tony had begun to tell him to name it when he interrupted himself: Wait a minute, why were you phoning me? This isn't about what I think it's about?

I'm as desperate as you are, Avery said.

There was a pause.

No. I'm sorry, I can't help.

So, what, it's OK you asking me to break a commandment, but not me asking you to break an oath?

You don't have to lie, you just have to make a phone call. I'll do the lying. And, anyway, this is someone's medical record. It's a criminal offence.

It's my condition, said Avery.

The pause this time was longer, the breath that scored it sulphurous.

All right, Tony said at last. What's the name?

11

Late November in Belfast, one day sun, the next day rain, the next day sun and rain and hurricanes. Ruth had woken with a bit of a cold. Avery told her to wait for him in the hall after breakfast then ran to the car, throwing it into reverse and starting a slow roll back towards the front door before he had even checked in the rear-view mirror . . . He jammed his foot on the brake. What on *earth*? All he could see in the mirror was ceiling upholstery. It had obviously got knocked, although he wondered as he wrestled it with both hands how he could have hit it such a whack without giving himself a bump to remember it by. First thing he saw when he had got the angle right was Ruth standing on the front step coughing into her quilted mitts. He rolled back the remaining few yards and got out to open the door for her. Didn't I tell you to wait in the hall?

We'll be late, she said.

No, we won't.

A boy was late and was sent to the headmaster.

Just for being late once? I'm sure that's not all it can have been for.

It is.

Well, I'm surprised at that. He was surprised at himself bickering.

Well, it's true.

Well, I'm surprised. Surprised but apparently unable to stop.

They arrived at the school gate, later in fact than Avery had anticipated, with barely a minute to spare before the bell rang. It was bin-collection day. The bottom of their street had been blocked by the council lorry and he had had to turn round and cut down the next side-street.

We'd have been quicker walking, he said aloud, as he turned out of the school and into a traffic jam. A bin lorry – the same bin lorry? – had strayed into the bus lane up ahead. A bus that had attempted to get round it hadn't enough room to complete the pass in the face of oncoming traffic. The lorry inched forward. The binmen strode their slowly unfolding stage, immune to the weather and the honking of horns, docking wheelie-bins to the back of their lorry, frisbeeing cardboard boxes *against the wind* into its jaws; accepting a crisps packet from an infant in a pushchair, pulverizing that.

The car behind Avery's was making small thrusts forwards and back as the driver tried to work herself room for a U-turn into a break that never materialized. Avery resisted the urge to switch on his own right indicator. He folded his hands in his lap and might have been staring at the dashboard for some seconds before he realized what it was there that was trying to claim his attention. He had missed the 90,000 miles coming up.

Someone whistled. A taxi driver leant from his cab, two vehicles ahead, to shout a greeting to a friend walking a collie on the far footpath. The friend told the dog to sit and picked his way through the traffic to the side of the taxi.

Avery looked again at the mileage display. Ninety thousand and eight. That was, what, seventeen miles since he had last looked at it? Which was when? Yesterday? The day before? No, he had just come out of the bank, it had flashed through his mind: book a service. Yesterday, definitely. He had no recollection of the drive home. All the routes east from the university were a little indirect, but though it was anyone's guess which one he'd taken, none of them came close to seventeen miles. You could have done the journey twice with a couple of laps of the city centre for good measure. There had to be another explanation. He flicked his finger off the Perspex cover. Could be a fault in there. Never mind the doubtful seventeen, there *were* 90,000 undisputed miles on the clock. And it did need a service.

The bin lorry moved a few feet. The bus edged a little closer to clear. The car in front of Avery moved. The taxi moved, the driver's friend keeping pace. On the footpath the collie stood, counted off half a dozen quick steps with its tail, sat again, looking at the road. Avery raised his left foot from the brake, the right from the clutch and let them sink again.

While he sat unmoving, before his very eyes, another tenth of a mile clicked up.

So there was a fault. Or maybe the fault was in his own understanding and what it was supposed to measure was the length of time the engine was running. Maybe it was *approximating* distance. He cast his mind back again to yesterday's journey home. The traffic had been heavy enough coming away from the university, he remembered that. He flicked the display cover again with his nail. Binmen were hopping from the footpath on to the tailboard of the lorry. Its rear end swung right into the centre of the road, then followed its nose left down a broad side-street. Engines revved. The trapped bus slipped back into its lane, pursued by two others travelling at speed along the cleared channel to confirm to people further down the road what they had always suspected: you wait half an hour then three come at once. The collie danced, light as a tennis player on the base line, trying to guess where exactly its owner was going to appear from. If he was ever going to.

At five o'clock on the dot Saturday evening – Frances's due date – Avery rang Tony and Michele's house. Michele was out of breath when she answered. She sounded disappointed when he told her he had no baby news to report. She had been in the middle of her yoga. She said she wasn't sure what Tony was at that he hadn't been able to get the phone. He heard her footsteps recede. Heard her turn Tony's name into a shouted question, his own into a sort of answer.

The footsteps returned. Make that woman of yours a good hot curry for her dinner tonight, she said.

Half a minute passed, then Tony came on. Avery was impressed by how much weary superciliousness he managed to pack into a simple hello. And there Avery had been thinking Michele was the theatrically minded one.

Well, Avery said, how long would you like me to talk for?

What? said Tony. No, don't worry.

A minute? Thirty seconds? Twenty seconds? Fifteen? Ten, nine, eight . . .

Oh dear. Yes, I see.

To be honest I didn't think this was going to work, but you're doing very well, acting up a storm.

No, of course, I understand, Tony said. I'll just have to have a word with Michele, but I'm sure there won't be any problem.

Brilliant.

Don't mention it.

Good luck.

Yes, see you later.

★

Avery was in the Minister's Room on Tuesday morning preparing for the last finance committee meeting of the year when Ronnie came to the door.

A couple of people to see you, he said, and Avery glimpsed over his shoulder the two police officers. Older woman, younger man.

Constables Jones and Ruddle, they said, stepping forward.

Avery was too used to people jumping to the wrong conclusion at the sight of him and his collar to be unduly concerned, though that didn't stop Jones telling him not to worry, nothing had happened to any of the family, after which neither she nor Ruddle said anything more till Ronnie had closed the door on his way out.

It had been a toss-up, Ruddle said then, watching his colleague place an A4 envelope on the edge of the desk, which would be less awkward for him, here or at home. The thing was, well, was the red Orion parked out front his car? Yes, said Avery. Registration number PXI . . . Yes, yes, yes, he said to each of the last three digits, almost before they were out.

We just have to be sure, said Jones, coolly.

It's been caught on one of our cameras, Ruddle said.

Speed trap? Avery asked himself, and was about to dismiss it when he thought of the dodgy mileometer. (In that instant there was no question in his mind the mileometer was dodgy.) If one reading was unreliable why not another? He could have been over the limit and never have known.

We've been receiving complaints from residents in the Joy Street area.

That pulled him up short. Joy Street was practically city centre, not somewhere Avery could imagine speeding, even unintentionally. I don't understand.

Cars causing a nuisance at night.

It was the weight on the word nuisance that caused him to sit forward. No, he said, I think there must be a mistake.

The constables exchanged glances: he would say that.

Jones turned the envelope over on the table and lifted the flap. She slipped out half a dozen images from an infrared camera. Front and back and left side: his Orion, all right, down to the Child on Board plaque. The way the street-light was hitting the windscreen it was impossible to make out the driver's face, even in the shot where he was talking to a woman crouching by his door. According to the figures in the bottom right-hand corner, the photographs had been taken between two and two twenty-five on Friday morning.

I don't understand this at all, he said.

There, I was wrong, said Ruddle. I said you'd tell us you were there on missionary work.

Avery turned in his seat to see was he having a rise taken out of him and decided to give the policeman's neutral expression the benefit of the doubt.

Does anyone else have access to the car? Jones asked.

My wife, he said, but I don't know what she'd be doing out in it at two in the morning. Unless.

He paused long enough for the policewoman to repeat the word. Unless?

Well, I suppose it's possible she didn't want to wake me.

You must be some sleeper.

We're in separate rooms at the moment. He clocked the look on their faces. She's expecting a baby any day now.

The looks grew more knowing.

He stared down at the photographs to stop himself saying anything rash. He stared at the windscreen, the light on the rear-view mirror. Someone took the car, he said.

You mean stole it?

Yes, he said. I got into it on Friday morning and the mirror was in a different position – I mean, it's not an easy mirror to move – and when I looked at the mileometer I noticed it was further on than it was the night before.

You check often? Ruddle asked.

It was just short of ninety thousand. I was going to book it in for a service.

Hold on, said Jones, and pressed a forefinger to each temple. This person, they took your car, went kerb-crawling, and then *left it back*?

Yes, said Avery, barely making it to the *s*.

The status of this conversation, Jones said, replacing the photographs in the envelope, was confidential, its character, she hoped he agreed, a friendly word of advice. But if his car turned up on their cameras again, Avery had better work on improving his story.

Ronnie was bleeding radiators in the corridor. He made a show of not seeing the police officers as Avery let them out his door. Avery waited until they were well out of sight. Have you a moment? he asked.

Ronnie pocketed the radiator key, wiped his hands: he could probably stretch to a moment.

Ronnie wouldn't sit in the Minister's Room, ever, though as a rule he spent every second looking resentfully at the seat he might have had. (Avery had long since stopped trying to insist.) Today he stood arms folded, looking straight at Avery, waiting.

Do you mind me asking, Avery said, have you ever noticed anyone messing about near my car?

You mean Wee Lads?

Wee Lads to Ronnie were even worse than Youngsters.

They were Youngsters' alien masters, not adults *in potentia* but a whole other life-form. He sniffed, he scowled, he practically snarled.

Wee lads, said Avery, big lads, anyone at all.

The whiff of more specific prey drifted away. Ronnie's tone changed from anger to affront. Not think maybe I'd've said something to you if I had? Not think I wouldn't've chased them the length of that road out there?

No, no, I know you would have. Avery rested his elbows on the table, his head on his hands.

Is that what they wanted, then? Ronnie asked. Did somebody phone them with a complaint? Clearly he felt that his vigilance and competence were in question here.

Avery knew it from sermons, from his own previous life, how one lie greased the path for another, how as each slipped out it met with less and less resistance. Three days ago he had lied to Michele by proxy, consoling himself he had been driven to it by reason of a greater good. This, in comparison, was direct, barefaced.

It was just a precaution, he said, with me parking here so regularly. There's been a bit of bother in the area, locks being tampered with, that sort of thing.

That'll be the minibus at risk too, Ronnie said.

No, I think it was just cars they were targeting. Anyway, like I say, just a precaution, nothing to worry about.

Ronnie's expression was that of a man who, until just a few minutes before, had had no more than the normal run of worries (Wee Lads, airlocks) and who was not going to let go of his new alarm as easily as that. There are signs you can get, I've seen them around the place: Beware, car thieves operating in this area.

I don't think we need to go down that route just yet.

It's only fair on the congregation.

I'll raise it with Session, said Avery, the words meeting next to no resistance at all.

He rang Des.

Can I come round?

12

Des held open the dining-room door for him. His sleeve was rolled, the hairs on his forearm were wet from the wrist up. A rubber glove hung, glistening, over the handle of the kitchen door opposite.

Mind the beast, he said, as the exercise ball rolled with a heavy bias across their path and under the table. It's my day cleaning the cage. Actually, yesterday was. I keep putting it off. Not a job for the faint-hearted.

Avery sat by the window, hands dug into his jacket pockets. The wind was giving the fruit trees a good going over. They looked like they were barely holding it together, like they had retreated deep into themselves, waiting for the assaults to pass. They looked like this got harder every year.

Can I not take your coat? Des asked.

I'm a bit chilled.

There's a draught round that window, all right. Move the chair back out of the road.

Avery shifted it an inch or two. Des sat facing him. So, he said, anything strange or startling?

The old Belfast opening gambit.

Avery's lips parted, but the only sound to emerge was a bleat. Even he couldn't tell at first if it was a laugh or a cry.

I'm sorry, he said then bleated again; a laugh definitely. (Strange? *Startling?*) He put his hand to his mouth, but it was no use, the laughter escaped out the sides then burst through the fingers. He had no idea where this was coming from and he had no way of stopping it.

Was it something I said? asked Des. He was laughing himself, uncertainly to begin with, but Avery was practically doubled over: you would have had to be made of stone not to join in.

The hamster ball came between them, which only made things worse. Des kicked his feet in the air. Avery had to stand finally to keep from hyperventilating. I'm really sorry, he said, each word a breath snatched.

Don't apologize, said Des. It's nice to be appreciated. At least, I'll tell myself it was appreciation.

Avery wiped his eyes. He couldn't kill the laughter in his voice entirely when he said, What's the best way to discredit a member of the clergy?

Vindictively? That's easy, accuse him of some sort of abuse. Don't even accuse, just let it be inferred, not rebutted.

What about kerb-crawling?

Oh, kerb-crawling would be right up there too, I would think, and hanging around in public toilets. Des stopped. Avery sat across from him dry-eyed. This isn't a suppose, is it?

I'm afraid not.

Kerb-crawling?

The police have been to see me. They have pictures of the car. You can't make it out, but I swear to you, it's not me driving.

Now Des's lips moved without forming words, without making any sound at all. There was no question that he believed Avery. That was why Avery had phoned him. No need to convince Des that someone could have helped themselves to the car for just a night.

Do you remember that insurance claim? Avery asked him.

I know, said Des.

That it was dropped?

I ran into Peter Lockhart who said he got it from someone in your church. We'd all been worried for you.

Avery nodded his gratitude, at the same time quelling his concern that church business was being bruited so freely. From what I can gather the wee lad's father and grandfather have connections, he said.

Connections connections?

UDA, UVF. I'm not sure which crowd exactly.

You think they did this?

Well, it crossed my mind all right. If we can't get you one way we'll get you another.

Des sucked air through his teeth, a sound that said this was a very dangerous development.

But then, said Avery, I started thinking about some of the other things that have been happening lately. That conversation we were having the last time I was round here.

Des seemed about to interject that they didn't have to go over all that again, but Avery stopped him. Just in the last few days, I found something out. I saw a couple of people I wasn't supposed to see together. I think somebody's trying to tell me to forget that I did.

Des frowned. I'm sorry, I know you have to be careful what you say, but I'm not sure I'm with you.

Well, put it like this, Avery said, did you ever lock your keys in the car?

Once, years and years ago.

And who were the first people you thought about phoning to help you break in?

Des drew back into his chair, appearing to weigh the likely effect on their friendship of any answer he might give. In the end he settled on the three safest words: You said it.

And if not out loud, Avery had indeed. Even to his pre-viously sceptical ear it did make perfect sense.

But still he resisted contacting Larry. The part of him that did not believe it was just coincidence that these photographs should have appeared – have been *produced* – days after he spotted Elspet and Blain was not yet inclined to alert anyone to his suspicions and draw who knows what further unwelcome attention.

Back home, he asked Frances if she had thought about going to her parents' after the baby was born.

What? Why on earth would I?

You wanted to after Ruth was born.

When Ruth was born we were living in a house without a bath. I only said it might make things easier the first few days. Besides, you nearly went through the roof.

When Ruth was born Avery was still in theological college. He was a home-owning student with a wife on maternity leave and no money to renovate. He remembered the nightmare of trying to bathe the baby in the kitchen sink, on the floor of their cramped bathroom; the hazardous lottery of carrying her into a shower that swung without reason or warning between freezing and scalding. And, yes, he remembered too, he did nearly go through the roof.

It was just a suggestion, he said.

Do you mean to tell me it's been on your conscience all this time? Frances asked. She massaged his frown lines with the tips of her middle fingers. She'd had a guarantee from the midwife the day before that they would take her in this weekend and induce her. She had good feeling to spare. Don't worry, she said, we'll be just fine here, all together.

The finance committee strove to end the calendar year on an upbeat note, but the removal of one worry only shifted the focus on to another one, or two, or ten. There might be no costly court action hanging over them, but the new year would be every bit as much of a struggle as the one now ending. If they had been a football club they could have sold their site at a healthy profit and relocated to the distant suburbs, confident that the faithful would follow. For better or for worse, though – for worse or for *worser* – this was their home. Still, if everyone connected to the church showed the same tenacity as Mervyn Armstrong, at the meeting a mere seven days after having his appendix removed, there was hope. Mervyn acknowledged the applause of his fellow committee members with a wince that might not have been purely of embarrassment, or of feigned pain at the several attempts to fashion a joke out of bust a gut.

Avery walked home and closed the driveway gates. The gates were wooden, eight feet high, and had only been closed once before in the time he had been in the house, when the three of them went to Donegal for a long weekend. They jibbed at this latest disturbance. He might as easily have moved a couple of the trees with which they had, in the interim, become entwined. He pushed, he pulled, he shouldered; he managed it eventually. He got into the car and aimed the nose towards the tightest angle of shrubbery and supermarket fence, where the gravel was least used and crunchiest. He double-checked the mileage then took the chain from the bag it had been in when he bought it and set it in the boot, eighteen months before, and wound it tight through the steering-wheel, under and over the clutch. He had to get out the passenger door.

He woke, it must have been, once every half-hour, that night and the next. Several times he tiptoed to the landing window. The car sat like some great otherworldly egg, colourlessly metallic in the night-light, nestling in its bed of gravel and leaves. He couldn't possibly miss its being driven away a second time.

On the third night Frances had to shake him awake.

Avery. *Avery.* Get up, she said. Get on you. It's started.

She was in the hallway before he had gathered even half his wits. Ten to – what was that his clock said? Two? Three? He heard her on the phone. No, she hasn't woken. Yes, if you could. No, we'll be another twenty minutes yet. Yes, I'm fine. No, I am. No, honestly.

Avery met her as she started back upstairs. He had made a complete hames of buttoning his shirt. He had only managed to find one sock.

Have you ever seen a dream walking? she half sang, a line inherited from her parents, from a musical neither she nor Avery had ever seen.

They sank down into a sitting hug. He kissed her brow and said a prayer that God might watch over her and the baby-to-be in the hours ahead. I love you, he said.

Me too you, said Frances, then dug her fingers into his back. Bad one?

She nodded, breathing through it.

There was a frost. The padlock burned cold in his palm as he struggled to remove the chain from the steering-wheel. The gates, which had been so reluctant to meet on Tuesday night, now screeched at being parted. Frances's parents were waiting on the other side of them, their four-wheel-drive fuming.

How is she? said Mrs Burns, leaning from the window.

I thought you were never going to get those blasted things open, Mr Burns said.

I didn't know you were here, said Avery.

We could hardly toot the horn at this hour. Since when have you started locking them anyway?

Frances's mother was trying to get out of the car. How *is* she?

Frances was sitting on the bottom stair with her delivery bag on her lap. Sanitary towels, breast pads, pants and night-dress. The last things of pregnancy. Her hospital bag was in the car, with the baby's bag. Though they had all supposedly been ready for weeks they were none of them where Avery thought they were, under the stairs, when he had gone looking for them.

I'm five days overdue, said Frances. What else have I got to do but take everything out and put it back in again? Look in the bathroom and bedroom.

Now it was the portable stereo was exercising him or, rather, the compilation tapes that should have been sitting beside it.

I put them in the baby's bag so we'd know where they were, Frances said.

I didn't see them.

You didn't know to look.

I didn't *hear* them.

Believe me, they're there. Can we go?

Will I take you in my car? Mr Burns said, walking with them on to the front step. It'd be quicker.

Thanks, the bags and all are in ours, said Frances.

Avery bit his tongue till they were out the gates. Honestly, anyone would think it was a flipping horse and cart we drove.

Two young women were brisk-stepping across Joy Street

as Avery came round by the Markets and into the city centre. Fun-fur jackets and handkerchief skirts. They glanced at the car, at Frances resting her cheek on the window.

Sorry, girls, you're out of luck, she said. You don't know how out of luck you are.

Avery applied his foot that little bit harder to the accelerator, even as he was telling himself that nothing improper could be read into just passing by, that he had his pregnant wife in the car, for pity's sake.

You have to hand it to them in a way, said Frances. Out there till all hours in all weathers. I mean, in terms of productivity.

I hope you're not mistaken about those tapes.

He felt her eyes slide round to him. Am I embarrassing you? she said.

Don't be silly.

They were stopped at a red light outside Avery's HQ, the Presbyterian Assembly Building. Not a single car in any direction.

Silly Frances, said Frances, straightening, pressing her hands on the dashboard. Avery placed a hand on top.

Sorry, I'm just trying to make sure we haven't forgotten anything.

And I'm just trying to take my mind off this baby pushing to get out of me. She nudged his hand.

The light was changing, and they had nothing but green lights from there right through to the maternity-unit car-park.

We'll take that as an omen, Frances said to her stomach.

She was four and a half centimetres. Amber light. By the time they got her up to the delivery suite the contractions were coming every three minutes. The labour lasted six more hours. Four full C90 tapes. (They were in the baby bag, with an elastic band round them to keep them from rattling.) The crown appeared to an Arvo Part cantus, the head and shoulders to Avery hadn't a clue what, such was the shouting and roaring in the delivery suite.

Oh, he's beautiful, he's beautiful, Avery kept saying, convinced by the face alone that they had a son. The proof soon followed, bunched between legs whose feet looked to have been confused with a bigger, purpler baby's.

Frances clutched the baby to her chest, kissing the tiny puncture marks where the monitor had been clipped to his scalp when she was first brought into the suite. Avery's hand trembled accepting the scissors to cut the cord between them.

David, he said. It was a name they had discussed. Beloved.

And now he tuned into the music again: 'If you should ever leave me,/Though life would still go on, believe me,/The world could show nothing to me, So/what good would living do me?'

'God Only Knows'.

It was why you made those tapes, after all, to be appropriate.

While Frances and the baby slept Avery called family from the phone at the end of the ward then filled a bag with dirty washing and drove back to the house. Streets that had been empty on the outward journey were now thronged. People queued, crossed roads, walked in, walked out of shops as though they had been summoned – the very light that shone on them had been summoned – by a baby's cry, and he thought that right at the heart of the Christian message was a restatement of what we all felt to be true. The world was born again into hope with each and every one of our children.

The day after tomorrow was Advent. Today and for all the days of his life this was David's city.

Frances's parents had tidied away much of the evidence of last night's confusion and haste. The guest room, though, had been left untouched. Clothes lay like the relics of an evaporated father of one. His notebook and Bible had tumbled to the floor, bringing with them a selection of his recent bedtime reading. He pushed the undercover book aside with his foot as he sat to unlace his shoes on the bed he had got out of ten hours ago with half as many responsibilities.

He sprang back up into a sitting position. His heart felt twisted in his chest. The phone stopped ringing. He looked at his watch, peeling the strap off the welts corrugating his wrist. Half two. Ruth. He was at the top of the stairs before he remembered the conversation in the early hours with Frances's mother. They'd collect Ruth and bring her home.

Down in the hall he picked up the phone and dialled 1471 but it was number withheld. The answer-machine had been left switched off. He switched it on and went out to the utility room to put on the washing. He just had time to clean his teeth and splash some water on his face before the front door was thrown open and Ruth burst in ahead of her grandparents. Is the baby here? she said, running up the hallway, looking in the rooms either side. Is it here?

Mrs Burns from the doorway said, I told you, sweetheart, he's still at the hospital.

Ruth launched herself into Avery's arms. Is the baby sick? she asked and, overwhelmed, began to cry.

No, he's not. He's just grand. His name's David.

David Avery, Mr Burns said, his mouth quirking.

David and Goliath, said Ruth, and wiped her eyes.

David and Goliath, Avery said back.

Only he's not sleeping in my room.

No, he's not sleeping in your room.

OK. Now can I go and see him?

We'll all go in mine, will we? said Mr Burns, keys already in his hand.

Yes, said Ruth. Granddad's big car!

The phone was ringing again as they were getting in.

It's OK, Mr Burns said. I switched on the answer-machine.

No, said Avery, I did.

But I thought I'd left it off the last time we went out.

You did, that's why I'd to turn it on, and now you've turned it off again.

The ringing stopped.

If it's anything important they'll call back, said Mrs Burns. Come on, I want to see this grandson of ours. And Avery was just too tired to argue.

The nurses had David away giving him a bath.

Frances, though she'd had a bath herself, looked more exhausted than she had right after the delivery. I'd a terrible time getting him to latch on, she said while her father frowned at the leaflet explaining the pay-TV system. They told me just to take a break and try again.

Of course, there's no saying you *have* to breastfeed, said her mother, as she had said when Ruth was born, lest there be any implied criticism of her for not breastfeeding her own. The bottle didn't do you a bit of harm.

Another woman passed the foot of the bed, her baby's head resting open-mouthed on her shoulder. Ruth had climbed on to the bed and burrowed in against Frances's side. She was getting upset again. What's *wrong* with wee David? When are they bringing him back?

In the end Frances's parents walked her down to the shop on the ground floor to find the baby a present.

Frances and Avery sat for a few minutes holding one

another, saying nothing. Frances broke the clinch to scratch her left arm, her leg, her arm again. The epidural hadn't taken properly and the anaesthetist had given her a shot of morphine just before the big push.

I meant to say – she was scratching her fingers now – Tony stopped by. You can't have been long away. I was so groggy, I didn't know for a minute who it was standing there in the white coat. Then when I remembered I was so relieved I forgot to be mad at him for being a pig to Michele.

Avery got up, cleared space on the top of her locker for the magazines her mother had brought with her. How is everything there, did he say?

What do you expect? He talked like everything was just hunky-dory. He's a serial adulterer, he knows how to keep up a front.

I suppose.

Suppose nothing, but I'll tell you something, it doesn't matter how clever he thinks he is, it's starting to take its toll. It wasn't just the drugs making me confused, he looks like he's aged about ten years since the summer.

Avery couldn't tell from this whether last Saturday night had been a success or a failure. Unable to think of a thing to say he poured his wife a glass of water.

Did he get you at home? asked Frances. He said he would try and phone you.

Avery began to explain about the mix-up with the answer-machine, but just then a baby cried out in the corridor. Frances sat to attention, cupping one engorged breast after the other. Left? Right? she muttered. Left? Right?

OK, Mummy, here's a nice wee clean one for you, said a nurse, coming round the corner, then seeing Avery handed the baby to him. Or maybe Daddy wants to take him a while.

The baby stopped crying and pursed his lips. *Frances's* lips. Avery's father's eyes looking out at him. What do you make of all this? they seemed to say.

And then Ruth and her grandparents were there with a blue teddy in noisy Cellophane wrap and David was passed from grandmother to grandfather to sister – carefully now, carefully – until he cried out again to be fed.

PART THREE

I

The congregation clapped Avery into church on Sunday morning.

The Sunday after, they barracked him as they made for the doors the moment he rose to his feet in the pulpit.

In between times he got himself in the *East Belfast Community News* again: front page; Frances brought the baby home from the hospital and left with him for her parents' three days later, twenty-four hours before Larry came to stay in Townsend Grange. And Tony, working back from second Sunday to previous Monday, Tony was ill but stable, still serious, improving, worsening, in a critical condition.

The first report said fighting for his life. Avery didn't really catch the details. He certainly didn't catch the name. Not then. The sun wasn't up and already he was in manic cleaning mode, trailing the vacuum from room to room, going at shelves and wooden mantelpieces with a duster cut from an old vest. As of yesterday afternoon Frances was breastfeeding unassisted. She could see no reason why she wouldn't be let home this morning and no reason why they shouldn't have a few friends and close family round this evening for a welcome-home party. Ruth had stayed the night again at her grandparents' to give Avery time to get the place in order. He had gathered up about a month's worth of papers that he wanted to take to the council yard for recycling. His plan was to get there for it opening at a quarter to eight then pick up some fresh bakery rolls for his breakfast.

Even at the second time of hearing the report, driving away from the council yard, he didn't quite take it all in, couldn't connect the words doctor and beating in the novel way that was being asked of him. A *doctor* was a person who pronounced that the *victim* was fighting for his life. He kept expecting to hear Tony's voice. Professional Tony. Distressed-to-be-having-to-tell-you-this-but-safe-in-my-own-world Tony. It was all he could do to keep control of the car when the connection was finally made. He was lucky, since he didn't look, that the side-street he pulled into off the urban clearway was one-way in his favour. He rested his head on the wheel through the morning's other headlines: foot-and-mouth, preparations for the Clinton visit; through traffic and travel and weather. A cold bright start, rain moving in slowly to western parts. He was nearly too numb to pray. He tried to squeeze a word out, any word.

The breakfast-programme anchor was returning to the morning's top story. Doctor found beaten in deserted car-park. This is an horrific incident, she said.

Indeed. The reporter who had given the bare bones in the bulletin went into more detail. It appears Dr Russell left the hospital shortly before midnight. His wife – who is six months pregnant – reported him missing at three a.m. His car was found a short time later at a supermarket car-park on the outskirts of the city after a passing motorist had reported seeing three men beating, as he thought, a dog or something. When police investigated they discovered Dr Russell in the boot of the car.

Dreadful, said the anchor.

Yes, quite, the reporter said. Police are stressing this was a particularly savage attack. They don't expect to be able to interview Dr Russell himself for some considerable time.

(Avery whimpered into the steering-wheel.) They are examining footage from the car-park's security cameras and in the meantime are appealing to anyone who saw his very distinctive silver Mazda car between midnight and three a.m. to contact them.

And what are the police saying about motive?

Well, obviously it's still a bit early. All they will say is that they are following a number of lines of inquiry.

But it must be a worrying development, nevertheless. This bears all the hallmarks of a paramilitary punishment beating and yet it happens in a supermarket car-park to a doctor?

Well, yes, there are a number of disturbing features to this incident, but again at the minute the police are refusing to rule anything in or out.

There was a gentle tap at the driver's side window. Avery leapt. A man staggered back from the car clutching a hand to his chest. The child beside him – young enough to be his grandson – started to scream. Avery got the door open. Are you all right? He didn't know whether to go to the child or the man first.

The man had steadied himself. Am *I* all right? His clutching hand became a fist, out of which a finger popped, pointing. I thought you were dead in there. Look at the state of this wee one. The child grabbed the man's leg. You have him scared stupid.

I'm sorry, Avery said.

Aye, sorry, said the man, and scooped the child up. He'd clearly have been happier if Avery had in fact been dead. You want your head looking at, carrying on like that.

I said I'm sorry. Avery turned back to the car but stopped short of getting in, suddenly recognizing the street he had pulled into. For much of the past eighteen months it had terminated a third of the way down in a stockade topped with cameras and estate agents' self-promotional hoardings. When exactly the fences had come down, Avery didn't know, though it couldn't have been that long ago for there was still cement dust on the surface of the road, which bounded, like sight regained, all the way to the next main road and its procession of city-bound cars, nose to tail in the narrow band of morning sunlight. On either side of the street new houses stood, neat and blank, and double-glazed; waiting. The terraces ended in a patch of ground heaped with rubble. Avery remembered coming at this patch from the other side when the street had still been two-way and the heap of rubble had still been a row of houses.

He drove the car in first gear, never straying more than a foot from the kerb, and parked again level with where Sheila Kirkpatrick's door had been, second from the end. There was no guesswork required, the doorsteps were intact; besides, he recognized the kitchen wallpaper, which had promiscuously tumbled into what was left of the sitting room. The bathroom sink, stripped of its taps, lay in two pieces either side of a section of chimney-breast.

The breakfast-programme anchor gave the time as eight thirteen. Avery didn't know when he had last felt so bleak. He backed the car up until he was abreast a turn-off. Left, he went, right, left, right, sticking to the lower gears and the less-used streets until he was facing the laundrette.

A light was on in the rear, rimming the door behind the counter yellow. Avery knocked for a couple of minutes off and on, but could hardly hear himself above the noise of the traffic. It was suddenly very important that he be admitted, however long he had to wait. He went and sat in the car again. A doctor was beaten on the news again, in brief. At eight thirty-one a woman stepped out from the back of the shop. A bus interposed itself, exchanging one old passenger for ten new ones and when it pulled out the sign on the door had been turned from closed to open.

The woman was crouched down behind the counter when Avery went in.

Be with you in a second, she said, standing up, catching her swinging braids. Then her face broke into a broad grin. Reverend Avery! It was Wendy. You're my first ever customer.

She didn't know anything about the woman who worked there before, except that she had family somewhere out about Newtownards. I suppose, she said, it's a long way to come for a wee job like this.

A friend of Dee's auntie had told her there was a vacancy coming up. She never thought she stood a chance when she put in for it, but Dee said he knew rightly she'd get it.

Avery asked her was Dee home again, then.

She laughed. Dee'll not be home for another eighteen months. Did you not hear? He's in Hydebank.

Hydebank was the young-offenders centre. Avery didn't try to hide his astonishment. What could he possibly have done? He couldn't have been out of hospital more than a few days.

No, you don't understand, she said. He hasn't done anything, or at least nothing new. This is for all the stuff he done before he got his hiding. The two of us talked about it when he was in the hospital. He did a deal. He gave the police a whole list of things, burglaries, stolen cars and that, and they promised they'd put in a word, get him a reduced sentence. He went straight from the hospital on to remand. See, all the trouble he was in, know with the ones that beat him, half of it was people whispering, making him out like he was worse than he was. The other half was them ones themselves, getting him to do things for them 'cause they thought he'd be too scared to go to the police. This way he gets it all out in the open and they don't have anything on him no more. Nobody has. They're lost without their wee secrets about you.

And what about you? Avery asked. Will you be OK?

She set her jaw, like she was *acting* acting-tough. Me? Sure why wouldn't I be? I'm not the one that's in jail.

The door opened. A woman came in carrying a large pink teddy-bear with a port-wine stain from left ear to right shoulder.

First real customer.

Is there anything you can do with this? she said.

The city centre was exactly half-way between the laundrette and the hospital. The first leg of the journey took him five times as long as the second. Heavy traffic in, light traffic out. All those tonnes of metal packed into a bare square-mile of streets each morning. Given the city's boggy origins it was a wonder the entire thing didn't just disappear down a hole in the ground. Avery switched between stations as he drove searching for news, but heard nothing that shed any more light on the attack.

Hospital is the clergyman's home from home. Avery, though, had been in this particular hospital so often lately for one thing and another that even without his collar no one gave him a second look that morning except to smile. He needed no directions to Intensive Care.

A policeman sat hunched over a magazine outside Tony's room. From the bottom of the corridor Avery was convinced it was Constable Rossborough, who had guarded Dee, whose parents attended Avery's church, but drawing nearer he realized that, hair colour aside, he was nothing like him. It must have been meeting Wendy unexpectedly had fooled him. He had begun to think there was a pattern to this day.

The policeman straightened, closing the magazine – it was *Auto Trader* – over his thumb.

Can I help you?

I'm a minister.

That's right, the policeman said, narrowing one eye, as though the deciding word was his, I've seen you before. He jerked his head to the room behind him. One of yours?

No, Avery said then thought better of saying, An old friend. The way we work it, sometimes if there's no one handy from the patient's own church another of us stops by to see if there's anything we can do.

The policeman nodded that this made sense, but Tony was just back from theatre; he didn't think there was anything Avery could do for a wee while yet.

They just took his wife away, he added in an undertone. Pregnant. Must have been rough on her. Terrible, terrible beating he got. Jaw smashed. Hardly a tooth left in his head. You'd think they'd been taking aim.

Avery remembered the conversation he'd had outside Dee's door about the literalness of the beatings. It was clear to him what concentrating on the mouth meant. Don't talk.

Look in again in a couple of hours, if you're still around, the policeman said, using his thumb to lever open the magazine.

I'll do that, said Avery, though already his mind was racing over the ground he hoped to have covered by then.

His mistake up to now was to have gone creeping about in the shadows. That was precisely where they preferred to operate. (Who are *they*? he'd asked Larry, months ago, and had been unimpressed by the vague reply. Now, however, he understood: nothing identified them like their deeds. They were the answer to the question *who benefits by this?*.) In the shadows you were at a double disadvantage: you could see nothing clearly and no one could see what was done to you.

Wendy had said it this morning: what was important was to get everything into the open. However uncomfortable to begin with, it was safer out there in the long run.

He had to make the calls from outside the main building, taking his place with the other mobile-phone users and the perpetual picket of smokers: a solidarity of visitors, patients and junior doctors. He called the newspaper first, asked for Barbara.

This is Barbara.

Of course. It had a staff of about four.

This is Ken Avery, he said. I don't know if you remember, but Barbara remembered all right.

How *are* you?

It's not really the best morning to ask, he said, but listen, I have something I think might interest you.

Larry wasn't picking up. He left a message: I believe you. Every word. Call me.

I don't believe you, Frances said when he broke the news about Tony. She sat back heavily on the bed. (Avery had had the foresight to take David from her before he spoke.) She hadn't heard a word about it. It was all Radio 1 on the ward. A beating in Belfast, even of a doctor, didn't register there.

What about Michele? What about the baby?

She looked at the bags packed on either side of her, at the cards and gifts and flowers, as though she was somehow abandoning her friend.

Michele's in the best of hands, you can be sure of that, Avery said.

Frances was trying to push the tears back into her brimming eyes. How am I going to say goodbye to the nurses like this? she said.

Here. He handed her the baby and went to the sink just inside the ward door to wet a piece of paper towel. Crouching before his wife he gently wiped her face.

It's just such a terrible shock, she said, and he said, I know, I know.

While Frances took David to thank the nurses, he gathered up the cards and envelopes from the top of her locker (Frances had the envelopes from her eighteenth-birthday cards) and divided them between the side pockets of two of the bags. They could sort them another time. The vases of flowers he placed on the counter next to the sink, and next to them an envelope of his own with a tip for the cleaners.

Frances was fighting tears again as they walked to the car, David asleep between them in the car seat they had carried Ruth out in five years before.

You know why he was beaten, don't you? she said.

Avery said he suspected he did, and it wasn't for the reason Frances thought. He told her it might be connected to a favour he had asked Tony to do involving a man who had come to the church looking for help. Frances stopped so abruptly the car seat caught her leg, causing the baby to stir and cry but – luckily – not to waken.

I don't believe you, she said.

The car-park attendant was leaning from his booth to make sure they were OK. Avery waved to him. I'll explain it to you in the car, he said.

I don't believe you, said Frances a third time when he got round to explaining that he was worried now about this man Larry's safety and that he wanted him to come and stay with them for a few days. What about *our* safety? What about the children?

Avery checked in his mirrors that nothing was coming up on his inside then turned right for the city centre past Spendlove C. Jebb plumbing supplies, though neither of them said, what either of them normally would have, The name's Jebb. Spendlove C. Jebb.

I've thought about this, Avery said. And this is the safest way.

So you are worried.

I was. I'm not any more. I've been in touch with that journalist who interviewed me during the summer.

Oh, well, then, Frances said, with scarcely a breath before the next salvo of objections: We have a four-day-old baby. He'll be waking up all hours of the day and night. I'll be walking around with my boobs permanently on display. You can't bring a complete stranger into the middle of that. We need time together as a family.

We need to do what's right.

That's trumps, is it? said Frances bitterly and didn't say another word for the rest of the journey. David slept on, facing back the way they had come, all he had so far known of the world receding. An unused delivery-suite compilation played in the tape deck, a Chopin nocturne segueing into Todd Rundgren as they turned the corner of their street. 'I Saw The Light'.

Frances hit the eject button. I really don't believe you.

They decided to go ahead with the party to welcome David home, more for Ruth's sake than anything. She worked her way round the sitting room with a bowl of olives and one, less forthcoming, of KP Skips, explaining to the several relatives and neighbours the significance of the name. It means Beloved, she said, from the Bible: For God beloved the world he only gave us his begotten son.

Like her father, it was the Bible's highlights Ruth remembered, in her own way.

The mood had been subdued to begin with, the word from the hospital still not being good on Tony, nor a whole lot better on Michele, who had been formally admitted at lunchtime for monitoring. Even so there was a head to be wetted and in time a cork was popped, and a toast drunk.

To David. Peace be with him and all our children and grandchildren.

A little later Michele's mother rang to say that Michele was being allowed home in the morning. The baby was going to be OK. By the time Ruth had finally consented to being put to bed word had come through that Tony was off the critical list. Frances had a second glass of champagne.

That'll guarantee the baby sleeps, her mother said, but Frances ignored her. She came to stand on the back doorstep next to Avery while volunteers took care of the dishes. Far out in the night's murky green a single star flickered on the point of visibility, like the last white dot of day. Somewhere closer at hand houses performed their party pieces. A heating unit did its dragon's roar; bathwater drained with a dirty chuckle.

There were Christmas-tree lights already in the windows of some maisonettes. No trace at all now of the summer's flags; no word this long time about the feud. Touch wood.

Avery grazed his knuckle on the doorframe as he put his arm round his wife's shoulders.

Not too cold? He felt her head move: no.

Did you ever think, she said, when I came into the bank with Michele that day?

They were words they often said when they were first married and still incredulous that they had found one another. Did you ever think?

No, he said, they always said. Never.

She laughed. Two children.

(They were then? They had now? He didn't know.) I know, he said.

The wind turned towards them, specks of rain mixed in, turned away. Frances's shoulders shook.

Sure you're all right?

Sorry, she said. That wasn't the cold. I was just thinking. I shouldn't have got on like that earlier in the car.

He pushed her away slightly, the better to turn and make his declaration and pull her back even closer.

Listen, I'm the one should apologize, springing everything on you.

Her arm went round his waist. Maybe it was the extent of his apology she mistook; maybe it was the mood that had brought him out here, glass in hand, in the first place. She was no better judge than he, after all, of how a man should act who feared he was the indirect cause of his friend being beaten half to death.

Why don't you hold off talking to that newspaper? she said, and he realized then that he had mistaken her mood too.

He relaxed his grip. She withdrew her arm and went indoors.

He woke at two to find her balanced on her elbow looking at him. He struggled to get up but sleep still had a hold on him, pinning his shoulders to the bed. David? he said, giving as much voice to the whisper as he dared.

David's fine, she whispered back. Avery gave up the

struggle. His eyes were closing. He'd had two and a half glasses of champagne himself.

What was the name of that girl you knew again? Frances asked. The one that was killed.

Avery's eyes were wide open. Frances knew the name rightly. Her knees were jigging against his ribs.

Joanna? Why?

No reason. Just I wonder sometimes was there something more there than you've told me.

It was back to the start of their relationship again: Tell me all the people you loved before you met me.

You know everything there is to know, he said. She helped me find God.

Sometimes I think I'd prefer it if you had just slept with her.

This was outrageous talk. He warned her to be careful what she said.

I know, Frances sighed, she's dead. And Peter Rogers is in Cape Town.

Peter Rogers was a former boyfriend with whom Frances had once indulged in anal sex. Several times down the years she had told Avery she was sorry she'd ever mentioned it. She worried he was becoming obsessed with Peter Rogers.

Can we finish this in the morning? Avery asked her.

Ten minutes later the baby woke, wanting fed. He woke again a little after five. When the alarm went for Ruth to get up for school Frances and Avery were nearly speechless with tiredness. They hadn't exchanged more than a dozen words by the time Barbara arrived at eleven. She had brought a Belfast Giants pennant for Ruth. (She had just added ice-hockey correspondent to her list of job titles at the *EBCN*.) She hadn't known about the new baby. While she fussed over David –

and got Frances's back up further by saying she didn't think she was cut out for motherhood: too much she wanted to do – Avery made coffee, then showed her up to his study. At the top of the stairs he was overcome by the urge to look back. Frances was holding the baby's head close to hers, waving his limp hand bye-bye.

The image of them stayed in his mind all the time he was talking to Barbara, so that on more than one occasion – was that the front door he heard closing? – he had to ask her to repeat what he had just said. Barbara did so, slowly, as though he had given the words without intending and might want to take them back, before she did what they both knew she must do with them.

Yes, sorry, he'd say before carrying on to the next stumble.

But Frances didn't leave that day, or the next. She didn't even leave when the *East Belfast Community News* began hitting the doormats on Thursday morning.

Has 'Forgetful' Minister discovered plot or lost it?

An east Belfast minister has accused security forces of going to extraordinary lengths to silence a terrorist killer he says they colluded with in the 1970s. Rev. Ken Avery, formerly of Holywood, Co. Down, might have been making a pitch to Hollywood, CA, with sensational claims of brain surgery and botched murder-bids. The details he gave, unfortunately, would not have filled the back of the proverbial envelope. 'It's not up to me,' he said. 'I just hope that by speaking out I can encourage the man concerned to come forward and tell his own story.' Rev. Avery is no stranger to controversy. Comments made earlier this year to the *EBCN* were interpreted by some as sacrilegious. Talking at his home this week he appeared tense and tired, though perhaps the birth recently of his second child (a son) had something to do with that!

According to police sources no allegations have so far been made to them. In response to reports that officers had been seen at Rev. Avery's church, the sources said that this was in connection with 'an unrelated matter'.

Only later that day when the rumours of what the unrelated matter might be had circulated to the school gates and the queues for the Tesco checkouts did Frances decide that life at the house was just no longer bearable.

(Avery had, of course, explained to her about the Joy Street photographs, but never mind for the minute what she thought of his story, it certainly would have cut no ice out on the street: Oh, it's nothing more lurid than kerb-crawling they're accusing him of. No, it wasn't even him driving. I know! Imagine!)

Even then she didn't sneak away.

I think I'll call my daddy, she said. Get him to come and pick us up before the traffic gets heavy.

She asked Avery to keep an eye on the baby while she took Ruth upstairs to pack.

Again? said Ruth.

Yes, sweetheart, *again*.

Avery said . . . Well, what was there to say? Frances shouted instructions to him over the banister. She'd need the Moses basket, the baby bath, the sterilizer, the monitor and the buggy. She'd need the baby seat and Ruth's seat out of the Orion. It didn't *feel* like a breaking-up and in a sense it was no more than he had suggested last week that she do. Her father, unpredictable as ever, maintained a respectful distance while they said their goodbyes.

You're a good man, Frances said into Avery's ear, but you're not always very smart. If you'd talked to me more this mightn't have happened.

Avery wanted to tell her that wasn't true, but knew it would only make matters worse.

I'll call you in the morning, if there's anything I've forgotten, she said. Assuming I can get through.

The phone had been ringing off the hook since late morning. Otherwise, Frances had said, it would have been easier to send him away and let her stay with the baby and his mountain of gear. The answer-machine, set to screen, was a box possessed. Spirits of a concerned congregation, in the main. Guy Broudie's was the dominant voice, requesting an emergency meeting of the Kirk Session one time, reminding Avery another that a meeting was only a courtesy to the Minister, he could and would go to the Presbytery without it. A researcher called from the radio phone-in programme. Would Reverend Avery be prepared to expand on his allegations on air? The information officer called from Church HQ. Would Reverend Avery care to discuss the allegations with him before saying anything further in public? Des wanted him to know he was in his prayers.

Avery sat against the radiator in the hall when Frances and the children had gone. When he was through crying he went and got himself a carton of orange juice and a banana from the kitchen. Later still he went upstairs for a blanket and pillow. The call he was waiting for came at half past ten. No message. No caller ID. His mobile rang the very next instant.

It's me, the voice said, and Avery said, I know.

I wasn't going to call at all.

I hoped and prayed you would.

Wherever he was ringing from it was beyond the reach of

the *East Belfast Community News*. It was pure coincidence he had phoned today and not yesterday or tomorrow. Avery told him what he had done, talking to the paper. It hadn't gone as well as it might have with Barbara, but that didn't matter now. The ball was rolling.

He couldn't impress on Larry the renewed danger he was in without mentioning Tony; he couldn't mention Tony without revealing what it was Avery had asked him to do.

How is the memory? he said.

Better every day.

Good. I have an idea. How soon can you get over here?

Tonight? It's half ten.

I can pick you up. You can stay the night. You can stay as long as you like.

2

Well   Wait   No   Sorry   Turn that off   I need a min

So   Am   Em   Sorry sorry   Rewind

*OK   OK   OK   Oh   You're not going to believe this
I need the toilet*

You running? Right.

You'll have to excuse me. There are still gaps. So if I

Anyway.

*There was a lot of grief at home. I remember that. Even when I
was a wee lad, my mum and my dad and me fought the bit out. I
couldn't wait to get out of there. Some people I knew had a house,
Cliftonville Road. Must've been twenty of them living there all told.
They offered me a bed. It made no difference, twenty, twenty-one,
there were always people coming and going. It wasn't a house, it
was a party, basically. You can imagine. The whole country's going
mad, bombings and shootings left, right and centre, and there we
are with Rory Gallagher and Thin Lizzy blasting out, having a
complete ball.*

*And ah   And ah   And ah And ah that went on a while and
then ah one day it, well, it just – I don't know what time it was
exactly, I'd just crawled into bed – there was this almighty crash
and the next thing I knew there were police and soldiers in the room,
grabbing the hold of me, trailing me down the stairs – trailing the
other fellas – slapping the girls to shut them up screaming, turning*

the whole place upside down. The front door was lying half-way up the hall, I don't know what they hit it with, a grenade, it looked like. A big splinter of it got caught in my sock – that's right, I'd these flipping socks, big Millets jobs, I wore them in bed over my ordinary socks, they were probably stinking, everything I was wearing was probably stinking – but, ah, but, ah, yeah, the splinter. It was jabbing into my foot, they had us right out on to the street, throwing our hands up against the wall, and all I'm thinking is how am I going to get this flipping thing out of my foot, and I'm sort of twisting round when a policeman comes down the front steps carrying a holdall with a gun poking out of it and then – slap! – this soldier hits me round the head and says, Face the wall, you IRA B. That's when I really started to get scared. I was shouting saying I knew nothing about any guns and then the fella beside me started shouting too and on down the line it went and the soldiers were whacking us and kicking us and telling us to shut the eff up and who did put them there, then, the fairies? They made us undo our trousers to stop us running away. There was a whole crowd gathered by this time out on the street and they were jeering the soldiers, spitting at them, so they piled us into a couple of Saracens and kicked us twice as hard till the doors were opened again and we were in the backyard of some sort of barracks with even more soldiers and lights and dogs barking. I don't know where they took everybody else, first thing they did was pull my jumper up over my head – I'd about three layers of T-shirts underneath that I slept in, they all got bunched up behind my ears, burning them – and I was trailed by the sleeves into this room and the door was shut behind me. I struggled to get my head out of the jumper. I couldn't see anything. I yelled. I thought it was my eyes. I actually touched them to make sure they were open. They were, but there was no light. You've never seen darkness like it. I lost it, I'm afraid. I cried I   I   I won't tell you what all I did in the hours before the light

*came on. What am I saying, light? It was like a junior-torch bulb,
but it near blinded me. There was a bed. There was a toilet, two
feet from where I'd been standing. I cried again.*

Wait   Stop   No   Don't   It's OK

*By the time they came to get me I just wanted to crawl into a hole
somewhere and die. They tossed me in a shower – freezing, of course
– and gave me somebody else's jeans to put on and took me into
another room with a table in it and two fellas sitting at it in leather
jackets and jeans. Only for their crewcuts they could have been some
of the ones from our house. They didn't say hello, or sit down or my
name's this or that or anything. One of them – he had an English
accent, Yorkshire, though I wouldn't have known that then – he had
a piece of paper in front of him and he started reading out all this
stuff about me, my rank in the IRA and so on. I stood there with
my mouth hanging open. Tell you the truth, I felt like laughing, I
was sure there'd been a big mistake. I said to them: You've made a
mistake, there's no way I'm in the IRA. I'm a Protestant. The fella
with the page, the Yorkshire fella – you called him Clark, but I
didn't know that then either – this fella shrugs. You're all effing
Micks to me, he says. (The other fella smirked.) Anyway, you
wouldn't be the first Proddie Provo I've had in here. And then the
other fella butts in: One of the weapons taken from your house was
used to kill a police officer, he said. I couldn't believe it – effing
Micks? – he was as Belfast as I was. I told him I didn't know how
the gun got there or who it belonged to for I never saw any guns
anywhere near the house, there was hardly even a knife you could
butter your toast with.*

*You calling us liars? Clark said. Hear that, Rob, he's calling you
a liar.*

I'm not calling anybody a liar, I'm just telling you what I saw.

Didn't see, Rob says.

That's what I meant, I says.

The piece of paper had got pushed across the table a bit. I could read dates, times. I thought maybe someone had been watching the house. They were upside-down, it took me a while to work them out. Wait, I said, most of those dates there are before I even moved in.

I didn't think they would take any notice, but then Clark, I think it was, one of them anyway, he pulled the page closer, put his elbows on the table looking at it. He slid it sideways to his mate. I thought, Brilliant, at last they're listening to me. I was gabbling away telling them how I only moved out of home because of the rows, how there was no way I'd have been living in that house up the Cliftonville Road otherwise, how as soon as this was all cleared up I was heading back to my own part of town.

Just as long as I didn't have to go back into that cell, that's what I was really thinking.

So the Belfast fella, Rob, he says, Maybe you're right. Maybe you're not mixed up in any of it. He says, All the same, I wouldn't be in too big of a hurry to move back over home, just in case, you know, it was to get around you'd been bunking up with a crowd of Provos.

Well, like, they must have been able to see how freaked out I was by that. Rob started saying, Let's see, who is it over your way are the big chiefs in the UVs? (It was always UVF round our way. Always.) They were throwing names out to me, him and Clark both. I told them I didn't know anything but, like, these two fellas, they knew what they were doing, they knew the signs to look for, they could tell from my face, the hairs on the back of my hand for all I know, when they'd hit the target.

Friend of yours, is he? Know him to see, do you?

I shrugged, twitched, tensed probably the odd time.

The two of them walked over to the corner of the room and

whispered. I don't know, pretended to whisper. Then Clark turns to
me and says, I'll tell you what we'll do.

Can we take a break a minute?

You OK?
  I think so.
  What about the splinter?
  What?
  The splinter from the door, I was just wondering. It was
sticking in your sock.
  I don't know.
  All the same, there aren't many gaps.
  No?
  No.
  I think maybe the locket, once I remembered that, it
unlocked everything. Unlocketed. Sorry.
  Do you feel up to talking about that?
  Another minute.
  Avery wound back a bit to check the recording: *and whis-*
pered. I don't know, pretended to. He wound on again, waited.
  The speed with which things were moving had taken him
by surprise. He had only suggested making a recording last
night to see if it would provide a different sort of focus.
  Anything's worth a try, Larry said.
  He had been sitting at the kitchen table this morning when
Avery came down, the blue sports jacket over the chair behind
him, shirt cuffs turned back twice. Let's get cracking here, the
look said.
  And they had got cracking.
  Avery would happily have waited the rest of the day for
more.

But Larry was turning back his cuffs again.
OK, he said. Record.

Am   Sorry   Stop a second

Where had I got to?
   Clark was about to put something to you?
   That's right. That's right. Go.

*I don't know how much of it they had planned, whether the whole
raid was part of it, or whether they just got lucky and improvised.
I moved back home for a while like I said I would, like Clark and
Rob said now that I should. I hung around a few places, you know
drinking clubs and that, where I knew I'd get noticed by the right
people. Well, I say 'right' . . . It was them suggested to me getting
more involved. I didn't have to volunteer. I mean there wasn't an
intensive training course or anything, but you know that, everyone
knows that, whatever the murals would have you believe. That's
what I'd love to see, by the way. An honest mural. No crests or
uniforms, no guns even. Four men round a table in drinking formation, glasses raised. Eff the Pope. Prods Out.*
   Anyway.
   *I'd meet Clark the odd time. I never knew whether that was a
Christian name or a surname. Clark. I'd a number I was to ring
and ask for him. I'd tell him who I'd seen, what I'd heard. You'd
hardly call it top secret, but Clark seemed happy enough, gave me a
fiver or a tenner, handy money in those days. And of course I wasn't
working. My da started up again, getting at me – like if ever there
was a case of the pot calling the kettle black – and in the end I just
thought, I can't stick this, if I don't get out of here once and for all
I'm going to do one of us damage. So I told Clark he could do what
he liked, I was finished, and he just said, Well, don't lose touch*

altogether, and he gave me another number and said, That one comes through practically to my bedroom. I can meet you at an hour's notice.

I could just have thrown it away, of course, the minute I was on my own. I wish I could say I was thinking it might come in useful if I was ever in trouble, because God – sorry – dear knows, you didn't have to go out of your way to find trouble then, but if I'm being really honest it was the excitement. If anybody's being honest they'll tell you that, no matter how unwilling they were to get into it in the first place, no matter how desperate they are to get out. You'd miss it.

I kept my head down for the next while. New area, new start, you know what I'm saying? But then, I don't know, I just started drifting back to the clubs and bars, and, of course, now I had a bit of a track record, names to drop, and the suggestion was made as before that maybe I'd like to be a bit more active, and before I knew it I was keeping this thing or that thing someone urgently wanted kept, letting someone else have a bed for the night, no questions asked, no recognition given if ever I was to bump into them again on the street.

It was months before I phoned Clark. You'd have thought he'd been sitting by the phone all that time. In his bedroom. Aye, right. He met me, must have been, in less than half an hour. Picked me up in his car. You want to have seen the smiles of him, I mean he didn't look like he was putting it on. Even shook my hand again. When I was getting out of the car he gave me twenty pound. After that it was always fifteen. I met him once a fortnight. Sometimes his mate, Rob, was there and I'd have to sit in the back. He'd turn in his seat and ask me a couple of questions, but normally on those days he'd either drive or sit and look out the window while Clark and I talked.

Rob wasn't his real name, but that was all I knew him by until he was shot dead and his name and his picture and everything was

in the papers. Provos. He'd a wee boy and a wee girl, five or six,
that sort of age. I never saw Clark as angry as the next time I met
him: A waste of space, the whole effing lot of you. If I'd my effing
way you'd all be put up against a wall and shot. I took exception, I
told him I'd have been perfectly happy to carry on playing my Thin
Lizzy records, getting drunk with my mates, if him and 'Rob' hadn't
decided to pay us a call. It was them had got me mixed up in this
not the other way around. And here he is, I'll tell you what's got
you mixed up in this, and he rubbed his fingers and thumb together.
Am I wrong? Am I wrong? Well, am I?

He wasn't entirely. Excitement and money. They were both
addictive.

He told me to get out of the car. I told him he didn't need to tell
me for I was getting out anyway. The door was still flapping when
he drove away. He stopped up the street and banged it shut.

Am   Ah   Can we stop do you think? Have a cup o

The doors must have been opened in the supermarket loading
bay. A radio was playing at a volume a shade off distortion.
Every second record was the Beatles or John Lennon or Bryan
Ferry singing John Lennon. Friday 8 December 2000. Twenty
years ago today.

Where were you? Avery asked.

Do you know – and actually Avery, if he'd given it even
half a moment's thought, might have guessed – I don't remember. You?

On the bus into school, the driver had a transistor hanging
from the mirror. He was in floods. He stopped taking fares. I
got off two stops early. I was worried he was going to crash.

From dead pop star it was an easy step to dead president
(where were they? 'School probably' and 'Not yet born'); from

there to the man who as a boy shook the soon-to-be-dead president's hand and who as president himself was in Belfast for one last round of handshakes in four days' time. The Odyssey. What better place to finish?

The thought seemed to occur to them both at once. They set down their teacups.

Will we start back and get this done?

So   Yes   I was in a pretty bad way. Nineteen seventy-six I'm talking now. I'd started hitting the drink big-time. I'd pick a different old-man's bar down the town and go and sit on my own in the corner getting quietly plastered night after night until someone, thinking they were doing me a kindness, decided to start up a conversation. Then I'd go and find another bar. The weird thing about Belfast in those days, the city centre – the dead centre – was more like the sticks than the sticks. Bars with next to no one in them. You could hear a glass being wiped. People came into town who didn't want to meet anybody. Old fellas and fugitives, that was about the height of it.

I recognized Davy from round and about the loyalist clubs. I'd always got the impression he was pretty well connected. I knew but, just from seeing him in Ellis's, he was trying to give his old associates a wide berth. I thought ten-to-one it was to do with the woman he was seeing. The two of them on their own were pretty quiet, but there was another woman with them the odd time and she'd be Roisin and Davying them left, right and centre. Roisin and Davy. It didn't take a genius. I caught him once or twice looking at me, trying to place the face. I smiled back at him, like don't worry about me.

I phoned Clark. I was skint. I thought maybe he'd be interested in Davy and his girlfriend, you know, put a bit of pressure on them, but he didn't think there was anything in it. Why would they talk

234

to him? They'd carved out a wee place for themselves and were careful not to stray outside it. Good luck to them.

He didn't give me a bean. A couple of days later I called him again. What if the two of them were to get a bit of a fright? Say someone was to let off a gun at them and only just miss? Do you think maybe then they'd be glad of an offer of protection? And Clark said something like, You're a bad wee so-and-so, do you know that?

It was Clark himself gave me the gun. He said I wasn't to worry, there'd be absolutely no trace on it, guaranteed. He went through some things about the action. I didn't let on to him that I'd never actually held a gun before. It looked fairly straightforward the way he described it. I was to meet him afterwards and he'd take the gun away, but it all went wrong from the start. I decided before I went in I'd get the bar takings while I was there. It wasn't part of the plan – one shot was the plan, in the door and out – but once you have a gun you get all kinds of ideas. And I was really, really skint. I'd the hood of my parka pulled up and a scarf over my mouth and nose. Your man behind the bar never clocked for a second who I was, but Davy did, don't ask me how, maybe I just stayed there too long. He was standing up pointing his finger. I was pointing the gun. I don't know when I'd raised it. It was like I'd a crane for an arm. Roisin said, Ach, now, son, don't. I think I was still looking for a place to shoot to miss, but they just seemed huge all of a sudden. I squeezed the trigger, it felt like it was cutting my finger in two, I wouldn't have been surprised if the thing had just toppled out of my hand on to the floor and then

then Roisin gave like a little hop. I wondered what she was doing, I was going to shout, Sit down before you get hit – I'd never seen anybody being shot, I'd no idea, no idea at all – then Davy slumped against the wall. I was deafened. It was like I was in a bubble. I kept walking forward with the gun out in front of me. I had to make sure it was done properly. Roisin's friend was lying to one side. I went to move her and that's when I saw the chain with the locket on it. I picked it up and felt it in my hand. Then the bubble burst.

I ran out of the bar. I ran and ran and ran. The gun was stuffed in my parka. I ran right past where Clark was parked. He got out of the car and came tearing after me. He should have let me go. I was hoping a car or bus would run me over and if nothing did I was going to throw the gun in the Lagan and myself with it. Next thing I felt this weight hit me just below the waist and my legs went: rugby tackle. He was on my back on the ground. He never said a word from the moment he opened the car door. I was trying to lift my head to shout, I shot them all! I shot them all! I was losing it. His hand was coming round on to my mouth and nose like a gag. I was desperate to get it out, I shot them all! It felt like it was my last chance.

And then I was opening my eyes in the hospital and there were doctors and people telling me how lucky I was to be alive and what a bad fall it was I'd had off the bike and there was this split second where I knew they were lying, where I could see everything that had happened dead, dead clearly, and then it just flicked out, like a dream getting away. From that day on I was never rid of the feeling that there was something just escaping me. A thousand times – more – a hundred thousand, I could almost feel it on the tip of my tongue, whatever the word was that would free all the other words I was certain were there.

I was wrong before when I said there were gaps. Blockages, I should have said. It was like whatever they did when they opened up my head, they made like a dam with all that stuff on one side. For years nothing got through. And then out of the blue there was a crack. I was listening to the radio. Someone said, Let every man be fully persuaded in his own mind. I knew I wasn't. I knew I wouldn't rest until I was. I am now.

I think that's it. I think that's all I have to say.

I'm sorry.

Avery's head had been bowed through the last sentences. He raised it now, swallowed before he spoke. How do you feel?
Better. Kind of. But also . . .
I understand. Stupid question.
Not stupid at all. Fire away, ask whatever you want.
Why do you think they operated? Really.
Because I wouldn't shut up any other way? As an experiment? Because they thought with everything else that was going on they could get away with it? I don't know.

3

Avery let himself in as usual by the door next to the Session Room at a quarter to eleven on Sunday morning. Ronnie, happening at that moment to turn into the corridor, nearly had kittens. His first instinct seemed to be to run but he checked himself in time. We weren't expecting to see you, he said, taking refuge in the plural.

Who else would lead the service? Avery asked, as he passed keys through his fingers until he had found the one to his own room.

The calendar hadn't been changed since before Remembrance Sunday. He tore off a month's worth of Sundays to Saturdays and dropped them in the bin. Underneath was a sign for the Midvale School for the Gifted. A boy at the top of the steps bent his full weight to pushing a door marked pull.

Avery sat at his desk with the *Lectionary* unopened before him. The second Sunday of Advent. Prophets' Sunday. He had already familiarized himself with the day's readings, sitting in his study last night long after Larry was asleep, poring over Ezekiel:

And he said unto me, Son of man, I send thee to the children of Israel, to a rebellious nation that hath rebelled against me: they and their fathers have transgressed against me, even unto this very day. For they are impudent children and stiffhearted. I do send thee unto them; and thou shalt say unto them, Thus saith the Lord God. And they, whether they will hear, or whether they will forbear, (for they are a rebellious house,) yet shall know there hath been a prophet among them . . . And when I looked, behold, an hand was sent unto me; and, lo, a roll of a book was therein; And he spread it before me; and it was written within and without: and there was written therein lamentations and mourning and woe.

He had picked up the cassette from on top of the recorder as he read, turning it in his hand, catching now and then that slight rattle which warned you not to expect this to keep for ever.

Moreover he said unto me, Son of man, eat that thou findest; eat this roll, and go speak unto the house of Israel.

He tapped the tape against his top lip, locked it in the study's desk drawer.

Several times he heard whispers in the corridor outside the Minister's Room, hurried footsteps, but no one came near the door. At eleven twenty he went to his cupboard to robe himself. A hood and bands day, he decided. Yes. A reminder to himself if nobody else of his learning. It was not by luck or fraud that he had arrived here, minister to this congregation. A minister should serve, but also lead. There were difficult truths about the past to be faced. He would urge the people gathered in the sanctuary this morning to face them with dignity that they might *go forward* with dignity.

The corridor was empty. He stood outside his room for a minute more to see would anyone appear and when no one did he walked as far as the sanctuary door where he waited again.

At first he thought there was no conversation at all – no

congregation possibly – but then he began to pick it up, pitched lower than a mumble: a grumble; a growl almost. He pushed open the door. The growl grew lower still but didn't disappear. The organ didn't start. Every creaking step of his walk across the front of the chancel was audible. As he climbed the steps he kept his eyes on the plaque on the pulpit door. To the Glory of God and in Grateful Remembrance of Ernest Arbuthnot. Door donor. There was a thumbprint, where the hand in gripping came naturally to rest, across Grateful. He added his own print to it and sat on a chair in the twin names of Hannah and Annalise Tiler, pinching the bridge of his nose, his entire body become prayer.

When he rose to his feet he saw that Michael Simpson was already standing, hands cupped around his mouth. Avery had an instant to wonder by what force of will he was remaining steady before he heard the shout.

Shame on you!

Michael, Avery said, but someone else had stood up now, on the opposite side of the aisle. Alan Rossborough, the father of the policeman he had spoken to at the hospital.

Shame!

Please. Both Avery's hands were extended, as though he had been tricked by the perspective into thinking he could still bring pressure to bear on them. And then two more people – one of them Avery didn't even recognize – got to their feet in the second last pew. Lorna Simpson stepped out into the aisle to unfold Michael's wheelchair.

They were standing now, too, in the gallery. The shouts had become a chant. *Shame, shame, shame.* Michael was leading it, arching back in his chair as he began to propel himself out of the church, Lorna keeping angry pace beside him. Hands were being clapped, feet were being stomped. It was the most noise the congregation had made in all the time Avery had been minister; in all the services put together. Some slapped each other on the back as they joined the procession. Out on the front steps someone tried to start up the national anthem, but was drowned by the gabble of more people arriving.

When the door swung shut on the last back there were three people left in the pews. Guy Broudie was sitting next to a white-haired man Avery recognized at once from the photographs in the Session Room as former minister, Moderator of the Presbyterian Church in Ireland, and self-styled prisoner of conscience, the Very Reverend Dr Arthur Talbot.

Dorothy Moore sat by herself in her usual position half-way down on the left-hand side. Avery smiled at her.

You needn't look at me, she said. I'm only sitting here because my lift doesn't come till twenty to one and there's no heat in that vestibule.

Avery leant his forearms on the lectern, hands limp over the pulpit fall.

You weren't returning our calls, said Guy, who unlike Ronnie was perpetually plural. Dr Talbot here volunteered to ensure that the gospel ordinances were supplied.

Talbot nodded with something like approval. At least you showed your face, he said. His voice came pre-amplified.

Why wouldn't I have? This is my church.

No, said Talbot, this is a building. Your church just walked out the door.

And that goes for me sat here, said Dorothy Moore, selfless as ever with her twopenceworth.

Avery gathered up his Bible and six-by-four cards and descended the pulpit steps.

Guy was walking down the aisle to check was there still a

demand outside to meet the supply of ordinances. Talbot rose up. He was about six foot five.

I want you to know I am not without sympathy, he said. I am after all a man of *conviction* myself. (Avery wondered how many times in the decades since his one-week sentence he had said that.) Some people, walking out's the only exercise they ever get, brain and body both. People have walked out of churches I've known over far less important matters: the siting of a font in one instance. Whatever happens tomorrow or the next day, or the next couple of weeks or years, the majority of them will shake your hand again eventually.

He held out his own. The hand was enormous, more symbol than limb-end. Avery's seemed parsimonious in comparison.

It was the most perplexingly Christian thing anyone had done for him in he didn't know how long. Still, he hesitated before grasping it.

Guy had opened the vestibule doors.

It would probably be a good idea if you left now, Talbot said.

Avery went.

Next morning when he left the house to buy milk a man stumbled from a car parked opposite the driveway gates and tried to take his picture.

Avery hurried back inside, bolted the door, and climbed the stairs two at a time to the landing window. The man from the car was ruffling his hair as though to rouse himself and talking to another man, dressed like him in a two-tone cagoule and like him carrying a camera.

Press, not police, unless police now operated the undercover double-bluff: officers sticking out like sore thumbs.

They glanced at the house and failed to spot him.

The second photographer lit a cigarette, tilting his chin to exhale, as if there was a height bylaw for smoke emissions. He dialled a number on his mobile phone and strolled off, phone to one ear, hand to the other, smoke curling up the side of his head. The first photographer got into the car again, yawned.

These two clowns did not a media circus make. Not with an American president arriving tomorrow and pre-visit briefings to attend and last-minute passes to be sorted and maybe last night's excesses – *Haven't seen you since the referendum!* – to sleep off. Still, it was a presence. And the fella in the car looked like he might have been there since the wee small hours. Avery would nearly have considered sticking his head out every so often to keep him there until the small hours of tomorrow.

He went into the study to try Frances. He got her mother.

She's still in bed, Mrs Burns said. I've told her, sleep when the baby sleeps.

Avery remembered Frances mimicking her mother telling her this when Ruth was a baby. If grandchildren were the reward for not giving your own children away, then licence to advise was surely compensation for the guilt you'd felt at ever being tempted.

He said, Tell her to call me just whenever. Tell her I love her.

Mrs Burns's silence suggested she would do no such thing.

We heard what happened at church yesterday, she said. Somebody from the radio phoned wanting to talk to Frances.

Did she talk to them?

What do you think?

No, he thought, she wouldn't have.

She's worried you'll lose the house, his mother-in-law said.

It'll not come to that.

You sound very sure.

I'm sure that I'm not in the wrong.

I think you'll find you're in a minority of one there.

Avery could have gone on. That's where *you* are wrong, he could have said. One hundred per cent verifiably wrong.

He didn't. I'll ring back later, he said.

Downstairs again, putting away last night's dishes, he heard his verification step into the shower directly above the kitchen. A shuffle of feet as he adjusted the temperature, an almost unconscious four-note whistle to signal the water was just right. *Plunk!* The drumming of water on the shower floor was interrupted as he bent to retrieve the soap. Five seconds later – *plunk!* – down went the soap again. Avery put the kettle on, conscious of the absurd, accelerated domesticity of the moment. He had – and just occasionally regretted it – no experience of one-night stands. Or two- or three-night, for that matter.

He opened the fridge for the milk, then remembered why he had been going out when the photographer ambushed him.

Doesn't matter, I can take my tea with or without, Larry said when he presented himself dried and dressed ten minutes later. (All he had brought with him on Thursday night was a small overnight bag. Avery had offered to go with him for the rest of his stuff, but he insisted he was fine as he was: It's not as if I'll be here much longer.)

I suppose when you've shared a house with – how many people was it you said?

Twenty.

With twenty people, you're used to there being no milk.

Larry was looking at him askance.

What? Avery asked.

You're a fly man. *How many people was it you said?*

It genuinely slipped my mind, said Avery. There's been so much to take in the last couple of days.

Larry at the table locked his hands round the mug of black tea, mood darkening. You know they'll just deny every word I say?

Avery pulled out the chair opposite. We'll call for an inquiry, he said. No: an examination. They can't deny a scar.

Larry's hair was flat from showering, the pointed strands chopping the scar into manageable sections. It was a little livid perhaps, but not much more remarkable this morning than the signs of wear and tear on an average forty-five-year-old's face. He sucked his top lip, as though it was Avery's respect he had just doubted.

I don't know, he said and looked off towards the window.

He jumped up, slopping tea.

Bloody hell, there's someone coming over the top of your hedge.

It was one of the photographers, the smoker. He was down in the corner where the hedge was sturdiest and reinforced by the metal palings round the electricity substation. Even so he was having to use both arms to cling on as the branches shifted beneath him. He hadn't a prayer of taking a picture. All the same, Avery knew his part. From the back door he shouted at the man he had thirty seconds before the hose was switched on. The head reared up, produced a grin, then grin, head and arms disappeared. There was a rustle, a yelp, the sound of something like a wheelie bin cowping over; a crystal clear *Fuck*, a murkier *Shit*.

He wants to watch he doesn't get himself electrocuted, Avery said.

Larry had backed off towards the hall door. I don't want to sound selfish here, but it's not him I'm worried about.

Avery could appreciate his alarm: what kind of hideaway was this, right under the noses of the press?

I think we're OK, he said. They don't know what it is they're looking for yet. Probably the most they're hoping is that one of the congregation will come and punch me on the nose, or that Frances will turn up and have a slanging match with me on the front doorstep. They don't realize it, but the longer they stay there the less is likely to happen. They're buying us time.

They spent the time that morning apart. Avery composed letters to the Chief Constable of the RUC, the General Officer Commanding Land Forces, the First and Deputy First Ministers of the Northern Ireland Assembly, the Prime Minister of the United Kingdom, the Queen, the Taoiseach, the President of the United States and – since he was on a roll – Nick Ross of *Crimewatch UK*, urging them to investigate. He didn't seal them into envelopes, they weren't that kind of letter. They were letters to be photographed being brandished, text turned out. The last people to know what was in them would be the people to whom they were addressed.

Larry, by the looks of him when next he and Avery met in the kitchen, had been lying down all the while, reading maybe, or sleeping. Keeping well clear of the windows was as much as he would say when Avery asked him.

He didn't offer to help as Avery got the cups ready for coffee (and in truth he hadn't often offered since his arrival), but sat at the table with his hands dug in his pockets, the picture of a teenager in the final week of school holidays.

Avery opened a tin. There's an end of a ginger cake here, he said. Will we go halfers? I'm afraid there's not much else till I get out to the shops.

Larry said he didn't have much of a sweet tooth, but ate his portion anyway, leaving only a scalp of lime-coloured icing at the side of his plate. He dabbed up the crumbs with the pad of his index finger.

The phone-in programme was starting on the radio. Item three in the contents announced at the top of the programme was a follow-up to Friday's story of the cryptic claims by a Presbyterian minister of security-forces' misconduct: a mass walkout by his east Belfast congregation.

More coffee? Avery said.

Larry shook his head. Avery picked up a spoon and dragged the handle across a cork mat a couple of times, then folded his arms and looked down at the table.

Clinton dominated the first ten minutes. Itinerary, security, impact on the political process. Then it was a problem with a locked disabled toilet in a flagship Belfast department store, a detour through the state of city-centre toilets generally, then it was the walkout.

Neither the minister nor anyone from the Presbyterian Church in Ireland had made themselves available for comment, the presenter said. (Avery was still screening his calls.) One senior member of the congregation was quoted as saying only that it was an internal matter, in more ways than one. – Avery could just hear him saying it too. – Conscience, he was sorry to disappoint people, made for a muted sort of drama.

A regular contributor to the programme, noted for his conservative views, wondered whether – without knowing the full details of the allegations, of course, and if listeners would excuse the gruesome pun – we weren't in danger of looking for feds under all our dead. Gruesome, perhaps, but not as ghoulish, he opined, as some of the recent judicial disinterments.

Strong views there, the presenter said, strong views, and he reminded listeners of the several ways they could register their own views on the subject. But there *was* a presidential visit in the offing. The vast majority of the callers who didn't have public-toilet horror stories to share wanted to know either what right Americans had interfering in our affairs – hadn't they trouble enough at home? – or whether Bill Clinton needed his head examined, spending the last days of his presidency in our benighted, begrudging neck of the woods.

There were items from the hotel where the president's entourage would be stopping. There was an interview with a chef and another with a barman, who claimed that if he'd used the same pint of Guinness for all the hundreds of dignitaries who'd been photographed in his bar taking a sip of one it still wouldn't be empty.

Avery made more coffee and cut some bread and cheese. Larry sat with his hands in his pockets. Then, shortly before the close of the programme, a north Belfast listener who preferred not to give her name called to say she knew the case that Reverend Avery was referring to. She said it involved the murder of two women and a man in Ellis's bar in 1976. She was married to the brother of one of the women.

Larry leapt out of his seat again. How could she know? How could she *know*?

Which was exactly what the presenter asked the caller.

She said she couldn't say, but she challenged the Reverend Avery to come on air and explain.

Well, the invitation has been made, the presenter said, but there you are, we'll keep trying.

I called at the house, said Avery. I made inquiries and I called round.

Larry stopped pacing the kitchen floor. You were checking on me.

I thought something might come out that would help you as well. Conclusive proof. I asked them about the necklace.

And?

They couldn't be sure. I couldn't be sure.

But I told you.

I know. What can I say? It was just after that I sent you the text message.

Larry sat again. Anything else I should know about?

Avery thought about it. Should was his get-out. No, he said.

Larry grunted, like this was scant consolation. There was some dreadful country-and-western programme on the radio. Northern Irish country-and-western. A car crash of terms. Avery switched to Radio 3 and, as often happened, hadn't the first clue what he was listening to. Minutes passed.

What were they like? Larry said at last.

Leo and Patricia? They were very nice. I mean, there was the odd awkward moment, but all things considered . . . like, it can't have been easy for them.

I suppose they wanted to see me strung up.

No, nothing like that. They didn't ask that much about you, to be honest.

Good.

I told them anyway I didn't know a whole lot.

But you do now.

I do now. Yes.

They managed not to cross each other's paths for the remainder of the afternoon. They met again at seven to eat pasta tossed in a tomato sauce that had made it to within five hours of the end of its use-by date. Avery would definitely have to shop.

Frances was feeding the baby when he rang. He spoke to Ruth instead. She had helped Granny and Granddad put up their Christmas tree. It was a real one and it smelt of the green stuff Mummy used to clean the toilet. David had blue lips when he wanted to do a burp. She had to go now, Granddad was giving her a story before bed.

He left it a while then phoned Michele. Hi, her answer-machine said. I can't come to the phone, but thank you, *everyone* who has been ringing to ask about Tony, and for all the cards and flowers. He's much better today. Fingers crossed he'll be able to have visitors by the end of the week.

Later, walking from the study to the bathroom, he saw a light on under the stairs. He called over the banister: You OK there?

After a second or two Larry's head appeared, looking up. Wrong turn, he said.

It's easily done.

You've a lot of videos here of comedians.

It's a hobby.

Strange hobby for a minister.

No stranger than golf.

Golf?

The clergyman's pastime of choice. Hadn't you heard? Some of the courses even offer special rates on Mondays.

You're not serious?

I'm telling you. You don't know the half of it. Like the big funeral homes? They put on a dinner every year: speakers, free diaries, the works. We're a major part of the economy. The country would face financial ruin if atheism was declared.

Larry had lifted down a videotape. This doesn't look like a bag of laughs. He handed it up through the spindles. *The Ballad of Lizzie Borden*.

Ah, but it did star Elizabeth Montgomery. The name clearly meant nothing to Larry. You know, *Bewitched*?

Larry appeared bewildered. You have a very generous definition of comedy.

We all have our blind spots. Actually there was a Larry in that. Darrin's boss.

Larry under the hall light closed his eyes and recited: 'Lizzie Borden took an axe, / Gave her father forty whacks.' One of my dad's favourite rhymes, which tells you all you need to know about him. 'When she saw what she had done, / She gave her mother forty-one.'

Probably, Avery said.

Worth watching?

Only if you're a fan of Elizabeth Montgomery.

They watched a wildlife programme instead before turning in and endured an uncomfortable twenty seconds, like a couple grown forgetful together, when a peacock and a peahen appeared and performed a spot of pea-porn.

The moment had passed for asking Larry where he had been heading when he found his way in under the stairs.

Avery woke from a nightmare, convinced someone was in the room with an axe. His eyes swept the darkness, high, low, under the wardrobe, up the side of the chest of drawers, and came to rest on the bedroom door. It was closed, exactly as he had left it. No, not exactly. It looked – how would you explain it? – too closed. Just closed. He listened. Absolute silence. He had never known a house, least of all this house, be *absolutely* silent. It was as though all natural sound was being withheld. He sat in bed, knees to his chest, a full minute longer, before a plane passing a mile overhead seemed to set his watch ticking again, agitate the water in the central-heating pipes. These he augmented with the creaking of the floorboards between his bed and the window, the rasp of runners on rail as he twitched the curtain.

His own car was in the driveway, but the photographer's car was gone from across the street. Instantly every noise assumed a sinister quality. He went over in his mind his bedtime ritual of checking and double-checking all the locks. Impossible he could have missed one. And then a terrible thought occurred to him. Perhaps what he had to fear most would not be coming from the outside in. He turned to the bedroom door again, certain now he understood what was different about it. It looked like a door that was being held to hide a person. He picked his steps with extra care, avoiding the least secure floorboards, and stopped with his hand inches from the door handle. Then he did something he never dreamt he would do in his own home. Very, very slowly he turned the key in the lock. The click was deafening.

Next time he opened his eyes it was light, and the locked door and all that had given rise to it was a total embarrassment. Only the fact that the key made no sound when he turned it the other way stopped him going straight across to the guest room to apologize.

Milk.

He put on his anorak and ventured outside, peering round the gates. Not a car he didn't know, not a camera or a cagoule in sight. No need to put his hood up so.

How quickly the abnormal became normal. He thought of Michele's breezy outgoing message. Much better, she'd said. Tony was still being drip-fed. His jaw was wired. He had a collapsed lung and a perforated eardrum. But he wasn't dead. He wasn't unconscious. Michele was right, he was much better in the circumstances, and where else had any of us to live but in the circumstances?

(Live *in* them, yes, but live *for* the One whose word and

law transcended whatever circumstances humankind could contrive.)

The photographer was waiting for him when he rounded the corner to Tesco's. They locked eyes, but a woman with twins in a buggy passed in front of Avery before the photographer could get a shot off. Avery took to his heels, shoulders hunched from silent, jubilant laughter.

Hold on a minute! the photographer shouted, the paparazzo's last resort. Hold on!

Larry was at the kitchen table.

Can you do without milk again?

Can you get the tape-recorder again? Larry asked. His face was ashen. There's something more I have to tell you.

Some days when I got out of the car from talking to Clark I would go to a certain place where there was another car waiting to pick me up. The fella driving it was am ah actually I would prefer not to say his name at this point in time, but he lived for a while in the house on the Cliftonville Road. He had come looking for me a few days after the police and army raided. I was already back home living. It wasn't a safe place for him to come, but he came anyway. I was out when he called. My mum brought him in and gave him a cup of tea. She'd no idea, of course. A friend of mine, that's all she knew. I near died when I came in and saw him. I took him through to the back garden for a cigarette. My mum never liked me smoking in the house. I said to him, You must be mad, and he said, No, not mad, just thorough. He asked me what I said at the barracks. I told him I'd said nothing because I knew nothing to say. He says, That's good, because you know you'd be a dead man if you had. He said it so matter-of-fact. He wasn't even looking at me. He was looking at my mum in the kitchen getting the dinner ready. What did you say?

I says. You heard, he said. One effing word – He made a clicking sound out the side of his mouth, like a gun being cocked, or a neck being snapped. I nearly laughed in his face. I was thinking all I had to do was lift the phone to Clark or Rob and they'd have him in Long Kesh like that, but it was like he was reading my mind for the next thing he says is, And by the way, anything happens to me after I leave here – any wee visits from the peelers or boys in hoods – and you're a dead man too. Come to think of it, you do anything other than what I tell you to do, you're dead.

A couple of weeks later he called back again. Been for any nice drives down to the Folk Museum recently? he said. The Folk Museum was one of the places where Clark drove me to. I hadn't a clue how this fella knew. He just said, I think it's about time you came and talked to some people I know. So I went and that was the start of it. They didn't give me any money, they just didn't kill me. They killed Rob, but. Maybe they would have killed him anyway. Who's to

Avery stopped the tape before he was asked.
    Are you telling me you were a double-agent?
    Correct.
    For the police, the army *and* the IRA?
    Correct.
    I don't know.
    You don't know what?
    Nothing. Just. Nothing.
    He switched the tape back on.

I have nothing else to say.

I heard him on the news this morning, Larry said, when the tape was off again, talking about his party's hopes for the president's visit.

The first voice Avery heard when he switched on the radio that lunchtime was Reverend Twiss's. He was talking about his church in Holywood. Yes, he supposed it was at the liberal end of the Presbyterian spectrum, the extreme liberal end, even. He made no apologies for that. His was a very cosmopolitan-minded congregation. Anyone who joined in their worship did so in a spirit of inquiry. That was what he hoped he had imparted to Ken Avery.

Avery guessed, from the emphasis on *hoped*, what was coming.

I'm afraid but, Twiss said, Avery seems to have forgotten that in order to stretch a point it helps to have one end of it *fixed*.

Avery walked out of the kitchen and phoned the radio station. The switchboard put him through to the researcher, who put him on to the producer, who wanted to put him straight on air.

Avery declined. Tomorrow everything would be revealed, he said, then people could decide for themselves what it was needed fixed.

By the time he reached the kitchen again the presenter was reading out his statement.

What do you make of that? he asked Twiss.

Whatever Twiss did make of it wasn't picked up by the microphone.

The presenter produced from his vast repertoire of sighs one that said he could just – *just* – bear to have to talk about this another day. I suppose we'll have to wait and see, he said, and after that it was wall-to-wall Clinton. The president's entourage was following its politically plotted route from Dublin, to Dundalk and finally to Belfast where, for the next two days, his star would outshine even the brightest Christmas lights.

*

Hunting in the freezer Avery found a pack of sausages, which he defrosted in the microwave for dinner. Larry said he wasn't a big pork fan and ate round them: baked beans sprinkled with curry powder and the last of the potatoes in the house. They had a beer together at the kitchen table. A filthy night outside. They watched themselves in the window tip the bottles to their lips, sleet swarming over their reflections. A poem he had learnt at school ghosted across Avery's mind. The drunkenness of something. Difference? Variousness? It slipped away from him. He tipped the bottle and felt the beer fizz on his tongue.

His final prayer that night was from the Tuesday evening order for daily devotion: O divine master, grant that we may not so much seek to be consoled as to console; to be understood as to understand; to be loved as to love. For it is in giving that we receive; in pardoning that we are pardoned; in dying that we are born to eternal life.

Amen.

4

The plan was not to go too early. They agreed the Odyssey would be mayhem. Presidential visits never did run to schedule and it was a brand new arena, open to the public for the first time. Even supposing only those with tickets turned up, the crowds would be huge, their focus irresistible. There would be stewards and security people everywhere, clearing anything that threatened to impede the flow.

Best to arrive while the president was already inside, create a commotion out the front. Rope in a couple of stray journalists to begin with, let the word find its way round.

That was the plan, it didn't need repeating; which was as well.

Avery had woken with a swirling headache that even extra-strength aspirin had failed to subdue. His calves and upper arms felt heavier than usual, heavy enough that he was aware of them, and once or twice in the course of the morning he was brought up short by a stabbing pain deep in his rectum. He really hoped he wasn't coming down with something.

Larry was understandably wrapped up in himself. By the end of the day he would have been revealed to the world as a killer. A victim, too, of course, of the grossest ethical and surgical malpractices, but a killer none the less: I did it. I shot those people in cold blood. Bang, bang, bang.

It was the end of a long, long journey for him, out of the darkness into the spotlight.

They went about their preparations in a silence punctuated

by Avery's burps, each more unpleasant-tasting than the last. Excuse me, he said, and, I do beg your pardon, then burped again.

He had assumed it was nerves had kept him down to a cup of tea at breakfast – nerves and the fact that the only bread left was rock-hard pitta – but the thought of lunch actually made him shiver. He was right off his food. He took some more aspirin and another cup of tea and for a time that seemed to do the trick.

In the study he slipped his open letters into a document wallet, and the wallet into an airplane carry-on bag he some-times used as a briefcase. He unlocked the desk drawer, took out the cassette and, after some deliberation, zipped it into the pocket of his anorak hanging on the back of the study door. Always better to have more than one egg-basket.

He spoke to Frances. I miss you, he said. I miss Ruth, I miss David. Can I come and see you tonight?

I'm sorry, she said. Not while all this is still going on. It's not fair on the children. It's not safe.

But it'll all be over by tonight, I promise you. My part in it at least will be done.

Frances took a moment to think about it. In the background David was building up a head of steam crying. Tomorrow, she said. Maybe. I have to go. Take care of yourself.

An elderly man in a baseball cap was coming down the stairwell of the maisonettes. Two steps, stop. Two steps, stop. Avery peered more closely, checking that it was the same man he had once watched taking out the garbage at dead of night. He felt cheered, seeing him again. It had been so long he had worried that the man might be ill, or worse. The man took two more steps then paused on the return and looked across at the house, as though he had been aware all along of being observed. Avery raised a hand in acknowledgement of the intrusion. The man's expression didn't change. His mouth opened and closed, opened and closed. Was he saying something? Just catching breath? Avery was beginning to wonder had the man spotted him after all when he noticed his hands. The heels had met in front of his crotch and the fingers were moving apart and back together, apart and back together. His mouth opened and closed, opened and closed, and then Avery got it. He was being a performing seal.

Avery took a step back and burped again. Tea and sausages. He stumbled into the toilet and placed his fingers at the back of his mouth, but all he managed was a dry heave, which stung his eyes. He wrung out a facecloth and wiped his forehead and the back of his neck. Tonight when he came home he would go straight to bed. His duty would be discharged. Even if Larry came back with him he would no longer be Avery's sole responsibility. In the morning, then, he would start refreshed. New circumstances, for him, for Frances, for everyone. Yes, his reflection mouthed to him. He reached further into his throat on the off-chance, but still nothing came up. He spat, passed the cloth across his face, went back into the study for his coat and bag.

Television pictures were starting to come through from the Odyssey. The rink had been covered and rows of seats laid out on it. Hundreds had already been filled, here and in the tiers rising up on three sides of the rink. And still there were many hundreds to be filled. Very Important Children played in an area roped off in front of the platform, while their parents looked around to see who else of importance was there. (Avery thought of his own plans, a month or a lifetime ago, to take Ruth along.) In another reserved area members of the new Belfast Giants ice-hockey team roamed around in their oversized shirts and, facing them, members of the Northern Ireland Legislative Assembly stood and chatted across party lines. All of a sudden, and to a tremendous cheer, the MLAs threw their hands in the air, surrendering to a Mexican wave.

Larry was looking on stony-faced.

Is your man among them? Avery asked.

Larry shook his head. Not that I can see, but he could be. Clark could be, for all I know, out back briefing the platform party on security.

The wave washed over the Very Important Children and their parents, over the Belfast Giants and citizens of more modest stature.

What do you think? Avery said. Will we go?

Larry watched the television for a few moments more then stood up. OK. He put on the sports jacket over his V-neck sweater.

Have you nothing heavier to wear? Avery asked. We're going to be right down at the water's edge.

I'll be fine.

You won't, you'll freeze. Avery left the room and returned with his duffel coat. You can borrow this.

Larry tried it. Too small, he said. It's catching me under the arms.

Avery wondered how he had never noticed before that Larry was the taller by two or three inches. He looked at the cuffs of his own anorak, reaching almost to his thumb knuckles.

This might be better, he said and took it off.

Really, I'm OK, let's just go.

Hang on to it at least, in case it gets really bad.

Maybe it was the flu, or whatever was ailing him, but Avery's concentration was such that he could not move on to the next thing until this thing was done. Larry took the anorak. The pocket rattled. Avery opened the front door.

Outside, street-lights were already coming on. The wind was picking up. A wind that didn't trouble with the extremities, but blew straight through you. Avery's hands trembled as he removed the chain from the steering-wheel. The palms were clammy and he wiped them on his trouser-legs. Larry got into the car beside him. He had the anorak on, the cuffs when he sat riding up his wrist.

Gates, he said and went to get out again.

No, let me. Avery was thinking of the photographers lying in wait. He didn't want any hitches at this late stage, not least because he didn't want to delay by even a minute getting home again to bed. They could snap him now to their hearts' content, but he couldn't risk Larry being unnerved.

He opened his door and tried to haul himself out of the seat, but it was as though all power had leeched away in the brief time he had been sitting there. Sweat had broken out on his brow.

Are you all right? Larry asked.

I don't know, he said. Those sausages last night.

Look, I'll get the gates.

No. This thing, he was thinking, then the next. I'll do it.

However he had managed it, he was upright on the gravel, but his legs now were shaking.

You're in no state to drive, Larry said.

He wasn't, he knew it. I'll be OK, he said.

You won't.

Larry was out of the car now too. I'll drive, he said.

Avery was nearly past caring, so long as they got there.

Sure. All right, then.

He had only gone a matter of yards towards the gates when

he thought to let Larry know about the rear-view mirror. He turned with the words *use both hands* somewhere between mind and mouth, in time to see Larry in the driver's seat raise both hands unbidden and wrench the mirror to his height.

At first his brain couldn't quite process what he was seeing. He wondered had the words escaped without his realizing, but then Larry seemed to sense he was being watched and looked out from between his arms, his hands detaching themselves from the mirror. A particle in search of a wave. And at once Avery knew, and Larry knew that he knew. His expression – Avery would have cause to describe it many times in the weeks ahead – suggested resignation, not panic, as though he was surprised he had managed to get this far without giving himself away.

He opened the car door and a foot came down below it on to the driveway. It looked wrongly positioned, like a comedy prop. He ought to have got out the opposite side, leaving the foot there on the gravel, but the other foot followed, bringing the rest of his body behind it.

It was you. You took my car, Avery said.

Of course I took your car. You were turning your back on me. I had to do something. You even left the door open.

No, said Avery – not a quarrel, but a simple marker: he wouldn't listen to any more. You're a liar.

I did what I had to do, said Larry.

Avery at that moment – and this was something else he would return to in the weeks, the months to come – wanted very much to make him suffer in some way. If he could have flown at him he would have. As it was he could just about swing one leg in front of the other.

Larry stood his ground a few seconds longer then turned and ran. No, jogged; maybe because he knew that Avery had no hope of catching him, maybe because he knew there was nowhere for him to run to. The house was locked. The hedge at the back was unclimbable. Avery – weak but not rooted to the spot – was between him and the gates.

The other possibility did not occur to Avery until he saw Larry grab hold of the palings round the electricity substation.

Now he summoned a jog of his own, but it was too little and too late. Larry's head was already level with the top of the fence. Avery went looking for another gear that just wasn't there. Even his voice seemed not to carry as he tried to shout a warning.

It was half hallucination. A man of Larry's age hauling himself up and over a fence of that height. It didn't seem possible that he could drop, as the man at the top did drop, down on to the other side without injury. Avery turned back to the gates, he would ask the photographers to please help him, before Larry could get away. But when he got the bolt out, the spike lifted and the gates pushed apart there was no one whichever way he looked on the street. And then – it appeared, from where he stood, across the whole city but perhaps it extended no further than his own field of vision – there was a blue flash and the lights winked out

and on again.

Avery pitched forward on to his hands and knees.

Still no one came.

5

Frances wanted to return home as soon as she heard, but Avery wouldn't let her anywhere near the house with the baby until he was certain it was food poisoning he was suffering from. By the time she arrived late on Friday he had nothing much left to sweat, vomit, or shit out of his system.

Des had sat with him that first, worst night, praying mostly, replenishing the water glass, emptying the basin at the side of the bed. In the early hours when Avery couldn't sleep for the cramps, for fear of what he might dream, Des fetched him the evening paper from the hall. (Even the late edition was too early for Larry.) Avery barely responded when he read the story under the page-five headline: Gambling Debt Theory in Doctor Case.

> Police investigating last week's assault on a Belfast doctor now think he may have fallen foul of paramilitary loan sharks. Dr Tony Russell (31) is believed to have led an extraordinary double-life of professional respectability and compulsive poker-playing. Insp. David Sloan, leading the investigation, said inquiries indicated that Dr Russell had been borrowing heavily in recent months. 'We know that there are all-night card schools out there at which extremely large sums are won and, sadly, as in this case, lost,' he said. 'We would appeal to anyone who came into contact with Dr Russell to phone us in confidence on the Crimestoppers line. Gambling on this scale is an addiction and as with other addictions there are

elements in this society who are all too ready to exploit the addict.' Dr Russell is still recovering in hospital where police are hoping that they will soon be able to interview him.

The police had already interviewed Avery about Larry, but he had kept breaking down (breaking down or throwing up) and they had left saying they would return when he was in better shape to talk. They were keen to stress this was purely routine. Despite the warning signs, it was not easy to *accidentally* electrocute yourself on one of those things. The deceased's estranged wife had explained to them that he had a history of delusion and depression. Sometimes in order to carry out the fatal act the would-be suicide needed to feel he was being pushed to it. Chances are, Larry had been looking for a corner to be backed into.

Avery told the police how he discovered the truth of his car being stolen. He told them how one day as he sat on a bench in the centre of town Elspet's address had been *accidentally* dropped at his feet; how he felt as though since then he was the one being pushed and pulled around. He had been played for a fool frankly.

I thought that was part of your job description, one of the policemen said. To give people the benefit of the doubt. No?

The tape in the anorak pocket was destroyed. (He had not thought it decent to ask and had let the police volunteer the fact.) Its contents, though, were vivid enough in Avery's mind for him to be confident, when he had regained a little of his strength and composure, of narrating passages, if not verbatim then at least with a degree of fidelity. He tried it out on Des, but got no further than the raid on the house on the Cliftonville Road when Des stopped him.

I'm sorry, he said, this will sound very strange coming from me, but did you ever see *In the Name of the Father*? Is that the one I'm thinking of? There's a scene at the start where – what's this you call him? – Daniel Day-Lewis and this other guy have to take their trousers down.

I don't remember.

I'm pretty sure that's it.

So?

I don't know. It's like, even you telling me it, the parties in the house and so on – there's another film – I can nearly hear the cameras running.

He cobbled it all together?

Like I say, it sounds strange coming from me.

But nothing sounded strange to Avery any more. All the same, the question remained: Why would he make it up?

Blain said he remembered a row – correction, he remembered no end of rows, but this particular one, there was a western on the TV, maybe Larry wanted to watch the other side, anyway he was keeping up this whole commentary, making fun of the acting, picking holes in the plot. The more their father shushed him, the louder Larry got. There was a big shoot-out, you know, guys taking tumbles off balconies, being dragged along the street by their stirrups. And every time somebody was shot Larry would ask their father the same question. What did you call that fella? What did you call that fella? He was goading him. Then all of a sudden, their father snapped: he grabbed Larry by the scruff of the neck and tried to run him out of the room. Their father could have buried Larry any time he wanted to and Larry knew it, but that only made Larry more demented. He was practically screaming: You know what that does to you, sitting there watching people being shot like they were rabbits or pigeons?

Of course, he might just have been winding his father up, but it had always stuck in Blain's mind. Rabbits or pigeons.

Blain it was who took care of the funeral arrangements. Almost the first thing he did when he talked to Avery was explain his relationship with Elspet.

It was all over, you know, with her and Larry before the two of us got together. Long before. I would call round on her every so often, see how she was getting on. She had been through a lot. My brother was a very difficult person to live with.

He had worried about what Larry might do when he found out. He had even tried to persuade Elspet, he was ashamed now to say it, to stop sending him money. It tied her to Larry as much as it tied Larry to her. Elspet ignored him. It was none of his business, she said. This was between her and Larry.

Other people's families, Avery said.

Other people's relationships, said Blain. Elspet pointed you out at the Dalai Lama thing. We were in the balcony. She wouldn't introduce me to you. We had an argument. She left before he'd finished speaking.

You ambushed me.

I didn't know when I started to follow you I'd go into the back of you like that. I hadn't even made up my mind that I wanted to speak to you. But, then, you know how it is when you're following someone.

Ah, said Avery, caught out all over again. Botanic Gardens. That's one vocation I clearly didn't miss.

I wouldn't be too sure. Only for Elspet making me stop the car we would never have known you were there as well.

As well as who? Avery asked.

Larry, of course.

No. Avery wondered which of them was getting mixed up. I was on my own that day.

Blain looked him in the eye, evidently saw no reason there to doubt him.

Well, he was standing about ten feet behind you. He had started turning up at the swimming-pool bothering her. I came down that day to warn him off. Elspet was furious with me. She was furious with you. She thought you were to blame somehow for his interest in her again all of a sudden, but of course it was the other way round. He was to blame for you. He must have known that sooner or later you'd see something that made you wonder could there be some truth in it, all these people conspiring to keep him silent.

I was only killing time that day, Avery said. I could just as easily have gone to the garage.

This isn't a city, it's a village, said Blain.

Elspet was too distraught to say anything much until the funeral was over. At the crematorium she and Blain sat separated by Blain and Larry's mother, a woman not so much advanced in years as far-distanced by them from everything that she would once have said made her who she was. She held a rose throughout the ceremony, held it as though her sole purpose in being brought here this morning was to hold a rose.

There were about twenty more people in the room, scattered rather than clustered, wanting neither to intrude nor be intruded on, their only connection the coffin poised above the trap-door. Leo and Patricia were at the very back, the seats beside the door, as close to out as in could get.

Avery acknowledged them with a gentle nod as he began to read aloud the Twenty-third Psalm, remembering the moment he first saw Larry, looking off towards the ceiling, while this same psalm was sung. He wondered had Larry known even then how it was all bound to end. Maybe that's what the drink he had smelt that Sunday had been for. Dutch courage.

Blain had only asked him the afternoon before would he say a few words.

It was the celebrity pint of Guinness in reverse. If Avery had added up all the few words he'd ever been asked to say it would have come to the best part of a Bible.

We weren't going to have anything religious, to be honest, Blain said. It didn't seem right, given what we knew of his beliefs, or lack of them. But maybe, at the end, when he was in the house there with you . . .

Avery would have been lying if he had said that was probable, but funerals were as much for the living as for the dead: For thou art with me; thy rod and thy staff they comfort me.

He did it strictly by the book: We affirm that none of us lives in vain, labours in vain, gives or receives or loves in vain. Within the eternal purpose each of us is worth more than we can ever calculate . . . And not for the first time the book got it just right. Blain thanked him, Elspet thanked him; outside in the corridor where the single wreath lay next to the card requesting donations in lieu of flowers to a brain-trauma charity, Leo and Patricia thanked him.

I was dead set against coming, said Patricia, but Leo was coming whether I was or not and I wouldn't have had him here on his own.

It helped me, seeing him, even if it had to be in a coffin, said Leo. I was raging to begin with. I'm still raging a lot of the time, but then other times I tell myself, well, he got people thinking about her again, even just for a day or two. Who knows? Maybe somebody's conscience really will get to them over the head of it.

The official police line was that the case of the murders in the bar remained open. They would carry on their investigations into all 1800 unsolved murders committed over the past three decades. It went without saying that Patricia didn't believe them. Avery doubted that many people did.

Most of the other mourners slipped away with no more than a word or two to Elspet or Blain or a squeeze of Blain's mother's hand.

Tragic.

Desperate sorry.

Bearing up?

Avery himself was walking to the car when a young man in a leather blouson jacket fell in beside him.

Excuse me, he said. You won't know me, but I was at the service.

Avery neither knew nor remembered seeing him. He offered his hand anyway. I'm sorry, he said. Were you a friend of Larry's?

Not me, the young man said, my granddad. He indicated a car parked three down from Avery's. He was wanting to know could he have a word with you?

The man who opened the passenger door to Avery was in his early seventies. His white hair was swept back, pomaded yellow at the crown. His fingers sported a deep Woodbine tan. He looked no more familiar than the grandson.

I'm sorry for sitting, he said. The old legs.

Never worry, said Avery, crouching.

You might want to get into the back a minute, the old man said. I'm Tommy Power. I managed the bar where those people were shot.

Oh, Mummy, no. Avery rocked back on to his heels, steadied himself, then opened the rear door and got in. The grandson wandered off on to the lawns to read the plaques at the foot of the memorial trees.

Tommy Power turned in his seat. His eye twitched, more apologetic wince than wink. Actually, the legs aren't as bad as I'm letting on. When it came to the bit I just couldn't face going in there. I sent the young fella to stand for me.

You did know him, then? Avery asked, and Tommy nodded.

I used to let him help me out in the bar. Collecting glasses, washing them, running errands. I'd a lad of my own around the same age living across the water. I hoped somebody would look out for him the same way if he was down on his luck. That night of the shooting he'd called in early and sat for a while reading the paper. It must have been going on eight, I told him it didn't look like there was anything doing and to away on and enjoy himself for a change. He was only a young fella, but sometimes you'd have thought he was carrying the weight of the world on his shoulders. I subbed him a couple of pound out of the till. I remember thinking I was leaving myself a bit short of notes if we'd a sudden run, not that there was a big likelihood of that and, like, some nights he'd helped out for just a pint and a sandwich.

The other three were walking in the bar as he was walking out. He held the door for them. Mairead grabbed hold of his arm, saying what a gentleman he was. She was rightly. They all were. She asked him where he was rushing off to, would he not stop and have a drink. Then she said maybe she'd go with him, leave the lovebirds – Davy and the other woman, Roisin, they were an item – leave the lovebirds on their own. Larry didn't know what to say. I think to tell you the God's honest he was scared of her. Roisin told her to sit down, let the wee fella alone, she yanked her by the collar, horsing around. Mairead had on her some sort of necklace and it got broke. So, of course, this was another big drama. Roisin was more upset than Mairead was, it was her had given Mairead the thing. She was going to get it mended for her, she was going to get her a brand new one . . . Mairead told her not to worry herself, it would all be all right. And then – I don't know if Roisin even noticed, for she had turned to give Davy her order – she slipped the necklace into Larry's pocket and said something to him. Look after this for me, maybe. Bring it back another time when I'm not as likely to lose it. I'm guessing, I was too far away to hear.

Half an hour later the boyo with the gun walked in. He wasn't too well pleased when I showed him the few pound I had in the till. I always wondered if that had something to do with what he did when I went out the back. You wouldn't know, would you, what could set them off? When the whole rest of the world's packed up and gone home we'll still have to account to ourselves for the things done here out of sheer malice.

Mourners had started arriving for the next cremation. A disproportionate number of teenage boys and girls. One of their own, must be. Some joked and smoked defiantly. Most looked stunned. *Even to us it can happen.*

Avery asked Tommy Power had he told all this to the police at the time.

Of course, he said. As much as I was able. You have to understand, my nerves were shattered. I wasn't right for a long time.

And did the police talk to Larry?

Talk to him? The way I heard it they'd to ask him in the end to stop coming in with all his theories. They'd God knows how many other murders on their plate. I mean these things were happening day and daily.

Two hearses arrived, the second so packed with white flowers they might have popped behind the glass, like corn, *en route*. A black car drew in behind carrying the broken parents. God help them.

Tommy's grandson returned and got into the driver's seat. I think we might have to make a move here.

I'm ready when you are, said Tommy.

Can I ask you one last thing? Avery said.

Go ahead.

If it had been Larry came back into the bar with his face covered?

I'd have known, said Tommy. No question. I knew him when I walked on to the hospital ward after his accident and saw his face all bandaged and bruised.

You visited him?

Every week. Nerves allowing. It was a shame for him he'd so few visitors, a young lad like that. Only other person I ever saw there was his mother. I was going to get out there now when I saw her leaving, say a few words, but I could tell straight off she didn't know herself any more, never mind me.

Granddad, the grandson said, and Avery said, Sorry, yes, and opened the door. He reached back in to give Tommy his hand.

Thank you, he said. For the story, he meant, but more than that. For looking out for Larry.

Blain and Elspet were having a small get-together at La Mon House hotel not far from the crematorium. Avery was expected. He asked Tommy and his grandson would they like to come with him. Tommy shook his head. Too close to home, he said.

Twelve people had died in a firebomb attack on La Mon more than twenty years before. Given that criterion, there couldn't have been many places in Northern Ireland that were far enough from home for Tommy Power to leave the door.

First thing he got back to the house, Avery took Ruth to the greengrocer's out on the road to choose a Christmas tree. A real, live, smelling-of-toilet-cleaner tree. There were cautious nods, half smiles from shoppers they passed on the street. Avery had been temporarily relieved of his ministerial duties pending a meeting of the Presbytery's Judicial Commission in the first week of the New Year, but perhaps Dr Talbot had been right. From the random sample encountered that afternoon it appeared that in time his congregation might be inclined to be forgiving.

Ruth chatted all the way to the greengrocer's and all the way back as though she had already put the disruptions of the previous weeks behind her. She was home, she was holding her daddy's hand, tonight they would decorate the Christmas tree. What else mattered?

Two and a half weeks into his life everything that mattered to David could still be accommodated on one half of a double bed, or in the Moses basket beside it. When not feeding or sleeping he seemed content to admire his fingers, which were admittedly exquisite. Avery himself lay propped up on his elbow for a full hour looking at them, at the hair so sparse you could nearly imagine the strands being planted by hand, at the lips kinking in sleep round a phantom nipple, while Frances very belatedly unpacked the bags she had last seen the bottom of the day she left the hospital.

The buff envelope was in a side pocket among the other, pastel envelopes and baby cards delivered to her on the ward.

Avery, she said.

His head swivelled on his palm. He could see his name on

the envelope. He sat up, saw whose handwriting it was, snatched it from her.

I'm sorry, she said. Avery was tearing at the seal. It went clean out of my head. He brought it round to the ward one night. I was nearly asleep. He said you'd know what it was about.

The envelope contained a page torn from a ring-bound pad and folded in two. On the outside of the fold Tony had written, *Remember, you didn't get anything from me*; and inside a single underlined word, *Nothing*.

Avery read it again, outside and in.

What is it? Frances asked.

What was it? An answer? A double-cross? Tony's idea of a joke?

I really can't say.

Frances paused midway between the case and the cupboard.

No, I mean really, I can't.

She stayed like that looking at him a long, long time.

Acknowledgements

Acknowledgement is due to the editors of *New Writing 12* (Picador), in which a version of Chapter 1 appeared; to Cathy McMenemy and Gerry Kelly at Donnelly & Wall Solicitors; to Ali FitzGibbon, first reader; and, above all, to Chris Glover, who gave me what I needed most, an understanding of the church as a place of work, while never leaving me in any doubt that to him it was infinitely more. All errors, as ever, are my own.